INSIDE THE MARGINS:

A Carleton Reader

selected and edited
by Tess Hurson

LAGAN PRESS

This publication has received support from
the Cultural Traditions Group of the Community Relations
Council and from Dungannon District Council.

PR
4416
.A4
1992
cop 1

ISBN No: 1 873687 02 8
Editor: Hurson, Tess
Title: Inside the Margins:
A Carleton Reader
Format: Paperback
First Edition: 1992

Lagan Press, PO Box 110 4AB

for my family

Contents

Chapter Four: Romance

Chapter Five: Little Worlds in Strange Places

Introduction

Many people have spoken of Carleton's 'world' and in so saying they catch one of his most important characteristics as a writer; that dual sense of, on the one hand, a comprehensive reality, rendered fully in all its dimensions of sound and sight and feeling and thought, and on the other hand, a frankly fictive universe, larger than life, lighter and darker than the real world.

We have the impression of a distinctive and encompassing reality partly, I think, because Carleton returns, again and again, to the same set of themes. The themes are integrally related and are all parts of his overarching subject—the condition of Ireland.

But the condition of Ireland is not, for Carleton, a set of remote national questions. He did not stop short at an examination of the impact of the major political, economic and religious issues of the time at local level; he realised that history had also to do with the whole culture of a people—their education, their attachment to place, their customs and beliefs, their hatches, matches and dispatches, what they eat and drink, what is on the dresser, how they entertain themselves, how they love and how they hate:

> I found them ... a class unknown in literature, unknown to their own landlords, and unknown by those in whose hands much of their destiny was placed. If I became the historian of their habits and manners, their feelings, their prejudices, their superstitions and their crimes; if I have attempted to delineate their moral, religious and physical state, it was because I saw no person willing to undertake a task which surely must be looked upon as an important one. I was anxious that those who ought, but did not understand their character, should know them, not merely for selfish purposes, but that they should teach them to know themselves and appreciate their rights, both moral and civil, as rational men, who owe obedience to law, without the necessity of being a slave either to priest or landlord.
>
> —William Carleton, *Introduction to Tales and stories of*

7

If Carleton has no merit at all as a literary figure, he must surely hold a strong position as one of Ireland's preeminent social historians. That he came from the people and knew 'the road of them' would not, in itself, entitle him to any great authority, and there were many men, even in his own time, who, as he acknowledged himself, were admirable chroniclers of the rural Irish, although far from it they were reared. What is significant is that, given his background and circumstances, Carleton made it into print at all, and what is equally significant is his political courage in refusing to rarify or compartmentalise his subject. The great national controversies of his time are there not apologetically but stoutly, meshed with wakes and weddings and sports and hedgeschools. What is also unique to Carleton is the range of his views. Some would dismiss this as political inconsistency, to which he would have brazenly responded, like Walt Whitman, "Do I contradict myself? Very well then, I contradict myself." Indeed, it may be argued that Carleton's contradictions are what makes him worth listening to. No mild-mannered advocate of live and let die, he thunders invective against Catholic and Protestant churches with equal brio, shovels vituperation on criminal and judge alike, rips apart the Janus face of sectarianism—Orangeism and Ribbonism, addresses a memorandum to Sir Robert Peel offering his services in the extirpation of Catholic sedition and twenty years later, with a similar mixture of utopianism and sarcasm, directs the preface of his grim famine novel *The Black Prophet* to the Prime Minister, Lord John Russell.

Was it because he himself 'converted' and converted with a vengeance—from the middle of one religion to the middle of another, that he could land the punches to all sides with special wickedness?

Carleton may have hated not wisely but well, but he was, arguably, more honest about the enormity of the divisions wrenching apart his own society, than the more 'balanced' of his countrymen. Out of division comes contradiction. And if he, at times, took matters by 'the thick end', he was also capable of a very great depth of compassion.

Carleton's style, like his handling of the central issues of his time, is frequently high-complexioned. Not for him the cool and measured tones of the objective historian. He was not objective;

neither were the historians, but Carleton is not, as some have contended, only a chronicler—he is a literary worker too.

Critics have often commented on his stylistic chiaroscuro (see Barbara Hayley's *Carleton's Traits and Stories and the 19th-Century Anglo-Irish Tradition* (1983)) and certainly he is a great man for the dramatic contrast; deep pathos tumbles into slapstick jollity in the space of a page, chilly didacticism swallows patient and quiet description, stilted romantic dialogue collapses under a deluge of dialect, sublime gorges and vertiginous vistas are yanked out of view to make way for coy courtships and homely firesides.

There are plots, like that of *Jane Sinclair*, which hirple along over vast tracts of Wagnerian enervation, others, like that of *The Black Baronet*, are so tortuous that their circumlocutions make Agatha Christie seem, by comparison, translucent and others too narratives like *Redmond, Count O'Hanlon* and *Rody The Rover*, which hurtle along with all the swash and buckle of an Erroll Flynn movie. There are quiet plots and ghoulish plots and fables and tidily crafted short stories and morality tales and mythological satires and books which mix two or three genres without allowing the tail to wag the dog. And curiously the physical and thematic backdrop remains recognisable and familiar, no matter what literary repertoire he engages.

Carleton's characters are perhaps, at times, more memorable than his plots. Like Dickens, he was, above all, the master of the thumb-nail sketch; who could forget the hedge schoolmasters, Buckram Back the Dancing Master, Raymond na Hattha. Beyond these vivid cameos are more extended character studies, equally powerful and succinct; Skinadre the Genius of Famine, Neal Malone, Fardorougha the Miser, the Lianhan Shee, the Black Prophet. It would not be quite true to say that there are no great heroes in Carleton's world. Rather, like many colonial writers, the writer's real sympathy lies with the ordinary man men and women living at the margins, dislocated, uncertain, ridiculous or pathetic. It does not take a lifetime with the deconstructionists to see that this kind of characterisation reflects the political reality as the writer sees it. Carleton was trying to enter into the centre ring figures never really seen and heard before, and at the same time to create a sense of an entire society with its gentry as well as its peasants.

That he did not study the gentry—the conventional heroes—is obvious in the marked contrast between their ludicrous stiffness and the 'felt life' which suffuses his portraits of the ordinary people. When he can get hold of an eccentricity in a landlord he can lay a better foundation and his most successful creations in this arena are themselves marginal and dislocated figures like the Black Baronet, the Black Spectre or Squire Foillard in *Willy Reilly* and Squire Squander. And they are not so much characters as atmospheres; the eerie malignity overshadowing *The Black Spectre* is an extension of the mood the 'hero' creates around himself, the rakishness which characterises the whole ambience of Castle Squander is a manifestation of the squire's ruling spirit; the paranoia and vehemence seen at every turn (and they are multitudinous) in *The Black Baronet* are engendered by the presiding cryptic neuroticism of the 'hero'.

The queer melange of Carleton's writing raises certain questions about the nature of his audience. Who was he writing for? Certainly not the 'plain people of Ireland', to use a Flann O'Brienism. For even if they were literate by kind permission of those gracious hedgeschools, the supply of books and periodicals reaching the tenantry, was, as Carleton himself testifies in his *Autobiography*, extremely light. Even by Kavanagh's time the houses of the ordinary country people had not much of a 'roughness' and books would have rated low in the hierarchy of needs. So Carleton, and well he knew it, was faced with a gap between audience and subject, the very first time he put pen to paper. What would they make of his peasantry and his gentry in the fashionable London coffee shops or at the elegant tables of the Anglo-Irish?

And he was not, nor ever would be, one of them. He was an outsider, a big scattery country boy, a dubious convert, a hack journalist, the father of an embarrassingly large family who could not keep them out of debt nor himself out of the seductions of the fist and bottle. How would he treat this audience? In truth, Carleton never really decided; he played to their gallery and gave them the comic safety of the stereotypical stage-Irishman, he barracked them for their profligacy and bigotry, he idealised their ladies into rice-paper paragons, and he delivered forth an Ireland with razor-sharp precision which brooked no dilution—writing like a man sure of his footing, talking to a secret and imaginary audience. Like the speaker in Heaney's 'Personal Helicon' he might have said "I rhyme/to see myself, to set the darkness echoing."

The uncertainty of attitude is clear not only in characterisation plot and tone but also, as Barbara Hayley has pointed out, in the handling of spoken language. Carleton, like most writers constrained or released by the tight deadlines of the journal and newspaper, worked at a pretty fast clip. One of his novels was, he tells us, written in eight or nine days. It may be surprising then to discover the amount of revision he undertook—particularly between the various editions of *Traits And Stories Of The Irish Peasantry*. While there was some reworking of plot and characterisation, a great deal of the recasting was done at the level of spoken dialect. The rendering in a written medium of the vocabulary, syntax and rhythm of spoken 'Irish-English' remained a key dilemma. How was he to meet the twin demands of authenticity and comprehensibility? He had no real models and no guarantee that the presentation of this strange idiom would even interest his readers. Nonetheless, he hammered away at it, insisting upon the margin, writing the unwritten.

Those who spoke the dialect wouldn't or couldn't read it, those who could read it couldn't or wouldn't speak it. And while he was eking out this uncharted territory he was also to be found hawking all the old stage-Irish and stage-English cliches.

Critics are right to point to Carleton's contradictions—or looked at more positively—his infinite variety. For contemporary deconstructionists, Billy Carleton, wearing a clutch of hearts upon his sleeve, could prove an attractive proposition. For he is perhaps the archetypal colonial writer; riven with instabilities, unsure of his attitude to his subject and to his audience, unable to smooth over the anxious chasm he has opened in his own political, religious, cultural and historical identity.

Not unconnected with this insecurity of tone is his highly compound or *ersatz* style. On the one hand Carleton's writing is shaped by the literary conventions of his time—principally Romantic melodrama. On the other, we see the attempt to forge a new style which would deliver the relatively uncharted territory of ordinary rural life viewed from the inside and yet make of this marginal backwater a magical universe whose colourful denizens could be found and not found in any parish in Ireland. To achieve

11

this new kind of writing, Carleton had to try and steer free from two other sets of conventions—the stage-Irish stereotype, of use to the professional writer stuck for a bout of comic relief and of use in more dubious ways to the ruling elite, and the perhaps equally suspect convention of ringfencing the 'natives' as scientific curios who could be rationalised into perfection.

Carleton did not always escape these off-the-peg treatments and the combination of melodrama, naive social utopianism, paddywhackery, and hollow sublimity at times overwhelms his truer instincts.

Nonetheless, it can be claimed, with the same kind of precarious irony characterising Stephen Dedalus' Icarian proclamation, that Carleton did set out to 'forge the uncreated consciousness of his race'. And more importantly—he often succeeded in somehow creatively manipulating the procrustean conventions available to him to the service of a quite different and highly original kind of writing; anchored in a rounded world of verisimilitude but more intense, more curious, more self-consciously fictive than realism.

Melodrama could be given a local habitation and a name and underlaid with political horror to produce work as powerful as 'Wildgoose Lodge'. Old forms like fable could be dusted down and filtered over local dialect in 'Neal Malone', local tales and legends could be whipped into rollicking adventure stories like *Count Redmond O'Hanlon The Irish Raparee*, Cuchulainn's wife could be made to talk like a nineteenth century labourer's wife and Cromwell's minions could find themselves 'snufflicated' at the hands of Tom Greasie the Irish Shanahus.

Not enough rigorous critical study of Carleton has yet been undertaken and his real worth as a writer has, consequently, not yet been determined.

It is to be hoped that the wider availability of his work through Colin Smythe's welcome reissue of *Traits And Stories Of The Irish Peasantry* and this Reader, will help to stimulate the critical debate that Carleton deserves.

Tess Hurson

A note on the texts

Carleton's work often appeared in periodical or serial form; where this is the case the first publication is cited, followed by the first appearance of the piece in book form. For further information on subsequent editions of the quoted works, see Barbara Hayley, ed. *A Bibliography Of The Writings Of William Carleton*, Gerrards Cross, Bucks: Colin Smythe, 1985.

Acknowledgements

Many people gave generously of their time, skill and encouragement in the making of this book: the staff of the Linen Hall Library, Belfast; Trinity College Library, Dublin; Belfast Central Library and the Irish Reference Library, Armagh; Paul Donaghy, Utopia Graphics; Gordon Guthrie; William O'Kane; Shona McCarthy; Kevin Smith; Kathy Whiteman; Damian Smyth; Noel Murphy; the Carleton School Committee and my family.

Biographical note

In the house at Springtown there is a radio set, made by a Canadian visitor for the Saddler's daughter. Over it a voice of the world comes to the quiet valley, mingling with the song of the blackbird in the hazel glen, with the confused contradictory voices of the past century. But if you listen carefully you will hear the one voice that matters most of all, speaking across a hundred years, speaking for the people of this valley, for the people of Ireland, for those who died, and those who live, for those who sailed over the sea, even for those who returned to camp where the soldiers of Cromwell once camped in the townland of Aughentain.

—Benedict Kiely, *The Poor Scholar* (1947)

William Carleton was born the youngest of fourteen children in a townland not far from Aughentain, in a place called Prillisk, near Clogher, Co. Tyrone, in 1794. The family shifted around the Clogher valley during his boyhood years with spells in Springtown and Towney. Carleton, like most ordinary country people of the time, got a patchy, if memorable, education through the travelling hedgeschool teachers. Also, as the son of a small farmer who spoke both Irish and English equally well, Carleton was handed down a wealth of folklore and folk tales to draw on in his later literary and journalistic career.

His early life, by his own account, was for the most part carefree and while he clearly had a strong liking for books when he could get hold of them, he was far from immune to the attractions of the wake, the dancing match or a bit of a jumping competition not unfortified with 'the native'.

Not enamoured of the idea of earning his living as a small farmer, Carleton began the preliminary studies required to fit him for entering Maynooth College in order to become a priest. However, following a visit to Lough Derg, he turned away from the idea and went to earn his living as a tutor for the family of a Co. Louth farmer.

Tired of the drudgery of teaching, in 1818 he drifted towards Dublin with, his *Autobiography* records, two shillings and ninepence in his pocket. Once again, he scratched together a living as a private tutor. After two years in the capital, he married, Jane Anderson, the niece of one of his early Dublin benefactors.

His rise to literary fame was not meteoric. Eventually, after a great deal of scrambling, he published his first stories in 1828 in the virulently anti-Catholic *Christian Examiner*. It is clear that by this time Carleton had renounced Catholicism, through the precise date and motivation for his conversion to evangelical Protestantism is still a matter of literary debate. Certainly the charge that he simply 'took the soup' has undergone some stout challenges. His most famous work, *Traits and Stories of the Irish Peasantry*, was published in 1830 and quickly went into several editions. The second series of the *Traits and Stories* published in 1833 was equally successful. In 1834 he published *Tales of Ireland* and between 1837-1838 *Fardorougha the Miser*, perhaps his most successful novel, was published in serialisation form. Among the best known of his many literary and journalistic works are *The Black Prophet* (1846), a novel written in the middle of the Great Famine, *The Tithe Proctor* (1849), *The Squanders of Castle Squander* (1852) *Willy Reilly and his Dear Colleen Bawn* (1855) and *Redmond, Count O'Hanlon, the Irish Rapparee* (1860). He died, aged 75, on 30 January 1869.

Chapter One:
RELIGION AND POLITICS

Preface

Two important aspects of Carleton's view of contemporary politics are illustrated here: his deep concern about the causes and effects of sectarian and agrarian violence and what he saw as the rampant abuses of the political system.

An Irish Election *demonstrates Carleton's talents as a journalist. Characteristically, it is the attention to the telling of comic detail which lifts the piece out of its stridently polemical straitjacket.*

Wildgoose Lodge *was one of Carleton's earliest stories and is based on historical fact. Carleton recalls in his* Autobiography *coming upon the rotting corpse of Paddy Devaun and the horrific impression it created upon him stayed with him all his life. He considered the story one of his best.*

Carleton is often glibly characterised as a writer of extremity and contradiction—he must needs have whole duck or no dinner. But this belies the many gradations of his religious attitude. While one would not wish to make claims for him as an Irish Aquinas, Carleton, perhaps because of his 'conversion', gave the matter no small degree of attention. If he 'took the soup' in conjoining himself to the gelid and anti-Catholic eloquence of Caesar Otway's Christian Examiner, *he took a long spoon to the task, as is evidenced by his fulminations against what he saw as the worldly excesses of the established church in his many sketches of parsons like Turbot in* The Tithe Proctor *and Lucre in* Valentine M'Clutchy.

Carleton's tone ranges from savage vituperation to energetic and affectionate mockery of 'superstitious pilgrims' and priests. The targets of his satire are the extremists, but he is equally generous in his tributes to the religious devotion of ordinary priests and people, who he regards as pawns in a political game played by those in authority. It is, centrally, the interconnection of politics and religion as a power base which he views as dangerous. Carleton's diagnosis of sectarianism and hypocrisy identifies this religious-political linkage as the recidivist virus. And consistently in his work he appeals for religious tolerance and justice, and not infrequently champions the case for his old religion.

In the extract from Valentine M'Clutchy *we catch Carleton in spry mood ridiculing one of his favourite targets—sectarianism.*

1.

from An Irish Election in the Time of the Forties,
Dublin University Magazine (1847)

IT IS UTTERLY impossible, upon principles of plain reason or common sense, to account for the preposterous insanity of ambition which prompts so many men of every party to seek, if possible, all those means which the ingenuity of the head and the blackest corruption of the heart united, can call into action, for a seat in the House of Commons. The fact, however, is too well known and admitted for us to philosophize upon it here, or to attempt any adjudication upon the nature and object of human ambition, as to whether it is founded upon principles that are selfish and corrupt, or disinterested and philanthropic ...

Elections present nearly the same features at all times and in all places; but as those which occurred during the existence of the Forty Shilling Franchise were perhaps somewhat more remarkable as manifestations of national manners that are now gradually disappearing, of systematic corruption equally gross and ingenious, and of gregarious and brutal degradation, which we trust superior education and more independent habits of thought may ultimately remove—we accordingly select it, not simply, however, as a mere record of the past, but with a view of startling the present generation, if it be yet possible, into something like common honesty and a sense of shame.

As is always usual, the moment a dissolution was determined on, or about to take place, an active canvass was resorted to by such as had resolved to contest the county or the borough, as the case may be. This canvass, as it was conducted in the olden time, was in general a great grievance to the people, inasmuch as it threw the whole country into a state of idleness, excitement, and excess, that banished industry, sobriety, and honesty from the land. From the moment it commenced, all those who possessed votes during the existence of the 'Forties,' as they were termed, became unsettled, and at once were seized upon by a spirit of licentiousness and tumult, that was agreeable to their reckless habits, their utter ignorance, the low moral standard by which they were regulated, as well as by the unparalleled political corruption which animated and characterized their superiors. If, however, the morals of the poorer classes were in those days at a low ebb, those of too many of the gentry, and of almost the whole class of vulgar and upstart Squireens, in particular, were still worse and more objectionable ... The whole population of the kingdom might, with truth, be divided into two classes—the lords of the soil—the squireens—and the buckeens—many of the two latter—middlemen, on the one side; and the ignorant, semi-barbarous, destitute, whipped, and trampled-on serfs, on the other. Such was the condition of the lower classes, as well as of those who drove them like unreasoning cattle to the hustings at the period laid in our description.

Parliament was at length dissolved, and those who had neglected the interests of the people began to make preparations for being reinvested with authority to neglect them again. Many fine speeches had been made—commissioners appointed to examine particular subjects, and reports printed in large blue books, having immense appendixes, with, as one might suppose, the special object of never being read or acted on—patriots had been provided for, or, at least, had their honesty placed in such a negociable position as vastly increased the manifestation of their love of country. The *Outs*, in fact, had been *in*, and the *Ins* had been *out* two or three times alternately. Many who had served their party at the expense of their country, had been pensioned off, and a few whose circumstances kept them free of the pension list were each rewarded by a peerage. In fact, all those circumstances which indicate the dissolution of parliament had taken place, and, amongst others, a writ had been issued to elect a member for a particular county, which it is not necessary to mention at present, inasmuch as every one of our readers has only to suppose it to be his own, and he will necessarily be right. There were two candidates, one of whom—he who had been the sitting member in the last parliament—was a liberal—the man who, although not in trade, dealt largely in promises that were never performed, and not unfrequently in performances that were never promised. Both candidates were absentees—a circumstance which was much in the favour of each; for it so happened that in those enlightened days our virtuous countrymen—from a principle, we suppose, of national generosity—always gave a preference to the man who possessed least opportunity of knowing his country, her people, or their wants. By absentees we do not mean individuals who merely were owners of property in the country, but persons who were Irishmen by birth and descent, and who had princely residences and lordly halls, in which they did not live, unless, perhaps, during a short visit, in order to look after their own affairs.

The liberal candidate, an emancipator, and strenuous advocate of popular rights, was a very honourable and disinterested gentleman, by name Alexander Egoe; and his rival, the Tory and Orangeman, was Robert Vanston, Esq., of Constitution House. The principles of the latter were, of course, those of Protestant Ascendancy in Church and State, and, consequently, of No Popery. In truth, the contrast, so far as principles—or, at least, professions—went, were sufficiently marked to give ample promise of a fierce and desperate contest.

Vanston was a large dark man, with a composed but saturnine cast of countenance and large limbs; whilst his rival was a shrewd-looking, thin little fellow, with a lively but circumspect and calculating eye, over which jutted a pair of projecting eyebrows, and a rapidly-retreating forehead. For two months previously the whole county had been traversed and canvassed by each, either in person, or through the medium of their friends. In this canvass, Mrs. Egoe, who was celebrated for her attachment to popular privileges, rendered essential service to her husband, by a very ingenious mode of testing at once the love of fatherland and gallantry of our countrymen. On experiencing any particular difficulty in the person canvassed, and especially when she had ascertained that he was attached to the enemy, being the most beautiful married toast of the day, she placed a golden guinea between her lips, which the voter was challenged to take between his: thus turning Cupid himself into a politician by a system of such irresistible and delicious bribery. Her husband, who was very proud of her, whenever he got deeply into his cups, expressed this feeling, and it was on one of those occasions that he was asked how he could be proud of a woman who had been kissed by more than half the county. The canvass on both sides having been concluded, the first day of the election at length arrived.

The town of Ballyticklem not only from an early hour, but from the previous night, was literally overflowing. The stream of human beings that flowed into it was almost equal in point of numbers to the multitudes which flock towards a fair. Equipages of every description, from the spanking four-in-hand to the one-horse jaunting-car, were all in rapid motion towards the scene of contest—most of them distinguished by the well-known colours of the opposing candidates, and covered by large placards, having printed on them 'Mr. Egoe's Friends,' or 'Mr. Vanston's Friends,' as the case might be. Egoe's colours were a grogram-grey, and those of Vanston a cutbeard; but some of their friends, not satisfied with so much moderation, had procured the old standing opponents of orange and green, which they kept ready for the close of the contest, when voters on each side might begin to get scarce. Indeed the appearance of the various grades, as they might be observed upon the two great thoroughfares that led to the town, was sufficiently striking. From the private jaunting car, and the spruce country squireen upon his bit of half-blood, to the common hack vehicle and the frieze-coated farmer; and from the latter to the struggling tradesman; and from the tradesman, somewhat out at the elbows, to the gregarious forty-shilling free-holder, clad in open multitudinous rags; from the highest link of corruption to the very lowest; from the conscious and deliberate profligate of rank, to the most unthinking, degraded and brutal slave, throughout the manifold gradations of bribery;—all were there—most of the latter eager for corruption, and all of the former anxious to corrupt. If there were any honesty at all among them, and there was indeed but little, it was to be found in the middle classes—the fact being that the gentry and higher ranks on the upper extreme, and the low, venal vagabonds on the lower, were precisely of the same moral standing, with the exception of an odd conscientious creature among the degraded wretches, for whom no corresponding case could be got among those who sought to degrade him ...

Every face was now filled with anxiety or importance. Those who knew how closely the chances on each side were balanced, felt in full force the desperate nature of the game that was about to be played; and those who were in possession of a vote, although on every other occasion looked upon only as perfect dirt under the feet of those who were now courting them with sugared words and ample promises, appeared with countenances in which could be read that spirit of the slave, that would wax insolent with tyranny, if it were entrusted with such power as it is qualified neither by education nor feeling to enjoy. Nothing, indeed, was more striking than this. The veriest profligate, abased in morals and brutal from ignorance, with an infinitesimal stride of earth on which to ground the perjured fiction of a vote, now swaggered about with a hardened consciousness of authority, and an utter abandonment of shame and decency, that prevented one from feeling surprise at the furious scramble for corruption, which characterised his class. Principle, manly feeling, a clear and conscientious perception of duty, were altogether out of the question, and could not, except in very rare instances, be seen at all. Conscience, a sense of what is due to religion, to civil freedom, or, as it is termed, political liberty, may, with but few exceptions, be sought for in vain at an election. On the contrary, the wretched people seem to forget every high and sacred feeling of honour, integrity, and truth, and to become subject for a moment to the worst and most debasing instincts of their nature. A shameless contagion of profligacy seems to prevail, which, descending, as every evil does from the high to the low, seems to fill the latter with an insolent gratification, in being able to rival and surpass their betters in this venal and demoralizing traffic. Some few, indeed, you might see, who came uninfluenced by the contagious insanity of this brief but corrupt epidemic. Such persons, however, kept themselves aloof from the crush and the scramble, and neither ran, nor rushed, nor shouted, nor fought, nor partook at all of the disgraceful spirit which prevailed around them. These were comfortable, independent-looking men, who either drove in quietly, and without any hurry, upon their own jaunting cars, or rode in upon their plump, sleek, well-fed horses, dressed either in warm superior frieze or comfortable broad-cloth ...

On every side now were seen men flying to and fro, some with letters, notes, and written communications in their hands, seeking out particular persons; others, again, were conversing in angry knots, or indulging in loud mirth, and according as a friend or an opponent passed, they greeted him with a cheer or a groan for their respective candidates. But above all that was remarkable, and sickening beyond the power of description, was the appearance and the incessant activity of the whippers-in, or agents, the potwallopers, and others, who are the organs or conduits through which the black and filthy streams of corruption flow, and which, like other sewers, are themselves certain to retain such an ample portion of its uncleanness.

At length the hour for commencing the proceedings arrived, and a headlong rush, such as always characterizes an election, took place into the courthouse ...

Mr. Egoe rose up amidst another storm of cheers and hisses, and for some time appeared to be engaged in pantomime. At length, after about fifteen minutes of dumb show, he was heard by a dozen or two of those who were nearest him, making a speech to the following effect:

"I know," he proceeded, "that it does not become a man to eulogise himself; but, under the circumstances in which I am placed, I feel that I would neglect an important duty to my constituents, if I were to overlook my exertions on their behalf in the House of Commons, where I have been placed by their independent votes. (Cheers and hisses.) Gentlemen, my political principles are not now a secret; they are, I trust, well known, for they have always been recorded on the side of liberty. Liberty, gentlemen, may be said to be my motto. Liberty to all; for what is or can the world itself be to a man who has it not? Gentlemen, liberty is that great principle which brings us here to-day, and which will bring my friends here also to-morrow. Liberty to the black as well as the white—liberty to the slave as well as to the freeman. Gentlemen, there is a house—a certain house which shall be nameless—but in that house, as it is at present constituted, there is, I regret to say it, no liberty, or, at least, comparatively little. There is, however, to be found in it a small band of patriots, who are fighting her battles, among which band, I am proud to say, is enrolled the name of Egoe. (Cheers, with much yelling.) Gentlemen, so long as any portion of my fellow subjects, who differ from me in religion, are not permitted to share in the rights of citizenship, so long shall my humble voice be raised against the policy which excludes them. (Outrageous cheering, with several bye-battles in different parts of the house.) I am not the man to bolster up a rotten and domineering ascendancy, by admitting the one portion of my fellow-subjects to the privileges which I would deny to the other. No; I am not the man who would advocate such exclusive dealing as that. Whatever be my faults—and I suppose I am not without my share—yet I may truly say that my lot is cast in the ranks of freedom. I am an advocate for civil and religious liberty over the universal world. (Monstrous cheers.) That is my political creed - universal liberty!—freedom to all! Slavery, as the great Roman orator said, is a bitter draught; and thousands have been made to drink of her, yet she is never a jot sweeter on that account. Gentlemen, there was an abominable law passed on the last session, laying the fine, wherever a poteen-still is found at work, upon the whole townland, by which means the innocent are generally punished, and the guilty escape. That law, gentlemen, shows us that the House of Commons itself is not what it ought to be. I opposed that law; I recorded my vote against it. Will my excellent friend say that he approves of it?—for I trust I may still be permitted to call him my excellent friend. (Here his honourable opponent rose and bowed, on which Mr. Egoe bowed again to him, and both met half way, and shook hands. Immense cheering.) Will my excellent friend say that he approves of it? ('No,' from Vanston.) Well, I am glad he says no; for, indeed, it is with great regret I differ from him on any subject; and if he lent his powerful aid to the great cause of universal liberty, nothing on earth would give me greater satisfaction. I trust, gentlemen, that the——. Well, my respected friend says he does not approve of the law in question; but will he permit me to ask him, if he does not approve of it, why did he vote for it? I trust, gentlemen, he will be able to answer that question in a satisfactory manner; not to me, but to the constituency of this great and important county. (From Mr. Vanston—'I pledge myself to answer it in a satisfactory manner.') I hope he may; no man will rejoice at it more than I shall. But will the honourable gentleman permit me to ask him another question, bearing on his claims to your confidence and your votes. Why is it that with liberty in his lips he can reconcile it to himself to vote against the rights of his Roman Catholic fellow-countrymen? Why is it that with freedom on his lips, but I fear on his lips only, he can have the courage to come here to-day, and expect to be supported by those whose civil thraldom he would help to perpetuate? These, gentlemen, are solemn and important questions, and must be solemnly and clearly answered. Will my honourable friend have the confidence to say, 'here are five millions of my fellow-countrymen in slavery—and here are a vast number at present around me—I have voted against their claims to freedom—I am pledged to vote against them, yet I have the hardihood to expect that they, by their votes, will enable me to perpetuate their slavery? This is the position in which he stands—let him get out of it if he can. Who is there here who will avow himself a friend to slavery? Who is there here who will support the man whose energies are devoted to the subjugation and debasement of his brother man? If there be any such, I care not for his vote—I disclaim it—I repudiate it—I renounce the support of the man who will support slavery—I will have no such companionship. 'Evil communication corrupts good morals.' Away with him—presto, be-gone—'get thee behind me, Satan'—'anathema, maranatha.' Gentlemen, I am detaining you too long (so you are—no, no—go on—cheers again and hisses.) Gentleman, I am not now speaking for myself, but for all of you—for as for me, *I* make no distinctions among you—God made none—you are all created with the same number of physical senses and qualities—all of your complexions are of the same stamp (except the yellow bellies)—you have the same number of limbs, the same number of faculties, both mental and bodily—why then, since God has created you all alike, should there be distinctions made among us in favour of one class, and against another? I should wish my honourable friend to answer that question—and I trust when he rises to address you, that he will reply to some others which, with all due respect, I have taken the liberty, from a strong sense of duty, to put to him. There is a talk, gentlemen, about depriving the Forty-shilling Freeholders of their franchise. Such a report is current. May I again ask my honourable opponent, whether he knows anything about such a rumour, or whether he is of opinion that it is founded in fact? Gentlemen, whatever I do shall be done above board—*coram populo*. If such a monstrous step be in contemplation, I for one shall most strenuously oppose it. Through every stage of its iniquitous progress, it shall meet my most decided and energetic hostility. Never shall I suffer—whilst I have a voice to support on the one side, nor to denounce on the other—the rights of the Forty-shilling Freeholders of Ireland to be bargained away for the sake of political convenience or personal corruption. What—a class of men so free, so honest, so independent, so incorruptible—yes, gentlemen, so incorruptible, that a friend of mine who was over here at the last election, and who is also at this, absolutely said that he knew of nothing which afforded him greater gratification than the mere attempt to bribe them, that he might more clearly perceive the extra-ordinary extent of their honesty. He would like to do so, he said, from principles of moral purity alone, in order to raise and confirm his good opinion of human nature, as exhibited in the high minded and unpurchaseable Forty-shilling Freeholders of Ireland! (Tremendous cheers from all parts of the house, accompanied with waving of caubeens and the dangling of rags, as before.) Do not be cast down, however, honest and high-minded Forty-shilling Freeholders;

"One faithful hand your rights shall guard"—

one voice at least shall be raised in your defence—one honest heart, honest as your own, shall be devoted to your interests, and one purse, should it be necessary, opened to protect your liberty. (The cheering here became perfectly astounding.) Gentlemen, what I say to the Forty-shilling Freeholders, I say to all, for I am the advocate of all; but I do not intend to stop here; I have no notion of merely defending your rights. This is a matter in which it is no man's duty to remain simply negative; I shall, therefore, not merely defend your rights, I shall extend them. It is my intention to bring in a bill in this session with a view to bring down the franchise from forty shillings, which, as it now stands, may be said to affect none

25

but the most respectable upper classes of the people, for the people, gentlemen, have their upper classes, and why should they not? And who are the upper classes of the people? I boldly say, without fear of contradiction, the Forty-shilling Freeholders of Ireland." (Deafening cheers, which lasted for several minutes.) ...

Here he sat down amidst a most extraordinary tumult. The high Tory party, consisting of Orangemen and staunch Presbyterians, who were also a vast number of them strong anti-Papists, groaned and hissed, and broke out into a most furious tumult, which was, on the other hand, as furiously and tumultuously opposed by the Roman Catholic party; so that another battle royal took place, as bitter and ruffianly on both sides as any of the preceding.

Egoe's announcement of the extension of the franchise, however, was by no means as well received as he had imagined it would have been. So far from that, the worthy Forties, on hearing that the franchise was about to be extended to other hands as well as their own, were by no means satisfied at seeing the principle of liberty, or, in other words, the prospect of gaining the wages of corruption, extended to the aforesaid other hands—hands which they knew the farther down the bribers went, were the more eager to catch at them.

Mr. Vanston now got up, and, after a fresh tumult, began to perform, for several minutes, the same description of dumb show that was exhibited by his opponent, until the cheering, yelling, and other indescribable sounds, had gradually subsided. At length he was permitted to proceed:—"Gentlemen," said he, "I thank you for the cordiality of this reception; and I trust that I shall soon be able to point to the future with as much confidence as I can to the past. At the same time that I say this, I do not wish you to understand that I am a man who deals very largely, in promises— that is to say, in mere promises, unsupported by good honest performance. Promises upon the hustings at an election are always rather suspicious, especially when they have been too frequently made, but very seldom kept. No, no, gentlemen; you may find persons who will be ready to give you enough of that commodity, and very little of anything else. I say you may find such persons, but I don't for a moment insinuate that my worthy and honourable friend is one of them—if he will allow me the honour of calling him my friend. (Here Mr. Egoe rose and bowed very politely to Mr. Vanston, who, on the other side, bowed again, after which they met each other half way as before, and very cordially shook hands. Immense cheering, &c.&c., as before.) Well, gentlemen, having stated to you that I won't promise, I now beg to let you know what I *will* perform. And, in the first place, I think it necessary to make a frank and fearless avowal of my principles—of those principles which have regulated my past life, and which shall also regulate my future; for, gentlemen, I beg to say that I am no trimmer. I and every member of my family are of the same political creed. Be assured there are no apostates among us. No, no. We do not divide ourselves in order to have a double chance of the good things that may be going among the Whigs and Tories." (Here Mr. Egoe rose and asked—' Does the honourable gentleman mean anything personal by these insinuations?")

To which Mr. Vanston replied—"Does my honourable friend feel that my words apply to him, or any member of his family?" Mr. Egoe.—"I beg to say, certainly not." Mr. Vanston.—"Then I beg, of course, to say, that I made no allusion of a particular nature—I spoke generally." Mr. Egoe.—"Then I beg to say, that if the honourable gentleman did not speak particularly, but generally, I am perfectly satisfied." (Great cheering.) Mr. Vanston proceeded "I am ... of my countrymen; and no man would or shall go farther to serve them than myself. I am a friend to my Roman Catholic fellow-countrymen, all of whom I would and shall serve, whenever and wherever I can; but I am at the same time bound to say, that whilst I like the man, I do not approve of his principles. I do not agree in, or sympathize with his creed, nor the politics which it teaches him—and why?—because the principles which it teaches him, and his party, are such as would establish, if they had the power, an oppressive and exclusively Catholic ascendancy, where the many would keep down the few, whereas I am—and I glory to say it—I am for a Protestant ascendancy, where the few, thank God, are able to keep down the many. These, gentlemen, are my principles so far; but it is monstrous for the Romish community to expect to put themselves in our places, which they would do if they could, but which I hope they will never live to accomplish. Church and state, then, gentlemen,—Church and State, and Protestant ascendancy, are my honest principles, with a fixed determination to support them at the hazard of my life, for I am one of

27

those men who have already fought to defend them, and who am ready and willing, should the occasion ever come, to fight as before, for the Protestant hearths and altars of my country. And, gentlemen, by G-d he is no honest Protestant who would not. No; I protest I would not sit with, or recognise as an acquaintance, much less as a friend, the cowardly knave, being a Protestant of course, who would not defend both with his life, for the sake of our holy religion. My honourable opponent, gentlemen, has put many questions to me in the course of his speech, which I said I would answer; for indeed I am not so churlish as to refuse information to any man who, because he is conscious of his ignorance, is not a whit ashamed to ask it. He asks me, for instance, how I voted on a certain question, and I reply, that I did not vote at all; and for the best reason in the world, because it so happened that I was not in Parliament when it came on, a circumstance which clearly proves to you all that the honourable gentleman, whatever he may be distinguished for, is at least not distinguished for a good memory. And I simply show this as a hint, that I think every man who deals largely in promises, ought to be gifted with the very thing which he wants, such a memory as will prevent him from forgetting, among other matters, the multitude of promises which he is in the habit of making. Gentlemen, he alludes to a law that has been made in the session that just closed, which imposes a fine upon the innocent instead of the guilty.

"It is true *he* opposed the law in parliament; but, gentlemen, there is a class of men who oppose certain measures, not I believe with a hope of defeating them, but because they know they will pass, and that they may, whilst they wish them well, enjoy at the same time all the credit of patriotism. Of course I do not say that this is the case, or was the case, with my honourable friend; all I can say is, that I have it from good authority that he helped to draw up the bill in private, which he so strongly and patriotically opposed in public. And further, gentlemen, I think I can say that a certain Commissioner of Excise, who shall be nameless, but who is not at least a perfect stranger to the honourable gentlemen, was the individual who got the bill alluded to drawn up, and had it introduced into the House of Commons. So much for that transaction; and I now beg to state in reply, that I would have *honestly* voted against so preposterous a bill, if I had been in

Parliament."

Mr. Egoe.—"May I beg to ask, why the honourable gentleman lays such a peculiar emphasis upon the word *honestly?*"

Mr. Vanston.—"Because it is my habit to do so. Honesty, especially political honesty, is so rare a thing in this world, that whenever we chance to meet with it, or even to hear of it, we are bound to speak of it with as much emphasis as possible." (Cheers.)

Mr. Egoe.—"Had the honourable gentleman no other motive?"

Mr. Vanston.—"I think we are here, not to explain motives, but to state principles. If the honourable gentleman is not satisfied with this reply, let him come to me at a proper time and place, and he shall have any further satisfaction that I can give, or he may require; but at this time, and in this place, I must decline to give him any further information on the subject. Gentlemen, the British constitution is a glorious constitution, and I for one am not, nor ever will be the man to strive, by forming a coalition with its enemies, to destroy the integrity, and diminish the strength of the empire. I am not a patriot, gentlemen, in the usual acceptation of that obnoxious word; but I trust I am what is still immeasurably better—an honest man, who feels neither afraid nor ashamed to avow my principles, and who, whatever may betide, will never be found voting *against* a bill which I privately aided in planning and drawing up, so as to meet all objections that might be urged against it. I name nobody, gentlemen, nor of course, you know, do I make any allusions—but the truth is that that worthy and maligned gentleman called Nobody, has more matters of this kind to answer for than all the anybodies and everybodies in the universe. Of course, gentlemen, Nobody did this, and it is only against him that I throw out the insinuation. But, gentlemen, I have already stated, that although I do not relish the religious or political principles of my Roman Catholic fellow-countrymen, yet this circumstance does not, nor ever shall, prevent me from rendering them, publicly and privately, both as a man and a politician, every service in my power that is consistent with the integrity of the British empire, and the safety of our glorious constitution, as it is established at present in Church and State. Is not this fair? Could any reasonable man expect me to vote, or in any other way work against my own principles—for, thank God, gentlemen, I *have* principles. And now, gentlemen, having fairly stated these opinions and principles,

I trust I may calculate upon your independent support. I am not, as you know, a man of promises, nor of mere words, but a plain man of work and action. As such I offer myself to you, and I have no doubt that the close of the election will find me where I aspire to be, and where I know your votes and support can place me."

Having concluded this harangue, a new row took place, more outrageous and fierce than any that had yet occurred. The pulling, the dragging, the knocking down, the throttling, and the barbarous ruffianism and violence which characterised the tumult, could not be described in suitable terms; nor would the description gratify the reader, even if it could. Several other speeches were made; but as they all have the usual and uniform characteristics of violence and recrimination, we shall pass them over, and proceed to describe the other general features of the Election.

In those fine old times there was a complication of machinery in the conduct of an election, which our readers will look upon with surprise, if not with incredulity. The friends, for instance, of the respective candidates had each their own peculiar task assigned them. The expenses of the whole election were generally divided between them, each man paying one-half; and in those days it usually happened that the longest purse was only another name for the best cause. The usual course was to select some experienced, ripe, old villain, to marshal all the organs of corruption according to their capacities, and, indeed, to conduct the Bribery Department in general. As, however, each candidate had a committee-room, where his friends were always assembled to issue orders, draw up addresses, concoct plans, and write squibs, we shall take the liberty of introducing the reader to that of our friend Egoe, in order that he may have an opportunity of becoming acquainted with the operations of the honest and independent electors who were there engaged. On that occasion, were assembled about two dozen, or perhaps thirty, of the late member's warmest supporters, including a sprinkling of priests, who forgot the peaceful spirit of their calling, and most of the decencies of life itself, in the headlong and insane violence of religious bigotry and party feeling. Egoe himself, we put out of the question, the truth being, that he on the one side, and Vanston on the other, were mere impersonations of political depravity, and simply stood forth as its representatives, rather than as men whom the people had honestly and freely approved.

Egoe's right-hand man was an old skilful manoeuverer, named Nicholas Drudge, of Gooseberry Lodge, who, having much practice in the best and safest methods of purchasing votes, was appointed to manage this difficult department, without either rule or stipulation, everything, of course, having been left to his own prudence and discretion ...

There was only another man in the county worthy of comparison with Nick, and that was Billy Burnside, a man who, in point of fact, was equally notorious with Drudge, for the adroitness and chicanery which are so essential in the management of an election. Burnside was supposed to be a still better economist that Nick, and able to bribe as many with thirty pounds, as Nick could with fifty. The two worthies, in fact, were not dissimilar, either in personal appearance or in political qualifications, and were consequently hand and glove with every man of note in the county, as well as with each other. Nick was a broad, weather-beaten, red-faced fellow, with a knowing, but by no means a sinister expression of countenance, unless when he became particularly confidential, and then his face puckered itself into such a varied and multitudinous exhibition of knavery as could seldom be witnessed. The mouth was small, but hard and unscrupulous; his chin and cheeks were intersected by the strong lines of cunning; move them as he might, there lurked in his eye such a disguised consciousness of his own successful duplicity, and the power of overreaching, as rendered his countenance, in connection with the habits of his life, absolutely a thing to be admired. He was a round, portly-looking man, and possessed a singular, indeed a peculiar facility, not merely of expressing himself, but also a felicity of insinuation, that rendered him almost beyond all price at an election.

Burnside, in figure, somewhat resembled him, as he did also in countenance, the only difference being, that nothing, so far as the eye could infer, but the blandest good humour, and the frankest honesty that ever broke in smiles from the sunshine of a good fellow's face, could be perused upon his. In fact, they looked very like counterparts of each other, and we question whether there could have been found in the country two persons capable of attributing, without a long discussion, any superiority in their respective qualifications to either one or the other. Next in importance to Drudge, was Captain Blaze, who, in common with most of the gentry on both sides, came duly prepared with a case of duelling-pistols. Blaze was a distinguished fire-eater, who had been concerned, either as principal or second, in about twenty-seven 'affairs', and was thought to be the most *au fait* in such matters, of any man in the kingdom. Blaze was what might not inaptly be termed, Chairman of the 'Intimidation Committee', that is to say, he undertook not only to fight himself, but to drill and regulate the rioters, so that the outrages might be most judiciously distributed in different parts of the town, with a view to produce the greatest possible quantum of intimidation upon the irresolute and timid.

Third in degree may be named Larry O'Ladle, who had been cook to old Egoe, but who, for several years, was proprietor of the 'Tare-an-ouns Tavern', an establishment long under the patronage of the Egoe family, who rewarded their faithful old domestic by installing him as its major-domo, in connexion with a good farm of land, which, to say the truth, made it an exceedingly comfortable thing for O'Ladle—whose province at elections was to regulate the potwallopers—to fall back upon...

On this occasion our friend Blaze seemed rather sulky and out of sorts, both with himself and every one about him.

"What the deuce is the matter, Captain?" asked a cousin of Egoe's; "you're pouting like a woman. What's wrong, you old fire-eater? I hope you're not afraid of 'fighting Grimes'. I'm told he won't allow this battle to pass without having a shot at you."

"I am not at all satisfied," returned Blaze; "I have been left in the dark too much. Curse me but Egoe's getting penurious; I fought three duels for him at the last two elections, and he had the meanness to refuse me his acceptance for three hundred pounds, after the thing was done." ...

"Mr. Drudge," said an agent, "I wish to have a few words with you."

"Come, Mark, my boy, something good's in the wind when you appear; what is it?"

"Why, the Forties from the Black Cosh are coming down on Thursday morning, about a hundred-and-twenty of them, to vote for Vanston; and you know if they do we're dished."

"Not a doubt of it; but what's to be done?"

"I don't know—I was thinking of a riot, and to get out the military."

"For what purpose?"

"Why, you see, by getting the military out, we might make the fellows take refuge in a lugger that's lying ready for them in the harbour; we might get them under hatches, you know, go out to sea, and keep them snug there till the election's over."

"But will you be able to manage all this?"

"Why, I'll try. Give me three hundred pounds; I want also about fifty intimidators, and I say, once and for all, that none but hardened fellows will do me—ruffians every one of them. You are not to suppose that fifty alone would do me, but these fellows must act as agitators and leaders, to influence the mob. It'll require nice management."

"It will; but it's in good hands, Mark, when it's in yours. I'll depend on you."

"If I fail, I can't help it—I want some flash notes." ...

It was on the second day that the business of the contest seriously commenced. On the first, Blaze, the fire-eater, had evidently been satisfied, as he appeared early the next morning on horseback, with a powerful cutting-whip in his hand. From this circumstance, it was perfectly well-known that shots would be exchanged, and the more so, as a champion, named 'Split-bullet Buxton', similarly equipped, was parading himself upon the other side.

One would imagine now, that two gentlemen so singularly bellicose as the pair we have described, would almost have set a-horsewhipping each other as soon as they met. Nothing, however, could be farther from their brave and honest hearts, than any such intention. They understood each other a great deal too well for that. Their first duty was, certainly, not to fight with each other in a spirit of wantonness and blood, but to intimidate and coerce, wherever they could, all such as were remarkable for a shrinking and timid character, and who wished to avoid notoriety.

"Buxton," said Blaze, when they met, "an even ten we beat you."

"No," replied Buxton, "I know it will be too close a contest to lay a wager on it; and, between you and me, Blaze, my dear fellow, I can't afford, no more than yourself, to lose a ten-pound rag now.

Do you expect any fighting on this occasion?"

"Why," replied Blaze, "I don't know. I should suppose so. Do you?"

"Begad, I can't exactly say. I think you ought to know best. Heaven forbid there should not be at least two or three little matters of the kind. Try and get me up a couple—will you, Blaze, like a good fellow?"

"Well, I don't know—perhaps I am—one good turn deserves another; you won't forget your friends on the other side, perhaps."

"Certainly not, if it's an understood case."

"Very well, then, let it be an understood case."

And with this mutual intimation of their intention, the two belligerent worthies separated, to support the cause of truth and liberty ...

The mail-coaches were stopped, the traces cut, the vehicles in many instances broken to pieces, and the respectable persons, on their way to vote, were seized upon with a fury that can hardly be accounted for at all, and treated with desperate and merciless outrage. To such a degree, indeed, did freedom of election prevail, that they were dragged about, and beaten, and trampled on, not as if they were men coming to exercise a legal and just privilege, in the possession of which they were all so clamorous, but as if every one of these unfortunate men had been a detected murderer, striving to escape, after having perpetrated some cruel and cowardly assassination. To hear the shouting and yelling, to witness the flying about of the excited multitude, broken into small masses, or larger mobs, as they were—to look on the wounded victims of blind popular fury—here a man borne away, amidst hisses, shoutings, and groans, in a state of insensibility—there, another kept on his limbs and protected by the police and in a different direction again, a band of twenty or thirty military putting to most shameful and cowardly flight no less than six or eight thousand of these brave and independent men; to witness, we say, and look upon such outrages as these with one's own eyes, was enough to make the spectator groan, at the bare idea of popular liberty, and wish in his heart that, instead of living under such a form of government as made them necessary, he were located under some honest and well-regulated despotism, where he could exercise his serfdom in quiet slavery, or be strung up, or Siberianized

34

in a manner that must be gratifying to his vanity, inasmuch as it shows him that he is considered of more importance in the eye of the autocrat, than those who are left behind him. After all, it is to be feared that poverty is only another name for guilt. Yet how, again, can we say so, especially when we reflect, that those who urged, excited, tempted, and goaded these starving wretches to such brutal and inhuman excesses, were not themselves in the slightest degree affected by poverty ...

To return, however. We said that the ingenuity exhibited in some of these atrocities was extraordinary, and a proof, that in whatever qualities our people are deficient, natural intellect is certainly not among them. As the electors came in, and voted either for this person or that, they were assailed by hissings and execrations, or by cheerings and exclamations, from the respective mobs. But this was not all; ruffians were stationed among the friends of the popular candidate, with pieces of red and white chalk in their hands, who, as the electors passed out, took care to score their backs with either colour, in proportion to the political enormity of their crime. A score of white chalk, for instance, was a signal to that portion of the crowd that the person thus marked had voted against the popular candidate, and deserved to be well beaten; whereas the red mark intimated a still more fearful punishment—to wit, that the individual bearing it might have his brains knocked out, or be beaten to death ...

On looking at the crowd, and reading the feeling of the occasion in their eyes, there was obvious an expression of outrageous excitement and delight, such as most significantly indicated the tenor of the whole proceedings. The brow seemed flushed with intoxication and passion, or pale with apprehension; the eye turbid and gleaming, the hands quivering with excitement, and the whole frame under the influence of those savage impulses, would enable any calm, disinterested person to perceive at a glance how far the practices usual at elections are calculated to promote the cause of civil liberty, or, what is equally high and important, that of social morality, and those humanities of life without which man is little better than an untamed animal howling in his jungle.

2.

'Dr. Turbot, Parson' from *The Tithe Proctor* (1840)

THE WORTHY RECTOR of Ballysoho was a middle-sized man, with coal-black hair, brilliant, twinkling eyes of the same colour, and as pretty a double chin as ever graced the successor of an apostle. Turbot was by no means an offensive person; on the contrary, he must of necessity have been very free from evil or iniquity of any kind, inasmuch as he never had *time* to commit sin. He was most enthusiastically addicted to hunting and shooting, and felt such a keen and indomitable relish for the good things of this world, especially for the luxuries of the table, that what between looking after his *cuisine*, attending his dogs, and enjoying his field sports, he scarcely ever might be said to have a single day that he could call his own. And yet, unreasonable people expected that a man whose daily occupations were of such importance to himself, should very coolly forego his own beloved enjoyments, in order to attend to the comforts of the poor, with whom he had scarcely anything in common. Many other matters of a similar stamp were expected of him, but only by those who had no opportunity of knowing the multiplicity of his engagements. Such persons were unreasonable enough to think that he ought to have occasionally appropriated some portion of his income to the relief of poverty and destitution, but as he said himself, he could not afford it. How could any man afford it who in general lived up to, and sometimes beyond, his income, and who was driven to such pinches as not unfrequently to incur the imputation of severity and oppression itself, by the steps he was forced to take or sanction for the recovery of his tithes?

In person he was, as we have said, about or somewhat under the middle size. In his gait he was very ungainly. When walking, he drove forward as if his head was butting or boring its way through a palpable atmosphere, keeping his person, from the waist up, so far in advance that the *a posteriori* portion seemed as if it had been detached from the other, and was engaged in a

36

ceaseless but ineffectual struggle to regain its position; or, in shorter and more intelligible words, the latter end of him seemed to be perpetually in pursuit of his head and shoulders, without ever being able to overtake them. Whilst engaged in maintaining this compound motion, his elbows and arms swung from right to left, and *vice versa*, very like the motion of a weaver throwing the shuttle from side to side. Turbot had one acknowledged virtue in a pre-eminent degree, we mean hospitality. It is true he gave admirable dinners, but it would be a fact worth boasting of, to find any man at his table who was not able to give, and who did give, better dinners than himself. The doctor's face, however, in spite of his slinging and ungainly person, was upon the whole rather good. His double chin, and the full, rosy expression of his lips and mouth, betokened, at the very least, the force of luxurious habits, and, as a hedge school-master of our acquaintance used to say, the smallest taste in life of voluptuosity; whilst from his black, twinkling eyes, that seemed always as if they were about to herald a jest, broke forth, especially when he conversed with the softer sex, something which might be considered as holding a position between a laugh and a leer. Such was the Rev. Jeremiah Turbot ...

3.

'A Most Religious Contention'
from *Valentine M'Clutchy* (1845)

IN SUCH ECCENTRIC speculations did Bob amuse himself, until, in consequence of the rapid pace at which he went, he overtook a fellow-traveller, who turned out to be no other than our friend Darby O'Drive. There was, in fact, considering the peculiar character of these two converts, something irresistibly comic in this encounter. Bob knew little or nothing of the Roman Catholic creed; and, as for Darby, we need not say that he was thoroughly ignorant of Protestantism. Yet, nothing could be more certain—if one could judge by the fierce controversial cock of Bob's hat, and the sneering contemptuous expression of Darby's face, that a hard battle, touching the safest way of salvation, was about to be fought between them. Bob, indeed, had of late been anxious to meet Darby, in order, as he said, to make him "show the cloven foot, the rascal;" but Darby's ire against the priest was now up; and besides, he reflected that a display of some kind would recommend him to the Reformationists, especially, he hoped, to Mr. Lucre, who, he was resolved, should hear it. The two converts looked at each other with no charitable aspect. Darby was about to speak, but Bob, who thought there was not a moment to be lost, gave him a controversial facer before he had time to utter a word:—"How many articles in your church?"

"How many articles in my church! There's one bad one in *your* church more than ought to be in it, since they got *you*:—but can you tell me how many sins cry to heaven for vingeance on you, you poor lost hathen?"

"Don't hathen me, you had betther; but answer my question, you rascally heretic."

"Heretic, inagh! oh, thin, is it from a barefaced idolather like you that we hear heretic called to us! Faith, it's come to a purty time o'day wid us!"

"You're a blessed convart not to know the forty-nine articles of your fat establishment!"

"And I'll hould a wager that you don't know this minute how many saikerments in your idolathry. Oh, what a swaggerin' Catholic you are, you poor hair-brained vagabone!"

"I believe you found some convincin' texts in the big purse of the bible blackguards—do you smell that, Darby?"

"You have a full purse, they say; but, by the time Father M'Cabe takes the price of your transgressions out of it—as he won't fail to do—take my word for it, it'll be as lank as a stocking without a leg in it—do you smell that, Bob, ahagur?"

"Where was your church before the Reformation?"

"Where was your face before it was washed?"

"Do you know the four pillars that your Church rests upon?

because if you don't, I'll tell you—it was Harry the aigth, Martin Luther, the Law, and the Devil. Put that in your pipe and smoke it. Ah, what a purty boy you are, and what a deludin' face you've got!"

"So the priest's doin' you—he's the very man can pluck a fat goose, Bob."

"Don't talk of pluckin' geese—you have taken some feathers out o' the bible blades, by all accounts. How do you expect to be saved by joinin' an open heresy?"

"Whisht, you hathen, that has taken to idolathry bekase Father M'Cabe made an ass of you by a thrick that every one knows. But I tell you to your brazen face, that you'll be worse yet than ever you were."

"You disgraced your family by turnin' apostate, and we know what for. Little Solomon, the greatest rogue unhanged, gave you the only grace you got or ever will get."

"Why, you poor turncoat, isn't the whole country laughin' at you, and none more than your old friends. The great fightin' Orangeman and blood-hound turned voteen!—oh, are we alive afther that!"

"The blaguard bailiff and swindler turned swaddler, hopin' to get a fatter cut from the bible blades, oh!"

"Have you your bades about you? if you have, I'll throuble you to give us a touch of your Padareen Partha. Orange Bob at his Padareen Partha! ha, ha, ha!"

"You know much about Protestantism. Blow me, but it's a sin to see such a knavish scoundrel professing it."

"It's a greater sin, you orange omadhawn, to see the likes o' you disgracin' the bades an' the blessed religion you tuck an you."

"You were no disgrace, then, to the one you left; but you are a burnin' scandal to the one you joined, and they ought to kick you out of it."

In fact, both converts, in the bitterness of their hatred, were beginning to forget the new characters they had to support, and to glide back unconsciously, or, we should rather say, by the force of their conscience, to their original creeds.

"If Father M'Cabe was wise he'd send you to the heretics again."

"If the Protestants regarded their own character, and the decency of their religion, they'd send you back to your cursed Popery, where you ought to be."

"It's no beef atin' creed, any way," said Darby, who had, without knowing it, become once more a staunch Papist, "ours isn't."

"It's one of knavery and roguery," replied Bob; "sure devil a thing one of you knows only to believe in your Pope."

"You'd bether not abuse the Pope," said Darby, "for fraid I'd give you a touch o' your ould complaint, the fallin' sickness, you know, wid my fist."

"Two could play at that game, Darby, and I say, to hell with him—and the priests are all knaves and rogues, every one of them."

"Are they, faith," said Darby, "here's an answer for that, any how."

"Text for text, you Popish rascal."

A fierce battle took place on the open highway, which was fought with intense bitterness on both sides. The contest, which was pretty equal, might, however, have been terminated by the defeat of one of them, had they been permitted to fight without support on either side; this, however, was not to be. A tolerably large crowd, composed of an equal number of Catholics and Protestants, collected from the adjoining fields, where they had been at labour, immediately joined them. Their appearance, unhappily, had only the effect of renewing the battle. The Catholics, ignorant of the turn which the controversy had taken, supported Bob and Protestantism; whilst the Protestants, owing to a similar mistake, fought like devils for Darby and the Pope. A pretty smart skirmish, in fact, which lasted more than twenty minutes, took place between the parties, and were it not that their wives, sisters, daughters, and mothers, assisted by many who were more peaceably disposed, threw themselves between them, it might have been much more serious than it was. If the weapons of warfare ceased, however, so did not their tongues; there was abundance of rustic controversy exchanged between them, that is to say, polemical scurrility much of the same enlightened character, as that in the preceding dialogue. The fact of the two parties, too, that came to their assistance, having mistaken the proper grounds of the quarrel, reduced Darby and Bob to the necessity of retracing their steps, and hoisting once more their new colours, otherwise their respective friends, had they discovered the blunder they had committed, would, unquestionably, have fought the battle a second time, on its proper merits. Bob, escorted by his Catholic friends, who shouted and hurraed as they went along, proceeded to Father M'Cabe's; whilst Darby and his adherents, following their example, went towards M'Clutchy's, and having left him within sight of Constitution Cottage, they returned to their labour.

4.

'Wildgoose Lodge' from *Traits and Stories of the Irish Peasantry,* Vol 2 (1833)

I HAD READ the anonymous summons, but from its general import, I believed it to be one of those special meetings convened for some purpose affecting the usual objects and proceedings of the body; at least the terms in which it was conveyed to me had nothing extraordinary or mysterious in them, beyond the simple fact, that it was not to be a general but a select meeting: this mark of confidence flattered me, and I determined to attend punctually. I was, it is true, desired to keep the circumstance entirely to myself, but there was nothing startling in this, for I had often received summonses of a similar nature. I therefore resolved to attend, according to the letter of my instructions, "on the next night, at the solemn hour of midnight, to deliberate and act upon such matters as should then and there be submitted to my consideration." The morning after I received this message, I arose and resumed my usual occupations; but, from whatever cause it may have proceeded, I felt a sense of approaching evil hanging heavily upon me: the beats of my pulse were languid, and an undefinable feeling of anxiety pervaded my whole spirit; even my face was pale, and my eye so heavy, that my father and brothers concluded me to be ill; an opinion which I thought at the time to be correct, for I felt exactly that kind of depression which precedes a severe fever. I could not understand what I experienced, nor can I yet, except by supposing that there is in human nature some mysterious faculty, by which, in coming calamities, the dread of some fearful evil is anticipated, and that it is possible to catch a dark presentiment of the sensations which they subsequently produce. For my part I can neither analyse nor define it; but on that day I knew it by painful experience, and so have a thousand others in similar circumstances.

It was about the middle of winter. The day was gloomy and tempestuous almost beyond any other that I can remember: dark clouds rolled over the hills about me, and a close sleet-like rain fell in slanting drifts that chased each other rapidly towards the earth on the course of the blast. The outlying cattle sought the closest and calmest corners of the fields for shelter; the trees and young groves were tossed about, for the wind was so unusually high that it swept in hollow gusts through them, with that hoarse murmur which deepens so powerfully on the mind the sense of dreariness and desolation.

As the shades of night fell, the storm, if possible, increased. The moon was half gone, and only a few stars were visible by glimpses, as a rush of wind left a temporary opening in the sky. I had determined, if the storm should not abate, to incur any penalty rather than attend the meeting; but the appointed hour was distant, and I resolved to be decided by the future state of the night.

Ten o'clock came, but still there was no change; eleven passed, and on opening the door to observe if there were any likelihood of its clearing up, a blast of wind, mingled with rain, nearly blew me off my feet. At length it was approaching to the hour of midnight; and on examining it a third time, I found that it had calmed a little, and no longer rained.

I instantly got my oak stick, muffled myself in my great coat, strapped my hat about my ears, and, as the place of meeting was only a quarter of a mile distant, I presently set out.

The appearance of the heavens was lowering and angry, particularly in that point where the light of the moon fell against the clouds, from a seeming chasm in them, through which alone she was visible. The edges of this chasm were faintly bronzed, but the dense body of the masses that hung piled on each side of her, was black and impenetrable to sight. In no other point of the heavens was there any part of the sky visible; a deep veil of clouds overhung the whole horizon, yet was the light sufficient to give occasional glimpses of the rapid shifting which took place in this dark canopy, and of the tempestuous agitation with which the midnight storm swept to and fro beneath it.

At length I arrived at a long slated house, situated in a solitary part of the neighbourhood; a little below it ran a small stream, which was now swollen above its banks, and rushing with mimic roar over the flat meadows beside it. The appearance of the bare slated building in such a night was particularly sombre, and to those, like me, who knew the purpose to which it was usually devoted, it was or ought to have been peculiarly so. There it stood, silent and gloomy, without any appearance of human life or enjoyment about or within it. As I approached, the moon once more had broken out of the clouds, and shone dimly upon the wet, glittering slates and windows, with a death-like lustre, that gradually faded away as I left the point of observation, and entered the folding-door. It was the parish chapel.

The scene which presented itself here was in keeping not only with the external appearance of the house, but with the darkness, the storm, and the hour, which was now a little after midnight. About forty persons were sitting in dead silence upon the circular steps of the altar. They did not seem to move; and as I entered and advanced, the echo of my footsteps rang through the building with a lonely distinctness, which added to the solemnity and mystery of the circumstances about me. The windows were secured with shutters on the inside, and on the altar a candle was lighted, which burned dimly amid the surrounding darkness, and lengthened the shadow of the altar itself, and those of six or seven persons who *stood* on its upper steps, until they mingled in the obscurity which shrouded the lower end of the chapel. The faces of the men who *sat* on the altar steps were not distinctly visible, yet their prominent and more characteristic features were in sufficient relief, and I observed, that some of the most malignant and reckless spirits in the parish were assembled. In the eyes of those who stood at the altar, and whom I knew to be invested with authority over the others, I could perceive gleams of some latent and ferocious purpose, kindled, as I soon observed, into a fiercer expression of vengeance, the additional excitement of ardent spirits, with which they had stimulated themselves to a point of determination that mocked at the apprehension of all future responsibility, either in this world or the next.

The welcome which I received on joining them was far different from the boisterous good-humour that used to mark our greetings on other occasions: just a nod of the head from this or that person, on the part of those *who sat*, with a *ghud dhemur tha thu?* in a suppressed voice, even below a common whisper: but from the standing group, who were evidently the projectors of the enterprise, I received a convulsive grasp of the hand, accompanied by a fierce and desperate look, that seemed to search my eye and countenance, to try if I were a person likely to shrink from whatever they had resolved to execute. It is surprising to think of the powerful expression which a moment of intense interest or great danger is capable of giving to the eye, the features, and the slightest actions, especially in those whose station in society does not require them to constrain nature, by the force of social courtesies, into habits that conceal their natural emotions. None of the standing group spoke; but as each of them wrung my hand in silence, his eye was fixed on mine, with an expression of drunken confidence and secrecy, and an insolent determination not to be gainsaid without peril. If looks could be translated with certainty, they seemed to say, "We are bound upon a project of vengeance, and if *you* do *not* join us, remember that we *can* revenge." Along with this grasp, they did not forget to remind me of the common bond by which we were united, for each man gave me the secret grip of Ribbonism in a manner that made the joints of my fingers ache for some minutes afterwards.

There was one present, however—the highest in authority— whose actions and demeanour were calm and unexcited. He seemed to labour under no unusual influence whatever, but evinced a serenity so placid and philosophical, that I attributed the silence of the sitting group, and the restraint which curbed in the out-breaking of passions to those who *stood*, entirely to his presence. He was a schoolmaster, who taught his daily school in *that* chapel, and acted also, on Sunday, in the capacity of clerk to the priest—an excellent and amiable old man, who knew little of his illegal connexions and atrocious conduct.

When the ceremonies of brotherly recognition and friendship were past, the Captain (by which title I shall designate the last-mentioned person) stooped, and, raising a jar of whiskey on the corner of the altar, held a wine-glass to its neck, which he filled, and with a calm nod, handed it to me to drink. I shrunk back, with an instinctive horror, at the profanity of such an act, in the house, and on the altar of God, and peremptorily refused to taste the proffered draught. He smiled mildly at what he considered my superstition, and added quietly, and in a low voice, "You'll be wantin' it I'm thinkin', afther the wettin' you got."

"Wet or dry," said I.—

"Stop, man!" he replied, in the same tone; "spake low. But why wouldn't you take the whiskey? Sure there's as holy people to the fore as you: didn't they all take it? An' I wish we may never do worse nor dhrink a harmless glass o' whiskey, to keep the cowld out, any way."

"Well," said I, "I'll jist trust to God and the consequences, for the cowld, Paddy, ma bouchal; but a blessed dhrop of it won't be crossin' my lips, avick; so no more ghosther about it; dhrink it yourself, if you like. Maybe you want it as much as I do; wherein I've the patthern of a good big-coat upon me, so thick, your sowl, that if it was raining bullocks, dhrop wouldn't get undher the nap of it."

He gave me a calm but keen glance, as I spoke.

"Well, Jim," said he, "it's a good comrade you've got for the weather that's in it; but, in the mane time, to set you a dacent patthern, I'll just take this myself,"—saying which, with the jar still upon its side, and the fore finger of his left hand in its neck, he swallowed the spirits—"It's the first I dhrank to-night," he added, "nor would I dhrink it now, only to show you that I've heart an' spirit to do the thing that we're all bound an' sworn to, when the proper time comes;" after which he laid down the glass, and turned up the jar, with much coolness, upon the altar.

During our conversation, those who had been summoned to this mysterious meeting were pouring in fast; and as each person approached the altar, he received from one to two or three glasses of whiskey, according as he chose to limit himself; but, to do them justice, there were not a few of those present, who, in despite of their own desire, and the Captain's express invitation, refused to taste it in the house of God's worship. Such, however, as were scrupulous he afterwards recommended to take it on the outside of the chapel door, which they did, as, by that means, the sacrilege of the act was supposed to be evaded.

About one o'clock they were all assembled except six: at least so the Captain asserted, on looking at a written paper.

"Now, boys," says he, in the same low voice, "we are all present except the thraitors, whose names I am goin' to read to you; not that we are to count thim thraitors, till we know whether or not it was in their power to come. Any how, the night's terrible—but, boys, you're to know, that neither fire nor wather is to prevint you, when duly summoned to attind a meeting—particularly whin the summons is widout a name, as you have been told that there is always something of consequence to be done *thin*."

He read out the names of those who were absent, in order that the real causes of their absence might be ascertained, declaring that they would be dealt with accordingly. After this, with his usual caution, he shut and bolted the door, and having put the key in his pocket, ascended the steps of the altar, and for some time traversed the little platform from which the priest usually addresses the congregation.

Until this night I have never contemplated the man's countenance with any particular interest; but as he walked the platform, I had an opportunity of observing him more closely. He was slight in person, apparently not thirty; and, on a first view, appeared to have nothing remarkable in his dress or features. I, however, was not the only person whose eyes were fixed upon him at that moment; in fact, every one present observed him with equal interest, for hither to he had kept the object of the meeting perfectly secret, and of course we all felt anxious to know it. It was while he traversed the platform that I scrutinised his features with a hope, if possible, to glean from them some evidence of what was passing within him. I could, however, mark but little, and that little was at first rather from the intelligence which seemed to subsist between him and those whom I have already mentioned as *standing* against the altar, than from any indication of his own. Their gleaming eyes were fixed upon him with an intensity of savage and demon-like hope, which blazed out in flashes of malignant triumph, as upon turning, he threw a cool but rapid glance at them, to intimate the progress he was making in the subject to which he devoted the undivided energies of his mind. But in the course of his meditation, I could observe, on one or two occasions, a dark shadow come over his countenance, that contracted his brow into a deep furrow, and it was then, for the first time, that I saw the satanic expression of which his face, by a very slight motion of its muscles, was capable. His hands, during this silence, closed and opened convulsively; his eyes shot out two or three baleful glances, first to his confederates, and afterwards vacantly into the deep gloom of the lower part of the chapel; his teeth ground against each other, like those of a man whose revenge burns to reach a distant enemy and finally, after having wound himself up to a certain determination, his features relapsed into their original calm and undisturbed expression.

At this moment a loud laugh, having something supernatural in it, rang out wildly from the darkness of the chapel; he stopped, and putting his open hand over his brows, peered down into the gloom, and said calmly in Irish, "*Bee dhu husth; ba nihl anam inh:*—hold your tongue, it is not yet time."

Every eye was now directed to the same spot, but, in consequence of its distance from the dim light on the altar, none could perceive the person from whom the laugh proceeded. It was, by this time, near two o'clock in the morning.

He now stood for a few moments on the platform, and his chest heaved with a depth of anxiety equal to the difficulty of the design he wished to accomplish:

"Brothers," said he—"for we are all brothers—sworn upon all that's blessed an' holy, to obey whatever them that's over us, *manin' among ourselves*, wishes us to do—are you now ready, in the name of God, upon whose althar I stand, to fulfil your oaths?"

The words were scarcely uttered, when those who had *stood* beside the altar during the night, sprang from their places, and descending its steps rapidly, turned round, and raising their arms, exclaimed, "By all that's sacred an' holy, we're willin'."

In the meantime, those who *sat* upon the steps of the altar, rose, and followed the example of those who had just spoken, exclaimed after them, "To be sure—by all that's sacred an' holy, we're willin'."

"Now boys," said the Captain, "ar'n't ye big fools for your pains? an' one of ye doesn't know what I mane."

"You're our Captain," said one of those who had stood at the altar, "an' has yer ordhers from higher quarthers; of coorse, whatever ye command upon us we're bound to obey you in."

"Well," said he, smiling, "I only wanted to thry yez; an' by the

47

oath ye tuck, there's not a captain in the country has as good a right to be proud of his min as I have. Well, ye won't rue it, maybe, when the right time comes; and for that reason every one of ye must have a glass from the jar; thim that won't dhrink it *in* the chapel can dhrink it *widout*, an' here goes to open the door for them."

He then distributed another glass to every man who would accept it, and brought the jar afterwards to the chapel door, to satisfy the scruples of those who would not drink within. When this was performed, and all duly excited, he proceeded:—

"Now, brothers, you are solemnly sworn to obey me, and I'm sure there's no thraithur here that 'ud parjure himself for a thrifle; but I'm sworn to obey them that's above me, manin' still among ourselves; an' to show you that I don't scruple to do it, here goes!"

He then turned around, and taking the Missal between his hands placed it upon the altar. Hitherto every word was uttered in a low precautionary tone; but on grasping the book, he again turned round, and looking upon his confederates with the same satanic expression which marked his countenance before, he exclaimed, in a voice of deep determination, first kissing the book! "By this sacred an' holy book of God, I will perform the action which we have met this night to accomplish, be that what it may; an' this I swear upon God's book, an' God's althar!"

On concluding, he struck the book violently with his open hand, thereby occasioning a very loud report. At this moment the candle which burned before him went suddenly out, and the chapel was wrapped in pitchy darkness; the sound as if of rushing wings fell upon our ears, and fifty voices dwelt upon the last words of his oath with wild and supernatural tones, that seemed to echo and to mock what he had sworn. There was a pause, and an exclamation of horror from all present: but the Captain was too cool and steady to be disconcerted. He immediately groped about until he got the candle, and proceeding calmly to a remote corner of the chapel, took up a half-burned peat which lay there, and after some trouble, succeeded in lighting it again. He then explained what had taken place; which indeed was easily done, as the candle happened to be extinguished by a pigeon which sat directly above it. The chapel, I should have observed, was at this time, like many country chapels, unfinished inside, and the pigeons of a neighbouring dove-cot had built nests among the rafters of the unceiled roof; which circumstance also explained the rushing of the wings, for the birds had been affrighted by the sudden loudness of the noise. The mocking voices were nothing but the echoes, rendered naturally more awful by the scene, the mysterious object of the meeting, and the solemn hour of the night.

When the candle was again lighted, and these startling circumstances accounted for, the persons whose vengeance had been deepening more and more during the night, rushed to the altar in a body, where each, in a voice trembling with passionate eagerness, repeated the oath, and as every word was pronounced, the same echoes heightened the wildness of the horrible ceremony, by their long and unearthly tones. The countenances of these human tigers were livid with suppressed rage; their knit brows, compressed lips, and kindled eyes, fell under the dim light of the taper, with an expression calculated to sicken any heart not absolutely diabolical. As soon as this dreadful rite was completed, we were again startled by several loud bursts of laughter, which proceeded from the lower darkness of the chapel; and the Captain, on hearing them, turned to the place, and reflecting for a moment, said in Irish, "Gutsho nish, avohelhee—come hither now, boys."

A rush immediately took place from the corner in which they had secreted themselves all the night; and seven men appeared, whom we instantly recognised as brothers and cousins of certain persons who had been convicted, some time before, for breaking into the house of an honest poor man in the neighbourhood, from whom, after having treated him with barbarous violence, they took away such fire-arms as he kept for his own protection.

It was evidently not the Captain's intention to have produced these persons until the oath should have been generally taken, but the exulting mirth with which they enjoyed the success of his scheme betrayed them, and put him to the necessity of bringing them forward somewhat before the concerted moment.

The scene which now took place was beyond all power of description; peals of wild, fiend-like yells rang through the chapel, as the party which *stood* on the altar and that which had crouched in the darkness met; wringing of hands, leaping in triumph, striking of sticks and fire-arms against the ground and the altar itself, dancing and cracking of fingers, marked the triumph of some hellish determination. Even the Captain for a time was unable to restrain their fury; but, at length, he mounted the platform before the altar once more, and with a stamp of his foot, recalled their attention to himself and the matter in hand.

"Boys," said he, "enough of this, and too much; an' well for us it is that the chapel is in a lonely place, or our foolish noise might do us no good. Let thim that swore so manfully jist now, stand a one side, till the rest kiss the book one by one."

The proceedings, however, had by this time taken too fearful a shape for even the Captain to compel them to a blindfold oath; the first man he called flatly refused to answer, until he should hear the nature of the service that was required. This was echoed by the remainder, who, taking courage from the firmness of this person, declared generally that, until they first knew the business that they were to execute, none of them would take the oath. The Captain's lip quivered slightly, and his brow again became knit with the same hellish expression, which I have remarked gave him so much the appearance of an embodied fiend; but this speedily passed away, and was succeeded by a malignant sneer, in which lurked, if there ever did in a sneer, 'a laughing devil', calmly, determinedly atrocious.

"It wasn't worth yer whiles to refuse the oath," said he mildly, "for the truth is, I had next to nothing for yez to do. Not a hand, maybe, would have to *rise*, only jist to look on, an' if any resistance would be made, to show yourselves; yer numbers would soon make them see that resistance would be no use whatever in the present case. At all evints, the oath of *secresy must* be taken, or woe be to him that will refuse *that*; he won't know the day, nor the hour, nor the minute, when he'll be made a spatch-cock of."

He then turned round, and, placing his right hand on the Missal, swore, "In the presence of God, and before his holy altar, that whatever might take place that night he would keep secret, from man or mortal, except the priest, and that neither bribery, nor imprisonment, nor death, would wring it from his heart."

Having done this, he again struck the book violently, as if to confirm the energy with which he swore, and then calmly descending the steps, stood with a serene countenance, like a man conscious of having performed a good action. As this oath did not pledge those who refused to take the other to the perpetration of any specific crime, it was readily taken by all present.

Preparations were then made to execute what was intended: the half-burned turf was placed in a little pot; another glass of whiskey was distributed; and the door being locked by the Captain, who kept the key as parish clerk and schoolmaster, the crowd departed silently from the chapel.

The moment those who lay in the darkness, during the night, made their appearance at the altar, we knew at once the persons we were to visit; for, as I said before, they were related to the miscreants whom one of those persons had convicted, in consequence of their midnight attack upon himself and his family. The Captain's object in keeping them unseen was, that those present, not being aware of the duty about to be imposed on them, might have less hesitation about swearing to its fulfilment. Our conjectures were correct; for on leaving the chapel we directed our steps to the house in which this devoted man resided.

The night was still stormy, but without rain; it was rather dark, too, though not so as to prevent us from seeing the clouds careering swiftly through the air. The dense curtain which had overhung and obscured the horizon was now broken, and large sections of the sky were clear, and thinly studded with stars that looked dim and watery, as did indeed the whole firmament; for in some places black clouds were still visible, threatening a continuance of tempestuous weather. The road appeared washed and gravelly; every dike was full of yellow water; and every little rivulet and larger stream dashed its hoarse murmur in our ears; every blast, too, was cold, fierce, and wintry, sometimes driving us back to a stand still, and again, when a turn in the road would bring it in our backs, whirling us along for a few steps with involuntary rapidity. At length the fated dwelling place became visible, and a short consultation was held in a sheltered place, between the captain and the two parties who seemed so eager for its destruction. Their fire-arms were now loaded, and their bayonets and short pikes, the latter shod and pointed with iron, were also got ready. The live coal which was brought in the small pot had become extinguished; but to remedy this, two or three persons from a remote part of the county entered a cabin on the wayside, and, under pretence of lighting their own and their comrades' pipes, procured a coal of fire, for so they called a lighted turf. From the time we left the chapel until this moment a profound silence had been maintained, a circumstance which, when I considered the number of persons present, and the mysterious and dreaded object of their journey, had a most appalling effect upon my spirits.

At length we arrived within fifty perches of the house, walking in a compact body, and with as little noise as possible; but it seemed as if the very elements had conspired to frustrate our design, for on advancing within the shade of the farm-hedge, two or three persons found themselves up to the middle in water, and on stooping to ascertain more accurately the state of the place, we could see nothing but one immense sheet of it—spread like a lake over the meadows which surrounded the spot we wished to reach.

Fatal night! The very recollection of it, when associated with the fearful tempests of the elements, grows, if that were possible, yet more wild and revolting. Had we been engaged in any innocent or benevolent enterprise, there was something in our situation just then that had a touch of interest in it to a mind imbued with a relish for the savage beauties of nature. There we stood, about a hundred and thirty in number, our dark forms bent forward, peering into the dusky expanse of water, with its dim gleams of reflected light, broken by the weltering of the mimic waves into ten thousand fragments, whilst the few stars that overhung it in the firmament appeared to shoot through it in broken lines, and to be multiplied fifty-fold in the gloomy mirror on which we gazed.

Over us was a stormy sky, and around us a darkness through which we could only distinguish, in outline, the nearest objects, whilst the wild wind swept strongly and dismally upon us. When it was discovered that the common pathway to the house was inundated, we were about to abandon our object and return home. The Captain, however, stooped down low for a moment, and, almost closing his eyes, looked along the surface of the waters; and then, raising himself very calmly, said, in his usual quiet tone, "Ye needn't go back, boys, I've found a way; jist follow me."

He immediately took a more circuitous direction, by which we reached a causeway that had been raised for the purpose of giving a free passage to and from the house, during such inundations as the present. Along this we had advanced more than half way, when we discovered a breach in it, which, as afterwards appeared, had that night been made by the strength of the flood. This, by means of our sticks and pikes, we found to be about three feet deep, and eight yards broad. Again we were at a loss how to proceed, when the fertile brain of the Captain devised a method of crossing it.

"Boys," said he, "of coorse you've all played at leap-frog; very well, strip and go in, a dozen of you, lean one upon the back of another from this to the opposite bank, where one must stand facing the outside man, both their shoulders agin one another, that the outside man may be supported. Then *we* can creep over you, an' a dacent bridge you'll be, any way."

This was the work of only a few minutes, and in less than ten we were all safely over.

Merciful Heaven! how I sicken at the recollection of what is to follow!

On reaching the dry bank, we proceeded instantly, and in profound silence, to the house; the Captain divided us into companies, and then assigned to each division its proper station. The two parties who had been so vindictive all the night, he kept about himself; for of those who were present, they only were in his confidence, and knew his nefarious purpose; their number was about fifteen. Having made these dispositions, he, at the head of about five of them, approached the house on the windy side, for the fiend possessed a coolness which enabled him to seize upon every possible advantage. That he had combustibles about him was evident, for in less than fifteen minutes nearly one half of the house was enveloped in flames. On seeing this, the others rushed over to the spot where he and his gang were standing, and remonstrated earnestly, but in vain; the flames now burst forth with renewed violence, and as they flung their strong light upon the faces of the foremost group, I think hell itself could hardly present anything more satanic than their countenances, now worked up into a paroxysm of infernal triumph at their own revenge. The Captain's look had lost all its calmness, every feature started out into distinct malignity, the curve in his brow was very deep, and ran up to the root of his hair, dividing his face into two segments, that did not seem to have been designed for each other. His lips were half open, and the corners of his mouth a little brought back on each side, like those of a man expressing intense hatred and triumph over an enemy who is in the death-struggle under his grasp. His eyes blazed from beneath his knit eye-brows with a fire that seemed to be lighted up in the infernal pit itself. It is unnecessary, and only painful, to describe the rest of his gang; demons might have been proud of such horrible visages as they exhibited; for they worked under all the power of hatred, revenge, and joy; and these passions blended into one terrible scowl, enough almost to blast any human eye that would venture to look upon it.

When the others attempted to intercede for the lives of the inmates, there were at least fifteen guns and pistols levelled at them.

"Another word," said the Captain, "an' you're a corpse where you stand, or the first man who will dare to spake for them; no, no, it wasn't to spare them we came here. 'No mercy' is the pass-word for the night, an' by the sacred oath I swore beyant in the chapel, any one among yez that will attempt to show it, will find none at my hand. Surround the house, boys, I tell ye, I hear them stirring. 'No quarther—no mercy', is the ordher of the night."

Such was his command over these misguided creatures, that in an instant there was a ring around the house to prevent the escape of the unhappy inmates, should the raging element give them time to attempt it; for none present durst withdraw themselves from the scene, not only from an apprehension of the Captain's present vengeance, or that of his gang, but because they knew that even had they escaped, an early and certain death awaited them from a quarter against which they had no means of defence. The hour was now about half-past two o'clock. Scarcely had the last words escaped from the Captain's lips, when one of the windows of the house was broken, and a human head, having the hair in a blaze, was descried, apparently a woman's, if one might judge by the profusion of burning tresses, and the softness of the tones, notwithstanding that it called, or rather shrieked, aloud, for help and mercy. The only reply to this was the whoop from the Captain and his gang, of "No mercy—no mercy!" and that instant the former, and one of the latter, rushed to the spot, and ere the action could be perceived, the head was transfixed with a bayonet and a pike, both having entered it together. The word "mercy" was divided in her mouth; a short silence ensued, the head hung down on the window, but was instantly tossed back into the flames!

This action occasioned a cry of horror from all present, except the *gang* and their leader, which startled and enraged the latter so much, that he ran towards one of them, and had his bayonet, now reeking with the blood of its innocent victim, raised to plunge it into his body, when, dropping the point, he said in a piercing whisper, that hissed in the ears of all: "It's no use now, you know; if one's to hang, all will hang; so our safest way, you persave, is to lave none of them to tell the story. Ye *may* go now, if you wish; but it won't save a hair of your heads. You cowardly set! I knew if I had tould yez the sport, that none of you, except my own boys, would come, so I jist played a thrick upon you; but remember what you are sworn to, and stand to the oath ye tuck."

Unhappily, notwithstanding the wetness of the preceding weather, the materials of the house were extremely combustible; the whole dwelling was now one body of glowing flame, yet the shouts and shrieks within rose awfully above its crackling and the voice of the storm, for the wind once more blew in gusts, and with great violence. The doors and windows were all torn open, and such of those within as had escaped the flames rushed towards them, for the purpose of further escape, and of claiming mercy at the hands of their destroyers; but whenever they appeared, the unearthly cry of "NO MERCY" rung upon their ears for a moment, and for a moment only, for they were flung back at the points of the weapons which the demons had brought with them to make the work of vengeance more certain.

As yet there were many persons in the house, whose cry for life was strong as despair, and who clung to it with all the awakened powers of reason and instinct. The ear of man could hear nothing so strongly calculated to stifle the demon of cruelty and revenge within him, as the long and wailing shrieks which rose beyond the elements, in tones that were carried off rapidly upon the blast, until they died away in the darkness that lay behind the surrounding hills. Had not the house been in a solitary situation, and the hour the dead of night, any persons sleeping within a moderate distance must have heard them, for such a cry of sorrow rising into a yell of despair was almost sufficient to have awakened the dead. It was lost, however, upon the hearts and ears that heard it: to them, though in justice be it said, to only a comparatively few of them, it appeared as delightful as the tones of soft and entrancing music.

The claims of the surviving sufferers were now modified; they supplicated merely to suffer death by the weapons of their enemies; they were willing to bear that, provided they should be allowed to escape from the flames; but no—the horrors of the conflagration were calmly and malignantly gloried in by their merciless assassins, who deliberately flung them back into all their tortures. In the course of a few minutes a man appeared upon the side-wall of the house, nearly naked; his figure, as he stood against the sky in horrible relief, was so finished a picture of woebegone agony and supplication, that it is yet as distinct in my memory as if I were again present at the scene. Every muscle, now in motion by the powerful agitation of his sufferings, stood out upon his limbs and neck, giving him an appearance of desperate strength, to which by this time he must have been wrought up; the perspiration poured from his frame, and the veins and arteries of his neck were inflated to a surprising thickness. Every moment he looked down into the flames which were rising to where he stood; and as he looked, the indescribable horror which flitted over his features might have worked upon the devil himself to relent. His words were few:

"My child," said he, "is safe, she is an infant, a young crathur that never harmed you, nor any one—she is still safe. Your mothers, your wives, have young innocent childre like it. Oh, spare her, think for a moment that it's one of your own: spare it, as you hope to meet a just God, or if you don't, in mercy shoot me first—put an end to me, before I see her burned!"

The Captain approached him coolly and deliberately. "You'll prosecute no one now, you bloody informer," said he: "you'll convict no more boys for takin' an ould gun an' pistol from you, or for givin' you a neighbourly knock or two into the bargain."

Just then, from a window opposite him, proceeded the shrieks of a woman, who appeared at it, with the infant in her arms. She herself was almost scorched to death; but, with the presence of mind and humanity of her sex, she was about to put the little babe out of the window. The Captain noticed this, and, with characteristic atrocity, thrust, with a sharp bayonet, the little innocent, along with the person who endeavoured to rescue it, into the red flames, where they both perished. This was the work of an instant. Again he approached the man: "Your child is a coal now," said he, with deliberate mockery; "I pitched it in myself, on the point of this," - showing the weapon—"an' now is your turn,"—saying which, he clambered up, by the assistance of his gang, who stood with a front of pikes and bayonets bristling to receive the wretched man, should he attempt, in his despair, to throw himself from the wall. The Captain got up, and placing the point of his bayonet against his shoulder, flung him into the fiery element that raged behind him. He uttered one wild and terrific cry, as he fell back, and no more. After this nothing was heard but the crackling of the fire, and the rushing of the blast: all that had possessed life within were consumed, amounting to either eight or eleven persons.

When this was accomplished, those who took an active part in the murder, stood for some time about the conflagration; and as it threw its red light upon their fierce faces and rough persons, soiled as they now were with smoke and black streaks of ashes, the scene seemed to be changed to hell, the murderers to spirits of the damned, rejoicing over the arrival and the torture of some guilty soul. The faces of those who kept aloof from the slaughter were blanched to the whiteness of death: some of them fainted, and others were in such agitation that they were compelled to lean on their comrades. They became actually powerless with horror: yet to such a scene were they brought by the pernicious influence of Ribbonism.

It was only when the last victim went down, that the conflagration shot up into the air with most unbounded fury. The house was large, deeply thatched, and well furnished; and the broad red pyramid rose up with fearful magnificence towards the sky. Abstractly it had sublimity, but now it was associated with nothing in my mind but blood and terror. It was not, however, without a purpose that the Captain and his gang stood to contemplate its effect. "Boys," said he, "we had better be sartin that all's safe; who knows but there might be some of the sarpents crouchin' under a hape o' rubbish, to come out an' gibbet us to-morrow or next day: we had betther wait a while, anyhow, if it was only to see the blaze."

Just then the flames rose majestically to a surprising height. Our eyes followed their direction; and we perceived, for the first time, that the dark clouds above, together with the intermediate air, appeared to reflect back, or rather to have caught the red hue of the fire. The hills and country about us appeared with an alarming distinctiveness; but the most picturesque part of it was the effect of reflection of the blaze on the floods that spread over the surrounding plains. These, in fact, appeared to be one broad mass of liquid copper, for the motion of the breaking waters caught from the blaze of the high waving column, as reflected in them, a glaring light, which eddied, and rose, and fluctuated, as if the flood itself had been a lake of molten fire.

Fire, however, destroys rapidly. In a short time the flames sank—became weak and flickering -by and by, they shot out only in fits—the crackling of the timbers died away—the surrounding darkness deepened—and, ere long, the faint light was overpowered by the thick volumes of smoke that rose from the ruins of the house, and its murdered inhabitants.

"Now, boys," said the Captain, "all is safe—we may go. Remember, every man of you, what you've sworn this night, on the book an' altar of God—not a heretic Bible. If you perjure yourselves, you may hang us; but let me tell you, for your comfort, that if you do, there is them livin' that will take care the lase of your own lives will be but short."

After this we dispersed every man to his own home.

Reader,—not many months elapsed ere I saw the bodies of this Captain, whose name was Patrick Devaun, and all those who were actively concerned in the perpetration of this deed of horror, withering in the wind, where they hung gibbeted, near the scene of the nefarious villainy; and while I inwardly thanked heaven for my own narrow and almost undeserved escape, I thought in my heart how seldom, even in this world, justice fails to overtake the murderer, and to enforce the righteous judgment of God—that "whoso sheddeth man's blood, by man shall his blood be shed."

Author's Note

This tale of terror is, unfortunately, too true. The scene of hellish murder detailed in it lies at Wildgoose Lodge, in the county of Louth, within about four miles of Carrickmacross ... The name of the family burned in Wildgoose Lodge was Lynch. One of them had, shortly before this fatal night, prosecuted and convicted some of the neighbouring Ribbonmen, who visited him with severe marks of their displeasure, in consequence of his having refused to enrol himself as a member of their body... Both parties were Roman Catholics, and either twenty-five or twenty-eight of those who took an active part in the burning, were hanged and gibbeted in different parts of the county of Louth.

Chapter Two:
THE BLACK LAND

Preface

In his relentless anatomisation of the land question, Carleton went right to the heart of the 'condition of Ireland'. Well ahead of his time in campaigning for agrarian reform, he saw, courageously, the manifold evils resulting from the landlord system and from British policy in Ireland. It did not lead him to join O'Connell's clamour for repeal of the union, possibly because he recognised that a parliament in Dublin would not in and of itself bring about a reduction in rack-renting, forced emigration, agrarian violence and the repeated horror of famine.

Characteristically, he brought the issues home, delineating the impact of the system on a small local community, digressing to create a wider context, only to return to his microcosmic village. Carleton was arguably unique in his ability to register the relationship between policy and practice, between the general and the particular, between Dublin and Clogher, between local and national. He excoriated without apology the landed gentry who were his readers, he lectured his own people for their fecklessness, but most often he held his powder for the middlemen— the tithe proctors, bailiffs, agents and usurers who were of the people but exploited and betrayed them even more rapaciously than the landlords themselves. In turning his anger upon these engines of destruction, he was able to write with a knowledge not available to him in the depiction of the landlords themselves— always remote and unconvincing in Carleton because he knew them not.

But there is something else in Carleton's portrayal of these men; by singling out these pivotal figures he can bridge microcosm and macrocosm and thus create a powerful focus.

Skinadre and Valantine and Solomon M'Slime tower like

malign spirits over their novels; their evil influence determines mood and imagery so that they become archetypal, human and yet titanic, their hypocritical and vampirish greed plucking the heart out of the people.

But, as is so often the case with Carleton, there is a humorous side, albeit caustic and Carleton's version of Edgeworth's classic Castle Rackrent, The Squanders of Castle Squander, emerges as a far earthier and less sentimental critique of the profligate landlord dynasty. Carleton's often bruited contention that the 'lower orders' take their cue from those who rule them is demonstrated with well-observed sarcasm in the extracts given here.

Was it from Carleton's The Hungry Grass that Seamus Heaney learned the tradition of the propiating scattered crusts, or was it, as is more likely, that the image of famine was etched so deeply into the cultural memory of the people that the exact ritual recurs over time and space with chilling resonance?

Down in the ditch and take their fill,
Thankfully breaking timeless fasts;
Then, stretched on the faithless ground, spill
Libations of cold tea, scatter crusts.

—Seamus Heaney, 'At a Potato Digging'

Carleton himself did not invent the image, he was merely reflecting the custom that stretched back behind his own childhood. Famine, as he notes in The Black Prophet was no new thing. Writing in 1845 in the middle of that disaster, he documents the effects of the 1820s famine, knowing as he dedicates his book to Lord Russell in scorn and optimism, that the catastrophe could have been avoided. It did not take a prophet to forsee it. And it is notable that the sinister O'Donnell is remarkable, not for revelation but for subterfuge—for the covering up of guilt-ridden history. There may, after all, be a metaphorical logic in the superficially unconnected narratives of the book. The causes and the manifestations of famine had been hidden away; in 1845 the ghost began to quicken that would haunt over a century later the quiet potato gatherers in Heaney's field.

Emigration was for Carleton as tragic as it was avoidable. The *pain of his own transplantation from the lovely open valleys of Tyrone to the dirty backstreets of Dublin may well have furnished the particularly poignant tone which suffuses* The Emigrants of Ahadarra. *He was a strong family man and when his own daughters left for Canada, his sorrow extended to a more general disenchantment. The emigrants, for Carleton, do not leave willingly but are driven out and those who stay may expect little better treatment as we hear in one of his few published poems* Taedate Me Vitae. *The theme of inner exile registered in the poem was to become a major issue for later Irish writers, principally Yeats, Joyce and Patrick Kavanagh. Characteristically, however, there is always a lighter side to Carleton's view, as can be seen in his hilariously localised version of the Finn M'Coul legend.*

1.

'The Agent of Doom' from *Valentine M'Clutchy* (1845)

NO MAN POSSESSED the art of combining several motives under the simple guise of one act, with greater skill than M'Clutchy. For instance, he had now an opportunity of removing from the estate as many as possible of those whom he could not reckon on for political support. Thus would he, in the least suspicious manner, and in the very act of loyalty, occasion that quantity of disturbance just necessary to corroborate his representations to government— free the property from disaffected persons, whose consciences were proof against both his threats and promises—and prove to the world that Valentine M'Clutchy was the man to suppress disturbance, punish offenders, maintain peace, and, in short, exhibit precisely that loyal and truly Protestant spirit which the times require, and which, in the end, generally contrived to bring its own rewards along with it.

2.

'The Very Genius of Famine'
from *The Black Prophet* (1846)

THERE IS TO be found in Ireland, and, we presume, in all other countries, a class of hardened wretches, who look forward to a period of dearth as to one of great gain and advantage, and who contrive, by exercising the most heartless and diabolical principles, to make the sickness, famine, and general desolation which scourge their fellow-creatures, so many sources of successful extortion and rapacity, and consequently of gain to themselves. These are Country Misers or Money-lenders, who are remarkable for keeping meal until the arrival of what is termed a hard year, or a dear summer, when they sell it out at an enormous or usurious prices, and who, at all times, and under all circumstances, dispose of it only at terms dictated by their own griping spirit and the crying necessity of the unhappy purchasers.

The houses and places of such persons are always remarkable for a character in their owners of hard and severe saving, which at a first glance has the appearance of that rare virtue in our country, called frugality—a virtue which, upon a closer inspection, is found to be nothing with them but selfishness, sharpened up into the most unscrupulous avarice and penury. About half a mile from the Sullivan's, lived a remarkable man of this class, named Darby Skinadre. In appearance he was lank and sallow, with a long, thin, parched looking face, and a miserable crop of yellow beard, which no one could pronounce as anything else than 'a dead failure;' added to this were two piercing ferret eyes, always sore and with a tear standing in each, or trickling down his fleshless cheeks; so that, to persons disposed to judge only by appearances, he looked very like a man in a state of perpetual repentance for his transgressions, or, what was still farther from the truth, who felt a most Christian sympathy with the distresses of the poor. In his house, and about it, there was much to mark the habits of the saving man. Everything was neat and clean, not so much from an innate love of neatness and cleanliness, as because these qualities were economical in themselves. His ploughs and farming implements were all snugly laid up, and covered, lest they might be injured by exposure to the weather; and his house was filled with large chests and wooden hogsheads, trampled hard with oatmeal, which, as they were never opened unless during a time of famine, had their joints and crevices festooned by innumerable mealy-looking cobwebs, which description of ornament extended to the dresser itself, where they might be seen upon most of the cold-looking shelves, and those neglected utensils, that in other families are mostly used for food. His haggard was also remarkable for having in it, throughout all the year, a remaining stack or two of oats or wheat, or perhaps one or two large ricks of hay, tanned by the sun of two or three summers into tawny hue—each or all kept in the hope of a failure and famine. In a room from the kitchen, he had a beam, a pair of scales, and a set of weights, all of which would have been vastly improved by a visit from the lord-mayor, had our meal-monger lived under the jurisdiction of that civic gentleman. He was seldom known to use metal weights when disposing of his property; in lieu of these he always used round stones, which, upon the principle of the Scottish proverb, that 'many a little makes a muckle,' he must have found a very beneficial mode of transacting business.

If anything could add to the iniquity of his principles, as a plausible but most unscrupulous cheat, it was the hypocritical prostitution of the sacred name and character of religion to his own fraudulent impositions upon the poor and the distressed. Outwardly, and to the eye of men, he was proverbially strict and scrupulous in the observation of its sanctions, but outrageously severe and unsparing upon all who appeared to be influenced either by a negligent or worldly spirit, or who omitted the least tittle of its forms. Religion and its duties, therefore, were perpetually in his mouth but never with such apparent zeal and sincerity as when enforcing his most heartless and hypocritical exactions upon the honest and struggling creatures whom necessity or neglect had driven into his meshes.

Such was Darby Skinadre; and certain we are that the truth of the likeness we have given of him will be at once recognised by our readers as that of the roguish hypocrite, whose rapacity is the standing curse of half the villages of the country, especially during the seasons of distress, or failure of crops.

Skinadre on the day we write of, was reaping a rich harvest from the miseries of the unhappy people. In a lower room of his house, to the right of the kitchen as you entered it, he stood over the scales, weighing out with a dishonest and parsimonious hand, the scanty pittance which poverty enabled the wretched creatures to purchase from him; and in order to give them a favourable impression of his piety, and consequently of his justice, he had placed against the wall a delf crucifix, with a semi-circular receptacle at the bottom of it for holding holy water.

This was as much as to say "how could I cheat you, with the image of our Blessed Redeemer before my eyes to remind me of my duty, and to teach me, as He did, to love my fellow creatures?" And with many of the simple people, he actually succeeded in making the impression he wished; for they could not conceive it possible, that any principle, however rapacious, could drive a man to the practice of such sacrilegious imposture.

There stood Skinadre, like the very Genius of Famine, surrounded by distress, raggedness, feeble hunger, and tottering disease, in all the various aspects of pitiable suffering, hopeless desolation, and that agony of the heart which impresses wildness upon the pale cheek, makes the eye at once dull and eager, parches the mouth and gives to the voice of misery tones that are hoarse and hollow. There he stood, striving to blend consolation with deceit, and in the name of religion and charity subjecting the helpless wretches to fraud and extortion. Around him was misery, multiplied into all her most appalling shapes. Fathers of families were there, who could read in each other's faces too truly the gloom and anguish that darkened the brow and wrung the heart. The strong man, who had been not long before a comfortable farmer, now stood dejected and apparently broken down, shorn of his strength, without a trace of either hope or spirit; so woefully shrunk away too, from his superfluous apparel, that the spectators actually wondered to think that this was the large man, of such powerful frame, whose feats of strength had so often heretofore filled them with amazement. But, alas! what will not sickness and hunger do?

There too was the aged man—the grand-sire himself—bent

with a double weight of years and sorrow—without food until that late hour; forgetting the old pride that never stooped before, and now coming with the last feeble argument, to remind the usurer that he and his father had been schoolfellows and friends, and that although he had refused to credit his son and afterwards his daughter-in-law, still, for the sake of old times, and of those who were now no more, he hoped he would not refuse his gray hairs and tears, and for the sake of the living God besides, that which would keep his son, and daughter-in-law, and his famishing grandchildren, who had not a morsel to put in their mouths, nor the means of procuring it on earth—if *he* failed them.

And there was the widower, on behalf of his motherless children, coming with his worn and desolate look of sorrow, almost thankful to God that his Kathleen was not permitted to witness the many-shaped miseries of this woeful year; and yet experiencing the sharp and bitter reflection that now, in all their trials—in his poor children's want and sickness—in their moanings by day and their cries for her by night, they have not the soft affection of her voice nor the tender touch of her hand to soothe their pain—nor has he that smile, which was ever his, to solace him now, nor that faithful heart to soothe him with its affection, or to cast its sweetness into the bitter cup of affliction. Alas! no; he knows that her heart will beat for him and them no more; that the eye of love will never smile upon them again; and so he feels the agony of her loss superadded to all his other sufferings, and in this state he approaches the merciless usurer.

And the widow—emblem of desolation and dependence—how shall *she* meet and battle with the calamities of this fearful season? She out of whose heart these very calamities draw forth the remembrances of him she has lost, with such vividness that his past virtues are added to her present sufferings; and his manly love as a husband—his tenderness as a parent—his protecting hand and ever kind heart, crush her solitary spirit by their memory, and drag it down to the utmost depths of affliction.

It is impossible, however, to describe the various aspects and claims of misery which presented themselves at Skinadre's house. The poor people flitted to and fro silently and dejectedly, wasted, feeble, and sickly—sometimes in small groups of twos and threes, and sometimes a solitary individual might be seen hastening with earnest but languid speed, as if the life of some dear child or beloved parent, of a husband or wife, or perhaps, the lives of the whole family, depended upon his or her arrival with food.

3.

'Taedet Me Vitae'* from *The Nation* (1854)

WRITTEN ON CHRISTMAS Eve, upon the occasion of the third of my daughters having emigrated with her husband to Canada to join her two sisters, already there.

(This poem will be among the most memorable ever published in *The Nation*. We fear it heralds an event that will be a reproach to Ireland, while the poverty of Burns, or the imprisonment of Tarso, are remembered against their people. Death and exile have stripped us bare of nearly all who will be remembered by posterity as belonging to this generation; but the man of most undoubted genius, born in Ireland in the 19th Century seemed still destined to live and die amongst us. Alas! even he is turning his eyes to a foreign shore.)

> Life's mysteries oppress me now—
> They wring my heart, they cloud my brow;
> My lonely spirit wails in vain—
> And I am sunk in grief and pain.
>   Taedet me vitae.

> Beloved ones, now that you are gone—
> The props my heart should lean upon—
> I feel the desert life I lead
> Approaching to the grave with speed.
>   Taedet me vitae.

---

* I am weary of life

For I had hoped to have you near
When I grew old and sad and sore—
To feel the whisperings of your breath
Pour sunshine on my bed of death.
                    Taedet me vitae.

But now the broad Atlantic rolls
Between us—between our souls—
For our affections, far more wide,
Can stretch beyond its giant tide.
                    Taedet me vitae.

Yet still the sad reflections press
On my bruised heart with dark distress—
A father's bitter sorrow fears
His grave will never have your tears.
                    Taedet me vitae.

I ask my memory, but in vain,
To find a fault—to find a stain
(It is but sorrow's selfish art)
To stay those wrenchings of the heart.
                    Taedet me vitae.

Yes, 'tis in vain, for when I look
O'er your young lives as in a book,
In their pure pages I can see
No record but your love for me.
                    Taedet me vitae.

Your love for two?—for sister, brother,
But dearer still, that Idol Mother,
Whose secret sorrow gives no sign,
Though tenderer, deeper still, than mine.
                    Taedet me vitae.

I look upon your vacant chairs—
I ask for *my* old *native* airs-
Airs ever heard with tearful eye—

Their music strings make no reply.
                    Taedet me vitae.

The memories of the coming Day,
Entwined with you now far away,
Will make, through all our future years,
To morrow's feast, "a Feast of Tears".
                    Taedet me vitae.

But no—my mind is changed—my heart
Was never made to live apart
From those it loves—my dear ones, I
Will lay my bones beneath *your* sky.
                    Taedet me vitae.

Ungrateful country, I resign
The debt you owe to me and mine—
My sore neglect—your guilt and shame—
And fling you back *your curse of Fame.*
                    Taedet me vitae.

Pain stricken Banim, lying low,
In friendless agony of woe,
Has his sad statue duly carved—
Cold recompense to him you starved? *
                    Taedet me vitae.

And Griffin, master of the heart,
In nature powerful as in art,
His holy path in gladness trod,

---

* Banim, for several years before his death, in consequence of a spine complaint, had
altogether lost the use of his lower limbs. He had, it is true, a poor pension from the
British government—and it was well for him that he had it. It is true that his affectionate
brother, Michael Banim—a man, it is said equally gifted—would not have have seen
him and his starve. But, suppose he had not had that miserable pension, nor that
affectionate brother—we dare not put the question—for we know what the melancholy
reply must be. His works are thoroughly Irish—all written in behalf of his country, and
full of the greatest originality and power.

From your ingratitude to God. *
                    Taedet me vitae.

For me, I scorn your love or hate—
I hold myself within my fate;
And, by a father's sacred vow,
My children are my country now.
                    Taedet me vitae.

I'll track them o'er the Atlantic wave;
Their tears shall consecrate my grave—
My heart will feel a brighter day,
And I again will never say,
                    Taedet me vitae.

4.

'The Cook's Norration'
from *The Squanders of Castle Squander*, Vol. 1 (1852)

"PLAISE YOUR HONOUR," replied the spokesman, throwing back his right foot, as if he were kicking at some one behind him, and attempting to bow—"you see the way of it is this—it dewolves upon me to state the full and satisfactory grievances of our whole party. My tongue, your honour, being smooth and oily, I undertake the task in a spirit of Tipperary independince, which is never to be afraid of stating your complaint to your oppressor behind his back; because you see that is always the manliest and most courageous coorse, especially when you're not afeard of layin' down the rights and wrongs of your purlimenary: ahem! Now, sir,

---

* Gerald Griffin stood on the pedestal with Banim. If weighted in opposite scales, a feather would turn the balance. Griffin's *Collegians* is, in the opinion of the writer of the above lines, one of the greatest, if not the greatest, Irish novel that ever was written. Yet, our judgment staggers when we think of 'Crofters of the Billhook'. Griffin's poems are exquisitely beautiful, and flow with such tenderness as we can scarcely find in any other Irish poetry. He took refuge, from a country that was unworthy of him, in a monastery in Cork, where he died prematurely of fever.

remimber that God—blessed be his name—has gifted you wid a concatenation of sich sarwints as not three noblemin in the land could be proud of (hear, hear), and that's a blessin', sir, for which you ought to go down upon your two knees—if it was only for the novelty of the thing—and be grateful, by offering up fifteen pathers, fifteen aves, and a creed to the Blessed Virgin, in ordher that the grease o'God might come down on you and make you duly thankful. I don't boast of my own religious gifts, although, God be praised for it, I'm nineteen stone weight, and a bad cook was never known to be fat, your honour, but is always the picture of hunger, and becoomze a libel on his purfission, glory be to God! ahem! The Lord knows, I never thought to see the day that your honest and respectable sarwints should be forced to tax you wid ongratitude, or feel ashamed of bein' in your employment (hear, hear). But whin a gintleman forgets the honour and respect that is due to his own sarwints, it's no wondher that he should forget himself as a punishment from Heaven for sich desate."

"Why, you confounded scoundrel, what have you to complain of?" asked his master, who, however, had now recovered his temper, and enjoyed the thing very much.

"Excuse me, sir," replied the cook, "I can answer no questions of that kind till I finish my norration; and it isn't fair, sir, to come acrass me that way—it's like burnin' me at the one side. No, sir, turn me round properly, and give me a fair advantage of the fire (Lord, how hot it is! I think I'm beginnin' to drip already)."

"Well," replied his master, "proceed with your grievances—go on with your 'norration'".

"I will, sir, but I must do so successfully (successively). You wouldn't have me roast a goose wid his feathers an him: no, sir, he must first be plucked."

"Egad! and you have plucked me to some purpose among you."

"He must first be plucked, then drawn, then skivered, and then spitted."

"By h—s, you scoundrels, you have put me through the whole process."

"Sir, we don't care a *traneen* about ourselves; we could ate burdock or nettle-tops, or parallelograms for that matter; but you forget that we have your *reputaytion* to look to; and that your name and fame in the country depinds upon uz. What 'ud you be widout us? Whew! Not that! (*snapping his fingers*) not that, sir. You are nothing—you are nobody—worse than nothing—worse than nobody—widout your illegant and respectable establishment. Isn't that what you're judged by? *We* are Mr. Squanders, sir, and not *you*; and we can appale to your whole past life for the trewth of this."

This was replied to by an indignant start, followed by a deep groan.

"Go on, sir, go on, you rascal; I feel the truth of it."

"Yes, sir, you do; and every rascal feels the truth of it. *I* feel the truth of it, and many another rascal as well as ourselves feels the truth of it. The butcher, the baker, the grocer, the wine-merchant, and every other such rascal, feels the truth of it. (Lord, I'm choking.) Yes, sir; but in the mane time I must purceed and state our case. The tratement we have resaved of late, sir, is onsufferable to jinteel people, sich as we are."

"What have you to complain of, I say?" asked his master, "have you not plenty to eat and drink for so far?"

"Plinty to ate an' dhrink! heavenly Father! and is *that* the view you take of it! Plinty to ate an' dhrink! to be sure we have. Good mutton, good beef, good lamb, excellent vale. I grant it: but sure, not a delicacy we've had these two months, and divil resave the dhrop of wine, barrin' a couple dozen bottles of dirty port and sherry. Where's the claret gone to? and where's the brandy gone to? If you have a conscience, sir, I believe I am ticklin' it to some purpose."

"You are, you scoundrel."

"Yes, sir; and there's not a scoundrel of us all but could tickle it if we said what we might say. Sir, I could take it to my solemn affidavy, that during the two or three last months there hasn't been more than a dozen parties given in the kitchen. We can scarcely ax a friend, be the same male or faymale, (*ha, you villain! from the fat she-cook without*) and when we do, the best we can offer them is plain beef or mutton, and whiskey punch! Is it come to this? We, that had puddins and pies, and sweetmates, and the best of wines to trate our friends wid, to be brought down to plain beef and mutton, and whiskey punch! Who, I ask, could live upon such coorse fare as this? Why, it's puttin' us upon low diet, as if we were in an hospital. Sir, think of this! Look to the honour of your establishment; look to its credit. In the eye of the world, sir, the establishment is the man. (*Ahem! from Mr. Squander*). Look to our desolate condition, look to our grievances, but don't *redress* them, for anything dressed a second time isn't worth atin'. Put us, thin, sir, upon the ould scale of livin'; let us have our usual dilicacies— a good glass of wine—enable us to be hospitable, and to see our friends, both male and faymale, (*ha, you villain!*) as we used to do, and then everything will be right—a blessing which I wish you all *in nomine Domini*. Amen!" (*Hear, hear, and cheers*).

Having finished his 'norration', the conclusion of which was an imitation of Father Fogarty's sermons, the cook looked about him with great satisfaction; and Mr. Squander, who felt both amused, and at the same time conscience-stricken, by certain allusions made in it, scarcely knew whether he should laugh or be angry. His determination, however, had been made, and he accordingly addressed them as follows:—

"Ladies and gentlemen; you could not have selected a more successful advocate, in order to get at least two-thirds of you sent about your business, than the fat and eloquent gentleman, Mr. Pat Bradley, the cook there, whose 'norration', if I had been before undecided upon the subject, has decided me now. I am perfectly aware of your affection for me, and of my ingratitude for it. I am to thank you—or, indeed, rather I am to thank my own senseless extravagance—for having been robbed and fleeced without scruple or conscience, for years. I neither now, nor at any other time, ever required such an establishment, and were it not that I acceded to the wishes of others, I never would have kept such an unprincipled set of dishonest profligates about me. My eyes, however, are now open to the folly of it, and I have come to the fixed and unalterable determination of dismissing two-thirds of you."

"The mistress will stand by us," said the cook. "Three cheers for the mistress! She's a lady anyhow, and won't see herself left widout an establishment. She's a lord's daughter, too! Oh, sweet Jasus! to lave her widout one to attind to her! That I may never, but that takes the froth off the pot! What's come over you, sir? Take care it's not a fit you're gettin'."

"It is, Mr. Bradley, a fit I'm getting—a fit of common sense—a complaint that I have been very little troubled with during my whole life."

"You always had good health, sir, glory be to God! and war free from fits. May God remove this from you in the mane time! Two-thirds of us, sir?"

"Two-thirds of you; and as the ladies and gentlemen of my establishment have so far honoured you as to make you their spokesman on this occasion, I also will honour you so far as to make you trot first."

"Sweet Savier! Is it to turn me out to the elements, afther having got so fat in the family. Let *her*—Molly Crudden—sir, the *she* one, go," and he pointed with his left thumb over his shoulder towards his female assistant. Here a strong bustle was heard outside, and the huge ladle was seen sweeping round in the hall, like the wing of a windmill, accompanied by the words, "Oh, the desateful vagabone; let me at him, will yez? If your honour only knew the loads of all kinds of mate and dhrink that he gives to Mary Corrigan, in the village beyant."

"Never mind her, your honour, she has been plundhering you night and day. There's Patsey, the stable-boy, and she stuffs him like a Christmas turkey. Let *her* travel, sir, and keep me, who, as I said, got so fat in the family."

"Why, sirra! upon that argument she has a better claim to be retained than yourself; of the two, she's fatter."

But it's not wholesome fat, sir—not honest fat—not the fat of this family, that you and yours have a right to feel proud of. No, sir! it's foreign fat; for she's only three years here from England, and she was as fat the first day she came as she is this minute, but not half so lazy. In my own opinion, it's dropsy she has. It's a common complaint with her, sir—one that comes and goes like a spring tide, your honour; at laste it has been so, by all accounts."

A scene now took place which it would be difficult, if not impossible, to describe. Mr. Squander contrived to pit them one against another with such dexterity that, ere the lapse of many minutes, a series of bitter recrimination, abuse, and mutual charges of dishonesty and fraud took place, that perfectly astounded him. Dick and Harry were about to intercede, each for a favourite of the softer sex; but perceiving at once, from their father's determined manner, and the indignation into which this mutual disclosure of villany had thrown him, that the exertion of their influence would rather injure than serve their *protegées*, they prudently withdrew from the scene of broil, and declined to interfere. On finding that he was firm, the persons—and he pricked off their names from a list—set apart for dismissal now turned boldly round and demanded their wages. This took him somewhat aback.

"You shall have your wages," he replied—"you shall have every farthing due to you; but you must wait until I get a large note changed."

5.

'The Magic of Home'
—Fin M'Coul, the Knockmany Giant,
from *Tales and Sketches* (1845)

WHAT IRISH MAN, woman, or child, has not heard of our renowned Hibernian Hercules, the great and glorious Fin M'Coul? Not one, from Cape Clear to the Giant's Causeway, nor from that back again to Cape Clear. And by the way, speaking of the Giant's Causeway brings me at once to the beginning of my story. Well, it so happened that Fin and his gigantic relatives were all working at the Causeway, in order to make a bridge, or what was still better, a good stout pad-road, across to Scotland; when Fin, who was very fond of his wife Oonagh, took it into his head that he would go home and see how the poor woman got on in his absence. To be sure, Fin was a true Irishman, and so the sorrow thing in life brought him back, only to see that she was snug and comfortable, and, above all things, that she got her rest well at night; for he knew that the poor woman, when he was with her, used to be subject to nightly qualms, and configurations, that kept him very anxious, decent man, striving to keep her up to the good spirits and health that she had when they were first married. So, accordingly, he pulled up a fir tree, and, after lopping off the roots and branches, made a walking-stick of it, and set out on his way to Oonagh.

Oonagh, or rather Fin, lived at this time on the very tiptop of Knockmany Hill, which faces a cousin of its own, called Cullamore, that rises up, half-hill, half-mountain, on the opposite side—east-

east by south, as the sailors say, when they wish to puzzle a landsman.

Now the truth is, for it must come out, that honest Fin's affection for his wife, though cordial enough in itself, was by no manner or means the real cause of his journey home. There was at that time another giant named Cucullin—some say he was Irish, and some say he was Scotch; but whether Scotch or Irish, sorrow doubt of it but he was a *targer*. No other giant of the day could stand before him; and such was his strength, that, when well vexed, he could give a stamp that shook the country about him. The fame and name of him went far and near, and nothing in the shape of a man, it was said, had any chance with him in a fight. Whether the story is true or not, I cannot say, but the report went that, by one blow of his fist, he flattened a thunderbolt and kept it in his pocket in the shape of a pancake, to shew to his enemies when they were about to fight him. Undoubtedly he had given every giant in Ireland a considerable beating, barring Fin M'Coul himself; and he swore by the solemn contents of Moll Kelly's Primer, that he would never rest, day or night, winter or summer, till he would serve Fin with the same sauce, if he could catch him. Fin, however, who no doubt was cock of the walk on his own dunghill, had a strong disinclination to meet a giant who could make a young earthquake, or flatten a thunderbolt when he was angry; so he accordingly kept dodging about from place to place, not much to his credit as a Trojan to be sure, whenever he happened to get the hard word that Cucullin was on the scent of him. This, then, was the marrow of the whole movement, although he put it on his anxiety to see Oonagh, and I am not saying but there was some truth in that too. However, the short and the long of it was, with reverence be it spoken, that he heard Cucullin was coming to the Causeway to have a trial of strength with him; and he was naturally enough seized, in consequence, with a very warm and sudden fit of affection for his wife, poor woman, who was delicate in her health, and leading, besides, a very lonely uncomfortable life of it (he assured them), in his absence. He accordingly pulled up the fir-tree, as I said before, and having *snedded* it into a walking-stick, set out on his affectionate travels to see his darling Oonagh on the top of Knockmany, by the way.

In truth, to state the suspicions of the country at the time, the

75

people wondered very much why it was that Fin selected such a windy spot for his dwelling-house, and they even went so far as to tell him as much.

"What can you mane, Mr. M'Coul," said they, "by pitching your tent upon the top of Knockmany, where you never are without a breeze, day or night, winter or summer, and where you're often forced to take your nightcap without either going to bed or turning up your little finger; ay, an' where, besides, there's the sorrow's own want of water?"

"Why," said Fin, "ever since I was the height of a round tower, I was known to be fond of having a good prospect of my own; and where the dickens, neighbours, could I find a better spot for a good prospect than the top of Knockmany? As for water, I am sinking a pump, and, plase goodness, as soon as the Causeway's made, I intend to finish it."

Now, this was more of Fin's philosophy, for the real state of the case was that he pitched on the top of Knockmany in order that he might be able to see Cucullin coming towards the house, and, of course, that he himself might go to look after his distant transactions in other parts of the country, rather than—but no matter—we do not wish to be too hard on Fin. All we have to say is, that if he wanted a spot from which to keep a sharp look-out—and, between ourselves, he did want it grievously—barring Slieve Croob, or Slieve Donard, or its own cousin, Cullamore, he could not find a neater or more convenient situation for it in the sweet and sagacious province of Ulster.

"God save all here!" said Fin, good-humouredly, on putting his honest face into his own door.

"Musha Fin, avick, an' you're welcome home to your own Oonagh, you darlin' bully." Here followed a smack that is said to have made the waters of the lake at the bottom of the hill curl, as it were, with kindness and sympathy.

"Faith," said Fin, "beautiful; an' how are you, Oonagh—and how did you sport your figure during my absence, my bilberry?"

"Never merrier—as bouncing a grass widow as ever there was in sweet 'Tyrone among the bushes.'"

Fin gave a short good-humoured cough and laughed most heartily, to shew her how much he was delighted that she made herself happy in his absence.

"An' what brought you home so soon, Fin?" said she.

"Why, avourneen," said Fin, putting in his answer in the proper way, "never the thing but the purest love and affection for yourself. Sure you know that's truth, any how, Oonagh."

Fin spent two or three happy days with Oonagh, and felt himself very comfortable considering the dread he had of Cucullin. This, however, grew upon him so much that his wife could not but perceive that something lay on his mind which he kept altogether to himself. Let a woman alone in the meantime, for ferreting or wheedling a secret out of her good man, when she wishes. Fin was a proof of this.

"It's this Cucullin," said he, "that's troubling me. When the fellow gets angry, and begins to stamp, he'll shake you a whole townland; and it's well known that he can stop a thunderbolt, for he always carries one about him in the shape of a pancake, to shew to any one that might misdoubt it."

As he spoke, he clapped his thumb in his mouth, which he always did when he wanted to prophecy, or to know any thing that happened in his absence; and the wife, who knew what he did it for, said, very sweetly,

"Fin, darling, I hope you don't bite your thumb at me, dear?"

"No," said Fin; "but I bite my thumb, acushla," said he.

"Yes, jewel; but take care and don't drae blood," said she. "Ah, Fin! don't, my bully—don't."

"He's coming," said Fin; "I see him below Dungannon."

"Thank goodness, dear! an' who is it, avick? Glory be to God!"

"That baste Cucullin," replied Fin; "and how to manage I don't know. If I run away, I am disgraced; and I know that sooner or later I must meet him, for my thumb tells me so."

"When will he be here?" said she.

"To-morrow about two o'clock," replied Fin, with a groan.

"Well, my bully, don't be cast down," said Oonagh; "depend on me, and maybe I'll bring you better out of this scrape than ever you could bring yourself, by your rule o' thumb."

This quieted Fin's heart very much, for he knew that Oonagh was hand and glove with the fairies, and, indeed, to tell the truth, she was supposed to be a fairy herself. If she was, however, she must have been a kind-hearted one; for, by all accounts, she never did any thing but good in the neighbourhood.

Now, it so happened that Oonagh had a sister named Granua, living opposite them, on the very top of Cullamore, which I have mentioned already, and this Granua was quite as powerful as herself. The beautiful valley that lies between them is not more than about three or four miles broad, so that of a summer's evening Granua and Oonagh were able to hold many an agreeable conversation across it, form the one hill-top to the other. Upon this occasion, Oonagh resolved to consult her sister as to what was best to be done in the difficulty that surrounded them.

"Granua," said she, "are you at home?"

"No," said the other; "I'm picking bilberries in Althadhawan" (Anglicé, the Devil's Glen).

"Well," said Oonagh, "get up to the top of Cullamore, look about you, and tell us what you see."

"Very well," replied Granua, after a few minutes, "I am there now."

"What do you see?" asked the other.

"Goodness be about us!" exclaimed Granua, "I see the biggest giant that ever was known, coming up from Dungannon."

"Ay," said Oonagh, "there's our difficulty. That giant is the great Cucullin; and he's now coming up to leather Fin. What's to be done?"

I'll call to him," she replied, "to come up to Cullamore, and refresh himself, and maybe that will give you and Fin time to think of some plan to get yourself out of the scrape. But," she proceeded, "I'm short of butter, having in the house only half a dozen firkins, and as I'm to have a few giants and giantesses to spend the evenin' with me, I'd feel thankful, Oonagh, if you'd throw me up fifteen or sixteen tubs, or the largest miscaun you have got, and you'll oblige me very much."

"I'll do that with a heart and a half," replied Oonagh; "and, indeed, Granua, I feel myself under great obligations to you for your kindness in keeping him off us, till we see what can be done; for what would become of us all if any thing happened Fin, poor man?"

She accordingly got the largest miscaun of butter she had— which might be about the weight of a couple dozen millstones, so that you may easily judge of its size—and calling up to her sister, "Granua," said she, "are you ready? I'm going to throw you up a

78

miscaun, so be prepared to catch it."

"I will," said the other, "a good throw now, and take care it does not fall short."

Oonagh threw it; but in a consequence of her anxiety about Fin and Cucullin, she forgot to say the charm that was to send it up, so that, instead of reaching Cullamore, as she expected, it fell half between the two hills, at the edge of the Broad Bog near Augher.

"My curse upon you!" she exclaimed; "you've disgraced me. I now change you into a grey stone. Lie there as a testimony of what has happened; and may evil betide the first living man that will ever attempt to remove or injure you!"

And sure enough, there it lies to this day, with the mark of the four fingers and thumb imprinted in it, exactly as it came out of her hand.

"Never mind," said Granua; "I must only do the best I can with Cucullin. If all fail, I'll give him a cast of heather broth to keep the wind out of his stomach, or a panada of oak-bark to draw it in a bit; but, above all things, think of some plan to get Fin out of the scrape he's in, otherwise he's a lost man. You know you used to be sharp and ready-witted; and my opinion, Oonagh, is, that it will go hard with you, or you'll outdo Cucullin yet."

She then made a high smoke on the top of the hill, after which she put her finger in her mouth, and gave three whistles, and by that Cucullin knew he was invited to Cullamore—for this was the way that the Irish long ago gave a sign to all strangers and travellers, to let them know they were welcome to come and take share of whatever was going.

In the meantime, Fin was very melancholy, and did not know what to do, or how to act at all. Cucullin was an ugly customer, no doubt, to meet with; and, moreover, the idea of the confounded "cake," aforesaid, flattened the very heart within him. What chance could he have, strong and brave though he was, with a man who could, when put in a passion, walk the country into earthquakes and knock thunderbolts into pancakes? The thing was impossible; and Fin knew not on what hand to turn him. Right or left—backward or forward—where to go he could form no guess whatsoever.

"Oonagh," said he, "can you do nothing for me? Where's all your invention? Am I to be skivered like a rabbit before your eyes, and to have my name disgraced for ever in the sight of all my tribe, and me the best man among them? How am I to fight this man-mountain—this huge cross between an earthquake and a thunderbolt?—with a pancake in his pocket that was once—"

"Be easy, Fin," replied Oonagh; "troth I am ashamed of you. Keep your toe in your pump, will you? Talking of pancakes, maybe we'll give him as good as any he brings with him—thunderbolt or otherwise. If I don't treat him to as smart feeding as he's got this many a day, never trust Oonagh again. Leave him to me, and do just as I bid you."

This relieved Fin very much; for, after all, he had great confidence in his wife, knowing, and he did, that she had got him out of many a quandary before. The present, however, was the greatest of all; but still he began to get courage, and was able to eat his victuals as usual. Oonagh then drew the nine woollen threads of different colours, which she always did to find out the best way of succeeding in any thing of importance she went about. She then platted them into three plats with three colours in each, putting one to her right arm, one round her heart, and the third round her right ankle, for then she knew that nothing could fail with her that she undertook.

Having everything now prepared, she sent round to the neighbours and borrowed one-and-twenty cakes of bread, and these she baked on the fire in the usual way, setting them aside in the cupboard according as they were done. She then put down a large pot of new milk, which she made into curds and whey, and gave Fin due instruction how to use the curds when Cucullin should come. Having done all this, she sat down quite contented, waiting for his arrival on the next day about two o'clock, that being the hour at which he was expected—for Fin knew as much by the sucking of his thumb. Now this was a curious property that Fin's thumb had; but, notwithstanding all the wisdom and logic he used to suck out of it, it never could have stood to him were it not for the wit of his wife. In this very thing, moreover, he was very much resembled by his great foe Cucullin; for it was well known that the huge strength he possessed all lay in the middle finger of his right hand, and that, if he happened by any mischance to lose it, he was no more, notwithstanding his bulk, than a common man.

At length the next day, he was seen coming across the valley, and Oonagh knew that it was time to commence operations. She immediately made the cradle, and desired Fin to lie down in it, and cover himself up with the clothes.

"You must pass for your own child," said she, "so just lie there snug, and say nothing, but be guided by me." This, to be sure, was wormwood to Fin—I mean going into the cradle in such a cowardly manner—but he knew Oonagh well; and finding that he had nothing else for it, with a very rueful face he gathered himself into it, and lay snug as she had desired him.

About two o'clock, as he had been expected, Cucullin came in. "God save all here," said he; "is this where the great Fin M'Coul lives?"

"Indeed it is, honest man," replied Oonagh; "God save you kindly—won't you be sitting?"

"Thank you, ma'am," says he, sitting down; "you're Mrs. M'Coul, I suppose?"

"I am," said she; "and I have no reason, I hope, to be ashamed of my husband."

"No," said the other; "he has the name of being the strongest and bravest man in Ireland; but for all that, there's a man not far from you that's very desirous of taking a shake with him. Is he at home?"

"Why, then, no," she replied; "and if ever a man left his house in a fury, he did. It appears that some one told him of a big basthoon of a giant called Cucullin being down at the Causeway to look for him, and so he set out there to try if he could catch him. Troth, I hope, for the poor giant's sake, he won't meet him, for if he does, Fin will make paste of him at once."

"Well," said the other, "I am Cucullin, and I have been seeking him these twelve months, but he always kept clear of me; and I will never rest night or day till I lay my hands on him."

At this Oonagh set up a loud laugh, of great contempt, by the way, and looked at him as if he was only a mere handful of a man.

"Did you ever see Fin?" said she, changing her manner all at once.

"How could I?" said he; "he always took care to keep his distance."

"I thought so," she replied; "I judged as much; and if you take my advice, you poor-looking creature, you'll pray night and day that you may never see him, for I tell you it will be a black day for you when you do. But, in the meantime, you perceive that the wind's on the door, and as Fin himself is from home, maybe you'd be civil enough to turn the house, for it's always what Fin does when he's here."

This was a startler even to Cucullin; but he got up, however, and after pulling the middle finger of his right hand until it cracked three times, he went outside, and getting his arms about the house, completely turned it as she had wished. When Fin saw this, he felt a certain description of moisture, which shall be nameless, oozing through every pore of his skin; but Oonagh, depending upon her woman's wit, felt not a whit daunted.

"Arrah, then," said she, "as you are so civil maybe you'd do another obliging turn for us, as Fin's not here to do it himself. You see, after this long stretch of dry weather we've had, we feel very badly off for want of water. Now, Fin says there's a fine spring well somewhere under the rocks behind the hill here below, an' it was his intention to pull them asunder; but having heard of you, he left the place in such a fury, that he never thought of it. Now, if you try to find it, troth I'd feel it a kindness."

She then brought Cucullin down to see the place, which was then all one solid rock; and after looking at it for some time, he cracked his middle finger nine times, and stooping down, tore a cleft about four hundred feet deep, and a quarter of a mile long, which has since been christened by the name of Lumford's Glen. This feat nearly threw Oonagh herself off her guard; but what won't a woman's sagacity and presence of mind accomplish?

"You'll now come in," said she, "and eat a bit of such humble fare as we can give you. Fin, even although he and you are enemies, would scorn not to treat you kindly in his own house: and, indeed, if I didn't do it even in his absence, he would not be pleased with me."

She accordingly brought him in, and placing half a dozen of the cakes we spoke of before him, together with a can or two of butter, a side of boiled bacon, and a stack of cabbage, she desired him to help himself—for this, be it known, was long before the invention of potatoes. Cucullin, who, by the way, was a glutton as well as a hero, put one of the cakes in his mouth to take a huge whack out of it, when both Fin and Oonagh were stunned with a noise that resembled something between a growl and a yell. "Blood and fury!" he shouted; "how is this? Here are two of my teeth out! What kind of bread is this you gave me?"

"What's the matter?" said Oonagh coolly.

"Matter!" shouted the other again; "why, here are the two back teeth in my head gone!"

"Why," said she, "that's Fin's bread—the only bread he ever eats when at home; but, indeed, I forgot to tell you that nobody can eat it but himself, and that child in the cradle there. I thought, however, that as you were reported to be rather a stout little fellow of your size, you might be able to manage it, and I did not wish to affront a man that thinks himself able to fight Fin. Here's another cake—maybe it's not so hard as that."

Cucullin at the moment was not only hungry but ravenous, so he accordingly made a fresh set at the second cake, and immediately another yell was heard twice as loud as the first. "Thunder and giblets!" he roared, "take your bread out of this, or I will not have a tooth in my head; there's another pair of them gone!"

"Well, honest man," replied Oonagh, "if you're not able to eat the bread, say so quietly, and don't be wakening the child in the cradle here. There, now he's awake upon me."

Fin now gave a skirl that startled the giant, as coming from such a youngster as he was represented to be. "Mother," said he, "I'm hungry—get me something to eat." Oonagh went over, and putting into his hand a cake *that had no griddle in it*, Fin, whose appetite in the meantime was sharpened by what he saw going forward, soon made it disappear. Cucullin was thunderstruck, and secretly thanked his stars that he had the good fortune to miss meeting Fin, for, as he said to himself, I'd have no chance with a man who could eat such bread as that, which even his son that's but in his cradle can munch before my eyes.

"I'd like to take a glimpse at the lad in the cradle," said he to Oonagh; "for I can tell you that the infant who can manage that nutriment is no joke to look at, or to feed of a scarce summer."

"With all the veins of my heart," replied Oonagh. "Get up, acushla, and show this decent little man something that won't be unworthy of your father Fin M'Coul."

Fin, who was dressed for the occasion as much like a boy as possible, got up, and bringing Cucullin out— "Are you strong?" said he.

"Thunder an' ounds!" exclaimed the other, "what a voice in so small a chap!"

"Are you strong?" said Fin again; "are you able to squeeze water out of that white stone?" he asked, putting one into Cucullin's hand. The latter squeezed and squeezed the stone, but to no purpose: he might pull the rocks of Lumford's Glen asunder, and flatten a thunderbolt, but to squeeze water out of a white stone was beyond his strength. Fin eyed him with great contempt, as he kept straining and squeezing, and squeezing and straining, till he got black in the face with the efforts.

"Ah, you're a poor creature!" said Fin. "You a giant! Give me the stone here, and when I'll shew what Fin's little son can do, you may then judge of what my daddy himself is."

Fin then took the stone, and slyly exchanging it for the curds, he squeezed the latter until the whey, as clear as water, oozed out in a little shower from his hand.

I'll now go in," said he, "to my cradle; for I'd scorn to lose my time with any one that's not able to eat my daddy's bread, or squeeze water out of a stone. Bedad, you had better be off out of this before he comes back; for if he catches you, it's in flummery he'd have you in two minutes."

Cucullin, seeing what he had seen, was of the same opinion himself, his knees knocked together with the terror of Fin's return, and he accordingly hastened in to bid Oonagh farewell, and to assure her, that, from that day out, he never wished to hear of, much less to see, her husband. "I admit fairly that I'm not a match for him," said he, "strong as I am; tell him I will avoid him as I would the plague, and that I will make myself scarce in his part of the country while I live."

Fin, in the meantime, had gone into the cradle, where he lay very quietly, his heart in his mouth with delight that Cucullin was about to take his departure, without discovering the tricks that had been played off on him.

"It's well for you," said Oonagh, "that he doesn't happen to be here, for it's nothing but hawk's meat he'd make of you."

"I know that," says Cucullin; "divil a thing else he'd make of me; but before I go, will you let me feel what kind of teeth they are that can eat griddle-bread like *that?*"—and he pointed to it as he spoke.

"With all pleasure in life," said she, "only as they're far back in his head, you must put your finger a good way in."

Cucullin was surprised to find such a powerful set of grinders in one so young; but he was still much more so on finding, when he took his hand from Fin's mouth, that he had left the very finger upon which his whole strength depended, behind him. He gave one loud groan, and fell down at once with terror and weakness. This was all Fin wanted, who now knew that his most powerful and bitterest enemy was completely at his mercy. He instantly started out of the cradle, and in a few minutes the great Cucullin that was for such a length of time the terror of him and all his followers, lay a corpse before him. Thus did Fin, through the wit and invention of Oonagh, his wife, succeed in overcoming his enemy by stratagem, which he never could have done by force; and thus also is it proved that the women, if they bring us *into* many an unpleasant scrape, can sometimes succeed in getting us *out of* others that are as bad.

6.

'A Land Fit for Heroes'—Easel's Portrait from *Valentine M'Clutchy* (1845)

"I HAVE *AMUSED* myself—you will see how appropriate the word is by and by—since my last communication, in going over the whole Castle Cumber Estate, and noting down the traces which this irresponsible and rapacious oppressor, aided by his constables, bailiffs, and blood-hounds, have left behind them. When I describe the guide into whose hands I have committed myself, I am inclined to think you will not feel much disposed to compli-. ment me on my discretion; the aforesaid guide being no other than a young fellow, named *Raymond-na-Hattha*, which means, they tell me, Raymond of the Hats—a sobriquet very properly bestowed on him, in consequence of a habit he has of always wearing three or four hats at a time, one within the other—a circumstance which, joined to his extraordinary natural height, and great strength, gives him absolutely a gigantic appearance.

This Raymond is the fool of the parish; but in selecting him for my conductor, I acted under the advice of those who know him better than I could. There is not, in fact, a field, a farm-house, or a cottage, within a circumference of miles, which he does not know, and where he is not also known. Poor Raymond, notwithstanding his privation, is, however, exceedingly shrewd in many things, especially where he can make himself understood. As he speaks, however, in unconnected sentences, in which there is put forth no more than one phase of the subject he alludes to, or the idea he entertains, it is unquestionably not an easy task to understand him without an interpreter. He is singularly fond of children—very benevolent—and consequently feels a degree of hatred and horror at anything in the shape of cruelty or oppression, almost beyond belief, in a person deprived of reason. This morning he was with me by appointment, about half-past nine, and after getting his breakfast—but no matter—the manipulation he exhibited would have been death to a dispeptic patient, from sheer envy—we sallied forth to trace this man, M'Clutchy, by the awful marks of ruin, and tyranny, and persecution; for these words convey the principles of what he hath left, and is leaving behind him.

"'Now, Raymond,' said I, 'as you know the country well, I shall be guided by you. I wish to see a place called Drum Dhu. Can you conduct me there?'

"'Ay!' he replied with surprise; ' *Why?* Sure there's scarcely any body there *now*. When we go on farther, we may look up, but we'll see no smoke, as there used to be. 'Twas there young Torly Regan died on that day—an' her, poor Mary!—but they're all gone from her—and Hugh the eldest is in England or America—but *him*—the youngest—he'll never waken—and what will the poor mother do for his white head now that she hasn't it to look at? No, he wouldn't waken, although I brought him the cock.' .

"'Of whom are you speaking now, Raymond?'

"'I'll tell you two things that's the same,' he replied; 'and I'll tell you the man that has them both.'

"'Let me hear, Raymond.'

"'The devil's blessin' and God's curse—sure they're the same—ha, ha—there now—that's one. You didn't know that—no, no; you didn't."

"'And who is it that has them, Raymond?'

"'M'Clutchy—Val the Vulture; sure 'twas he did *that* all, and is doin' it still. Poor Mary! Bryan will never waken; she'll never see his eyes again, 'tany rate—nor his white head—oh! his white head! God ought to kill Val, and I wondher he doesn't.'

"'Raymond, my good friend,' said I, 'if you travel at this rate, I must give up the journey altogether.'

"'The fact is, that when excited, as he was now by the topic in question, he gets into what is termed a sling trot, which carries him on at about six miles an hour, without ever feeling fatigued. He immediately slackened his pace, and looked towards me, with a consciousness of having forgotten himself, and acted wrongly.

"'Well, no,' said he, 'I won't; but sure I hate *him*.'

"'Hate whom?'

"'M'Clutchy—and *that was it*; for I always do it; but I won't agin, for you couldn't keep up wid me if I spoke about him.

"We then turned towards the mountains; and as we went along, the desolate impresses of the evil agent began here and there to become visible. On the roadside there were the humble traces of two or three cabins, whose little hearths had been extinguished, and whose walls were levelled to the earth. The black fungus, the burdock, the nettle, and all those offensive weeds that follow in the train of oppression and ruin were here; and as the dreary wind stirred them into sluggish motion, and piped its melancholy wail through these desolate little mounds, I could not help asking myself, if those who do these things ever think that there is a reckoning in after life, where power, and insolence, and wealth misapplied, and rancour, and pride, and rapacity, and persecution, and revenge, and sensuality, and gluttony, will be placed face to face with those humble beings, on whose rights and privileges of simple existence they have trampled with such a selfish and exterminating tread. A host of thoughts and reflections began to crowd upon my mind; but the subject was too painful—and after avoiding it as well as I could, we proceeded on our little tour of observation.

How easy it is for the commonest observer to mark even the striking characters that are impressed on the physical features of an estate which is managed by care and kindness—where general happiness and principles of active industry are diffused through the people! And, on the other hand, do not all the depressing symbols of neglect and mismanagement present equally obvious exponents of their operation, upon properties like this of Castle Cumber? On this property it is not every tenant that is allowed to have an interest in the soil at all, since the accession of M'Clutchy. He has succeeded in inducing the head landlord to decline granting leases to any but those who are his political supporters— that is, who will vote for him or his nominee at an election; or, in other words, who will enable him to sell both their political privileges and his own, to gratify his cupidity or ambition, without conferring a single advantage upon themselves. From those, therefore, who have too much honesty to prostitute their votes to his corrupt and selfish negociations with power, leases are with-held, in order that they may, with more becoming and plausible oppression, be removed from the property, and the staunch political supporter brought in in their stead. This may be all very good policy, but it is certainly bad humanity, and worse religion. In fact it is the practice of that cruel dogma, which prompts us to sacrifice the principles of others to our own, and to deprive them of the very privilege which we ourselves claim—that of acting according to our conscientious impressions. 'Do unto others,' say Mr. M'Clutchy and his class, 'as you would *not* wish that others should do unto you.' How beautifully here is the practice of the loud and headlong supporter of the Protestant Church, and its political ascendancy, made to harmonise with the principles of that neglected thing called the Gospel? In fact, as we went along, it was easy to mark, on the houses and farmsteads about us, the injustice of making this heartless distinction. The man who felt himself secure and fixed by a vested right in the possession of his tenement, had heart and motive to work and improve it, undepressed by the consciousness that his improvements to-day might be trafficked on by a wicked and unjust agent to-morrow. He knows, that in developing all the advantages and good qualities of the soil, he is not only discharging an important duty to himself and his landlord, but also to his children's children after him; and the result is, that the comfort, contentment, and self-respect which he gains by the consciousness of his security, are evident at a glance upon himself, his house, and his holding. On the other hand, reverse this picture, and what is the consequence?

Just what is here visible. There is a man who may be sent adrift on the shortest notice, unless he is base enough to trade upon his principles, and vote against his conscience. What interest has *he* in the soil, or in the prosperity of his landlord? If he make improvements this year, he may see the landlord derive all the advantages of them the next; or, what is quite as likely, he may know that some Valentine M'Clutchy may put them in his own pocket, and keep the landlord in the dark regarding the whole transaction. What a bounty on dishonesty and knavery in an agent is this? How unjust to the interest of the tenant, in the first place—in the next to that of the landlord—and, finally, how destructive to the very nature and properties of the soil itself, which rapidly degenerates by bad and negligent culture, and consequently becomes impoverished and diminished in value. All this was evident as we went along. Here was warmth, and wealth, and independence staring us in the face: there was negligence, desponding struggle, and decline, conscious, as it were, of their unseemly appearance, and anxious, one would think, to shrink away from the searching eye of observation.

"'But here again, Raymond; what have we here? There is a fine looking farm-house, evidently untenanted. How is that?'

"'Ha, ha,' replied Raymond, with a bitter smile, 'ha, ha! Let them take it, and see what *Captain Whiteboy* will do? *He* has the possession—ha, ha—an' who'll get *him* to give it up? Who dare take that, or any of Captain Whiteboy's farms? But sure it's not much—only a coal, a rushlight, and a prod of a pike or a bagnet—but I know who ought to have *them*.'

"The house in question was considerably dilapidated. Its doors were not visible, and its windows had all been shivered. Its smokeless chimnies, its cold and desolate appearance, together with the still more ruinous condition of the out-houses, added to the utter silence which prevailed about it, and the absence of every symptom of life and motion—all told a tale which has left many a bloody moral to the country. The slaps, gates, and enclosures were down—the hedges broken or cut away—the fences trampled on and levelled to the earth—and nothing seemed to thrive—for the garden was overrun with them—but the rank weeds already alluded to, as those which love to trace the footsteps of ruin and desolation, in order to show, as it were, what *they* leave behind them. As we advanced, other and more startling proofs of M'Clutchy came in our way—proofs which did not consist of ruined houses, desolate villages, or roofless cottages—but of those unfortunate persons, whose simple circle of domestic life—whose little cares, and struggles, and sorrows, and affections, formed the whole round of their humble existence, and its enjoyments, as given them by Almighty God himself. All these, however, like the feelings and affections of the manacled slave, were as completely overlooked by those who turned them adrift, as if in possessing such feelings, they had invaded a right which belonged only to their betters, and which the same betters, by the way, seldom exercise either in such strength or purity, as those whom they despise and oppress. Aged men we met, bent with years, and weighed down still more by that houseless sorrow, which is found accompanying them along the highways of life—through its rugged solitudes, and its dreariest paths—in the storm and in the tempest:—wherever they go—in want, nakedness, and destitution—still at their side is that houseless sorrow—pouring into their memories and their hearts the conviction, which is most terrible to old age, that it has no home here but the grave—no pillow on which to forget its cares but the dust. The sight of these wretched old men, turned out from the little holdings that sheltered their helplessness, to beg a morsel, through utter charity, in the decrepitude of life, was enough to make a man wish that he had never been born to witness such a wanton abuse of that power which was entrusted to man for the purpose of diffusing happiness, instead of misery. All these were known to Raymond, who, as far as he could, gave me their brief and unfortunate history. That which showed us, however, the heartless evils of the clearance system in its immediate operation upon the poorer classes, was the groups of squalid females who traversed the country, accompanied by their pale and sickly looking children, all in a state of mendicancy, and woefully destitute of clothing. The system in this case being to deny their husbands employment upon the property, in order to drive them, by the strong scourge of necessity, off it, the poor men were compelled to seek it elsewhere, whilst their sorrowing and heart-broken families were fain to remain and beg a morsel *from those who were best acquainted with the history of their expulsion*, and who, consequently, could yield to them and their little ones, a more cordial and liberal sympathy.

Chapter Three:
THE EDUCATION OF A LIFETIME

Preface

It was an education, sometimes with lethal literalness, in the 'school of hard knocks'. Among the attainments required for completion of the curriculum, Carleton stressed the importance of the scholar graduating from the hedge school proficient in the use of the cudgel.

There was on the syllabus also Latin, Greek, Mathematics and English. The classrooms were liberally endowed with furniture—stones or the butt of a tree—and the main teaching aids were poteen and a blackthorn stick. Continuity of employment was not de rigueur for the masters of these gracious and illegal establishments; they went where they could get pupils and some place to sleep.

Sometimes, like Paddy Devaun in Wildgoose Lodge, *they captained secret societies. But they have one thing common in their many avatars through Carleton's pages; their importance in small rural communities. For Carleton's schoolmasters are not only teachers; they are inditers of letters, makers and settlers of quarrels, men who knew everything that went on in the place—shrewd, frequently pedantic, soft-hearted and seldom sober.*

In his Autobiography, *Carleton recounts with obvious affection his first encounters with these exotic creatures, and it is clear that it was under their tutelage that he first acquired a lifelong and incurable love of words; Ciceronian, excessive, rich, comically off-key to the dull metronome of standard English, a fantastical melody akin rhythmically to the dialect of the people but opening out to them a world of erudition and splendour and accomplishment, to be respected and mocked in equal measure.*

Recalling his youth, Carleton describes himself as a big-boned athletic lad, not overly fond of work and game for any devilment that could be got up, whether it was leaping a river or out-dancing the company or beating the miller for who could raise the heaviest weight.

The prospect of labouring was gall and wormwood and after forsaking the road to Maynooth, his prospects were poor enough. The 'leap' is recounted with enormous relish, but lying close under the surface is the sobering recognition that it could be his last, for he was to go as apprentice to a stone-cutter the next day. Years after, he was to recapture the early exuberance through writing which did its share of leaping and dancing and the shouldering of weights.

Carleton's attitude to folk belief in a supernatural order was ambivalent. In the series of sketches he wrote for the Irish Penny Journal *(1840-41), the authorial tone tends to be dismissive, but the stories illustrating the 'superstition' are invested with considerable conviction. He wrote two sustained works on the subject:* The Evil Eye or Black Spectre *and* Fair Gurtha or The Hungry Grass, *but perhaps his most powerful treatment of the theme is* 'The Lianhan Shee' *with its powerful blending of intimacy and the macabre. The poignancy, as real as its horror, is masterfully rendered.*

Carleton often incorporates anecdotes and 'tall stories' into his narrative and the mischievousness and sprightliness of tone certainly indicates his relish for the popular oral form. He discovered his own skill in yarn spinning quite accidentally, in his early days in Dublin, and it was to the lay the foundation for his literary career. Heroic and mock heroic feats, legends, local history, good-humoured chicanery and romance are the main ingredients of such tales, which form a contrast to Carleton's more sombre concerns. The Castle of Aughentain *as told by Tom Gracie the Shanahus is a prime example.*

Buckram Back the Dancing Master is probably one of Carleton's most memorable characters, revealing the writer's shrewd craftsmanship in the thumb-nail sketch and typical of his unique blending of poignancy and comedy. Like the Hedge Schoolmasters and Raymond a Hattha, he is almost, but not quite, a caricature, and for all their antics, we do not fail to believe in the essential humanity of such figures. Buckram Back makes a number of appearances in Carleton's writings.

Carleton's inside knowledge of the lives of country people is well-evidenced in his precision in describing vernacular architecture and small domestic activities. The extract from The Black Spectre *is a particularly good example, but there are countless others which give to his work great concreteness and credibility, especially when, as is the case here, they enliven otherwise abstract and rambling narratives. His memory for minute detail is, in itself, noteworthy. Sometimes, Carleton uses this talent for observation for comic purposes and the humour is largely dependent upon the physical accuracy of his descriptions.*

Carleton has mixed success in describing landscape. At his worst he teeters into a bookish vacuity or tiresomely vertiginous 'sublimity' doubtless borrowed from the English Romantics. The extract from Rody the Rover or The Ribbonman *illustrates a less literary landscape.*

1.

'The Schoolmaster's Letter'
from *The Emigrants Of Ahadarra* (1848)

"WORTHY MR. HYACINTHUS,—

"A FRIEND unknown to you, but not altogether so to fame, and one whom no display of the subtlest ingenuity on behalf of your acute and sagacious intellect could ever decypher through the medium of this epistle, begs to convey to you a valuable portion of anonymous information. When he says that he is not unknown to fame, the assertion, as far as it goes, is pregnant wid veracity. Mark that I say, as far as it goes, by which is meant the assertion as well as the fame of your friend, the inditer of this significant epistle. Forty-eight square miles of good sound fame your not inerudite

93

correspondent can conscientiously lay claim to; and although there is, with regret I admit it, a considerable portion of the square superficies alluded to, waste and uncultivated moor, yet I can say, wid that racy touch of genial and expressive pride which distinguishes men of letters in general, that the other portions of this fine district are inhabited by a multitudinity of population in the highest degree creditable to the prolific powers of the climate. 'Tisn't all as one, then, as that thistle-browsing quadruped, Barney Heffernan, who presumes, in imitation of his betters, to write Philomath after his name, and whose whole extent of literary reputation is not more than two or three beggarly townlands, whom, by the way, he is inoculating successfully wid his own ripe and flourishing ignorance. No, sir; nor like Gusty Gibberish, or (as he has been most facetiously christened by his Reverence, Father O Flaherty) Demosthenes M'Gosther, inasmuch as he is distinguished for an aisy and prodigal superfluity of mere words, unsustained by intelligibility or meaning, but who cannot claim in his own person a mile and a half of dacent reputation. However, *quid multis?* Mr. Hyacinthus; 'tis no indoctrinated or obscure scribe who now addresses you, and who does so from causes that may be salutary to your own health and very gentlemanly fame, according as you the same, not pretermitting interests involving, probably, on your part, an abundant portion of pecuniarity.

"In short, then, it has reached these ears, Mr. Hyacinthus, and between you and me, they are not such a pair as, in consequence of their longitudinity, can be copiously shaken, or which rise and fall according to the will of the wearer, like those of the thistle-browser already alluded to; it has reached them that you are about to substantiate a disreputable—excuse the phrase—co-partnership wid four of the most ornamental villains on Hibernian earth, by which you must understand me to mane that the villains aforesaid are not merely accomplished in all the plain principles and practices of villany, but finished off even to its natest and most inganious decorations. Their whole life has been most assiduously and successfully devoted to a general violation of the ten commandments, as well as to the perpetual commission of the seven deadly sins. Nay, the *"reserved cases"* themselves can't escape them, and it is well known that they won't rest satisfied wid the wide catalogue of ordinary and general iniquity, but they must, by

94

way of luxury, have a lick at blasphemy, and some of the rarer vices, as often as they can, for the villains are so fastidious that they won't put up wid common wickedness like other people.

I cannot, however, wid anything approximating to a safe conscience, rest here. What I have said has reference to the laws of God, but what I am about to enumerate relates to the laws of man and to the laws of the land. Wid respect, then, to them, I do assure you, that although I myself look upon the violation of a great number of the latter wid a very vanial squint, still, I say, I do assure you that they have not left a single law made by Parliament unfractured. They have gone over the whole statute-book several times, and I believe are absolutely of the opinion that the Parliament is doing nothing. The most lynx-eyed investigator of old enactments could not find one which has escaped them, for the villains are perfectly black letter in that respect; and what is in proper keeping wid this, whenever they hear of a new Act of Parliament they cannot rest either night or day until they break it. And now for the inference: be on your guard against this pandemonial squad. Whatever your object may be in cultivating and keeping society wid them, theirs is to ruin you—fleece was the word used—and then to cut and run, leaving Mr. Hycy—the acute, the penetrating, the accomplished—completely in the lurch. Be influenced, then, by the amicitial admonitions of the inditer of this correspondency. Become not a smuggler—forswear poteen. The Lord forgive me, Mr. Hycy—no, I only wished to say forswear—not the poteen—but any connexion wid the illegal alembic from which it is distillated, otherwise they will walk off wid the 'doublings' or strong liquor, leaving you nothing but the *residuum* or feints. Take a friend's advice, therefore, and retrograde out of all society and connexion wid the villains I have described; or if you superciliously overlook this warning, book it down as a fact that admits of no negation, that you will be denuded of reputation, of honesty, and of any pecuniary contingencies that you may happen to possess. This is a sincere advice from

"Your Anonymous Friend,

"PATRICIUS O'FINIGAN, Philomath"

2.

'Irish Superstitions—Ghosts And Fairies'
from *The Irish Penny Journal* (1840)

WE HAVE MET and conversed with every possible representative of the various classes that compose general society, from the sweep to the peer, and we feel ourselves bound to say that in no instance have we ever met any individual, no matter what his class or rank in life, who was really indifferent to the subject of dreams, fairies, and apparitions. They are topics that interest the imagination in all; and the hoary head of age is inclined with as much interest to a ghost-story, as the young and eager ear of youth, wrought up by all the nimble and apprehensive powers of early fancy. It is true the belief in ghosts is fast disappearing, and that of fairies is already almost gone; but with what new wonders they shall be replaced, it is difficult to say. The physical and natural we suppose will give us enough of the marvellous, without having recourse to the spiritual and supernatural. Steam and gas, if Science advance for another half century at the same rate as she has done the last, will give sufficient exercise to all our faculties for wondering. We know a man who travelled eighty miles to see whether or not it was a fact that light could be conveyed for miles in a pipe underground; and this man to our own knowledge possessed the organ of marvellousness to a surprising degree. It is singular, too, that his fear of ghosts was in proportion to this capacious propensity to wonder, as was his disposition when snug in a chimney corner to talk incessantly of such topics as were calculated to excite it.

In our opinion, ghosts and fairies will be seen wherever they are much talked of, and a belief in their existence cultivated and nourished. So long as the powers of the imagination are kept warm and active by exercise, they will create for themselves such images as they are in the habit of conceiving or dwelling upon; and these, when the individual happens to be in the appropriate position, will even by the mere force of association engender the particular

Eidolon which is predominant in the mind ... the first which I shall narrate may possess some interest, as being that upon which I founded the tale of the 'Midnight Mass'. The circumstances are simply these:—

There lived a man named M'Kenna at the hip of one of the mountainous hills that divided the county of Tyrone from that of Monaghan. This M'Kenna had two sons, one of whom was in the habit of tracing hares of a Sunday, whenever there happened to be a fall of snow. His father it seems had frequently remonstrated with him upon what he considered to be a violation of the Lord's day, as well as for his general neglect of mass. The young man, however, though otherwise harmless and inoffensive, was in this matter quite insensible to paternal reproof, and continued to trace whenever the avocations of labour would allow him. It so happened that upon a Christmas morning, I think in the year 1814, there was a deep fall of snow, and young M'Kenna, instead of going to mass, got down his cock-stick—which is a staff much heavier at one end than at the other—and prepared to set out on his favourite amusement. His father seeing this, reproved him seriously, and insisted that he should attend prayers. His enthusiasm for the sport, however, was stronger than his love of religion, and he refused to be guided by his father's advice. The old man during the altercation got warm; and on finding that the son obstinately scorned his authority, he knelt down and prayed that if the boy persisted in following his own will, he might never return from the mountains unless a corpse. The imprecation, which was certainly as harsh as it was impious and senseless, might have startled many a mind from a purpose which was, to say the least of it, at variance with religion and the respect due to a father. It had no effect, however, upon the son, who is said to have replied, that whether he ever returned or not, he was determined on going; and go accordingly he did. He was not, however, alone, for it appears that three or four of the neighbouring young men accompanied him. Whether their sport was good or otherwise, is not to the purpose, neither am I able to say; but the story goes that towards the latter part of the day they started a larger and darker hare than any they had ever seen, and that she kept dodging on before them bit by bit, leading them to suppose that every succeeding cast of the cock-stick would bring her down. It was observed afterwards that she also led them into the recesses of the mountains, and that although they tried to turn her course homewards, they could not succeed in doing so. As evening advanced, the companions of M'Kenna began to feel the folly of pursuing her farther, and to perceive the danger of losing their way in the mountains should night or a snow-storm come upon them. They therefore proposed to give over the chase and return home; but M'Kenna would not hear of it. "If you wish to go home, you may," said he; "as for me, I'll never leave the hillside till I have her with me." They begged and entreated him to desist and return, but all to no purpose; he appeared to be what the Scotch call *fey*—that is, to act as if he were moved by some impulse that leads to death, and from the influence of which a man cannot withdraw himself. At length, on finding him invincibly obstinate, they left him pursuing the hare directly into the heart of the mountains, and returned to their respective homes.

In the mean time, one of the most terrible snow-storms ever remembered in that part of the country came on, and the consequence was, that the self-willed young man, who had equally trampled on the sanctions of religion and parental authority, was given over for lost. As soon as the tempest became still, the neighbours assembled in a body and proceeded to look for him. The snow, however, had fallen so heavily that not a single mark of a footstep could be seen. Nothing but one wide waste of white undulating hills met the eye wherever it turned, and of M'Kenna no trace whatever was visible or could be found. His father now remembering the unnatural character of his imprecation, was nearly distracted; for although the body had not yet been found, still by everyone who witnessed the sudden storm and who knew the mountains, escape or survival was felt to be impossible. Every day for about a week large parties went out among the hill-ranges seeking him, but to no purpose. At length there came a thaw, and his body was found on a snow-wreath, lying in a supine posture within a circle which he had drawn around him with his cock-stick. His prayer-book lay opened upon his mouth, and his hat was pulled down so as to cover his face. It is unnecessary to say that the rumour of his death, and of the circumstances under which he left home, created a most extraordinary sensation in the country—a sensation that was the greater in proportion to the uncertainty occasioned by his not having been found either alive or dead. Some affirmed that he had crossed the mountains, and was seen in Monaghan; others, that he had been seen in Clones, in Emyvale, in Fivemiletown; but despite all of these agreeable reports, the melancholy truth was at length made clear by the appearance of the body as just stated.

Now, it so happened that the house nearest the spot where he lay was inhabited by a man named Daly, I think—but of the name I am not certain—who was a herd or care-taker to Dr. Porter, then Bishop of Clogher. The situation of this house was the most lonely and desolate-looking that could be imagined. It was at least two miles distant from any human habitation, being surrounded by one wide and dreary waste of dark moor. By this house lay the route of those who had found the corpse, and I believe the door was borrowed for the purpose of conveying it home. Be this as it may, the family witnessed the melancholy procession as it passed slowly through the mountains, and when the place and circumstances are all considered, we may admit that to ignorant and superstitious people, whose minds even under ordinary occasions were strongly affected by such matters, it was a sight calculated to leave behind it a deep, if not a terrible impression. Time soon proved that it did so.

An incident is said to have occurred at the funeral which I have alluded to in the 'Midnight Mass', and which is certainly in fine keeping with the wild spirit of the whole melancholy event. When the procession had advanced to a place called Mullaghtinny, a large dark-coloured hare, which was instantly recognised, by those who had been out with him on the hills, as the identical one that led him to his fate, is said to have crossed the road about twenty yards or so before the coffin. The story goes, that a man struck it on the side with a stone, and that the blow, which would have killed any ordinary hare, not only did it no injury, but occasioned a sound to proceed from the body resembling the hollow one emitted by an empty barrel when struck.

In the meantime the interment took place, and the sensation began like every other to die away in the natural progress of time, when, behold, a report ran about like wildfire that, to use the language of the people, "Frank M'Kenna was *appearing*!" Seldom indeed was the rumour of an apparition composed of materials so strongly calculated to win popular assent or to baffle rational investigation. As every man is not a Hibbert or a Nicolai, so will many, until such circumstances are made properly intelligible, continue to yield credence to testimony which would convince the judgment on any other subject. The case in question furnished as fine a specimen of a true ghost-story, freed from any suspicion of imposture or design, as could be submitted to a philosopher; and yet, notwithstanding the array of apparent facts connected with it, nothing in the world is simpler or of easier solution.

One night, about a fortnight after his funeral, the daughter of Daly, the herd, a girl of about fourteen, while lying in bed saw what appeared to be the likeness of M'Kenna, who had been lost. She screamed out, and covering her head with the bed-clothes, told her father and mother that Frank M'Kenna was in the house. This alarming intelligence naturally produced great terror; still, Daly, who notwithstanding his belief in such matters possessed a good deal of moral courage, was cool enough to rise and examine the house, which consisted of only one apartment. This gave the daughter some courage, who, on finding that her father could not see him, ventured to look out, and she *then* could see nothing of him herself. She very soon fell asleep, and her father attributed what she saw to fear, or some accidental combination of shadows proceeding from the furniture, for it was a clear moonlight night. The light of the following day dispelled a great deal of their apprehensions, and comparatively little was thought of it until the evening again advanced, when the fears of the daughter began to return. They appeared to be prophetic, for she said when night came that she knew he would appear again; and accordingly at the same hour he did so. This was repeated for several successive nights, until the girl, from the very hardihood of terror, began to become so far familiarised to the spectre as to venture to address it.

"In the name of God," she asked, "what is troubling you, or why do you appear to me instead of to some of your own family or relations?"

The ghost's answer alone might settle the question involved in the authenticity of its appearance, being, as it was, an account of one of the most ludicrous missions that ever a spirit was dispatched upon.

"I'm not allowed," said he, "to spake to any of my friends, for I parted wid them in anger; but I'm come to tell you that they are quarrelin' about my breeches—a new pair that I got made for Christmas day; an' as I was comin' up to thrace in the mountains, I thought the ould ones 'ud do betther, an' of coorse I didn't put the new pair an me. My raison for appearin'," he added, "is, that you may tell my friends that none of them is to wear them—they must be given in charity."

This serious and solemn intimation from the ghost was duly communicated to the family, and it was found that the circumstances were exactly as it had represented them. This of course was considered as sufficient proof of the truth of its mission. Their conversations now became not only frequent, but quite friendly and familiar. The girl became a favourite with the spectre, and the spectre on the other hand soon lost all his terrors in her eyes. He told her that whilst his friends were bearing home his body, the handspikes or poles on which they had carried him had cut his back, and *occasioned him great pain!* The cutting of the back was also found to be true, and strengthened of course the truth and authenticity of their dialogues. The whole neighbourhood was now in a commotion with this story of the apparition, and persons incited by curiosity began to visit the girl in order to satisfy themselves of the truth of what they had heard. Everything, however, was corroborated, and the child herself, without any symptoms of anxiety or terror, artlessly related her conversations with the spirit. Hitherto their interviews had all been nocturnal, but now that the ghost found his footing made good, he put a hardy face on, and ventured to appear by daylight. The girl also fell into states of syncope, and while the fits lasted, long conversations with him upon the subject of God, the blessed Virgin, and Heaven, took place between them. He was certainly an excellent moralist, and gave the best advice. Swearing, drunkenness, theft, and every evil propensity of our nature, were declaimed against with a degree of spectral eloquence quite surprising. Common fame now had a topic dear to her heart, and never was a ghost made more of by his best friends, than she made of him. The whole country was in a tumult, and I well remember the crowds which flocked to the lonely little cabin in the mountains, now the scene of matters so interesting and important. Not a single day passed in which I

101

should think from ten to twenty, thirty, or fifty persons, were not present at these singular interviews. Nothing else was talked of, thought of, and, as I can well testify, dreamt of. I would myself have gone to Daly's were it not for a confounded misgiving I had, that perhaps the ghost might take a fancy of appearing to me, as he had taken to cultivate an intimacy with the girl; and it so happens, that when I see the face of an individual nailed down in the coffin—chilling and gloomy operation!—I experience no particular wish ever to look upon it again.

Many persons might imagine that the herd's daughter was acting the part of an imposter, by first originating and then sustaining such a delusion. If any one, however, was an imposter, it was the ghost, and not the girl, as her ill health and wasted cheek might well testify. The appearance of M'Kenna continued to haunt her for months. The reader is aware that he was lost on Christmas day, or rather on the night of it, and I remember seeing her in the early part of the following summer, during which time she was still the victim of a diseased imagination. Everything in fact that could be done for her was done. They brought her to a priest named Donnelly, who lived down at Ballynasaggart, for the purpose of getting her cured, as he had the reputation of performing cures of that kind. They brought her also to the doctors, who also did what they could for her; but all to no purpose. Her fits were longer and of more frequent occurrence; her appetite left her; and ere four months had elapsed, she herself looked as like a spectre as the ghost himself could do for the life of him.

Now, this was a pure case of spectral illusion, and precisely similar to that detailed so philosophically by Nicolai the German bookseller, and to others mentioned by Hibbert. The image of M'Kenna not only appeared to her in daylight at her own house, but subsequently followed her wherever she went; and what proved this to have been the result of diseased organization, produced at first by a heated and excited imagination, was, that, as the story went, she could see him with her eyes shut. Whilst this state of mental and physical feeling lasted, she was the subject of the most intense curiosity. No matter where she went, whether to chapel, to fair, or to market, she was followed by crowds, every one feeling eager to get a glimpse of the girl who had actually seen, and what was more, spoken to a ghost—a live ghost.

Now, here was a young girl of an excitable temperament and large imagination, leading an almost solitary life amidst scenery of a lonely and desolate character, who, happening to be strongly impressed with an image of horror—for surely such was the body of a dead man seen in association with such peculiarly frightful circumstances as filial disobedience and a father's curse were calculated to give it—cannot shake it off, but on the contrary becomes a victim to the disease which it generates. There is not an image which we see in a fever, or a face whether of angel or devil, or an uncouth shape of any kind, that is not occasioned by cerebral excitement, or derangement of the nervous system, analogous to that under which Daly's daughter laboured. I saw her several times, and remembered clearly that her pale face, dark eye, and very intellectual forehead, gave indications of such a temperament as under her circumstances would be apt to receive strong and fearful impressions from images calculated to excite terror, especially of the supernatural. It only now remains for me to mention the simple method of her cure, which was effected without either priest or doctor. It depended upon a word or two of advice given to her father by a very sensible man, who was in the habit of thinking on these matters somewhat above the superstitious absurdities of the people.

"If you wish your daughter to be cured," said he to her father, "leave the house you are now living in. Take her to some part of the country where she can have companions of her own class and state of life to mingle with; bring her away from the place altogether; for you may rest assured that so long as there are objects before her eyes to remind her of what happened, she will not mend on your hands."

The father, although he sat rent free, took this excellent advice, even at a sacrifice of some comfort: for nothing short of the temptation of easy circumstances could have induced any man to reside in so wild and remote a solitude. In the course of a few days he removed from it with his family, and came to reside amongst the cheerful aspect and enlivening intercourse of human life. The consequences were precisely as the man had told him. In the course of a few weeks the little girl began to find that the visits of the spectre were like those of angels, few and far between. She was sent to school, and what with the confidence derived from human society, and the substitution of new objects and images, she soon perfectly recovered, and ere long was thoroughly set free from the fearful creation of her own brain.

Now, there is scarcely one of the people in my native parish who does not believe that the spirit of this man came back to the world, and actually appeared to this little girl. The time, however, is fast coming when these empty bugbears will altogether disappear, and we shall entertain more reverend and becoming notions of God than to suppose such senseless pranks could be played by the soul of a departed being under his permission. We might as well assert that the imaginary beings which surround the couch of the madman or hypochondriac have a real existence, as those that are conjured up by terror, weak nerves, or impure blood.

The spot where the body of M'Kenna was found is now marked by a little heap of stones, which has been collected since the melancholy event of his death. Every person who passes it throws a stone upon the heap; but why this old custom is practised, or what it means, I do not know, unless it be simply to mark the spot as a visible means of preserving the memory of the occurrence.

Daly's house, the scene of the supposed apparition, is now a shapeless ruin, which could scarcely be seen were it not for the green spot that was once a garden, and which now shines at a distance like an emerald, but with no agreeable or pleasant associations. It is a spot which no solitary schoolboy will ever visit, nor indeed would the unflinching believer in the popular nonsense of ghosts wish to pass it without a companion. It is under any circumstances a gloomy and barren place, but when looked upon in connection with what we have just recited, it is lonely, desolate, and awful.

3.

'Quantum Leaps' from *Autobiography* (1896)

THE RIVER AT which the scene of my crossing the weir occurred is there called the Karry; and the reason why I thought of leaping it is easily told. About a quarter of a mile above that spot was a portion of the same river which ran through the meadows of a man called David Aikins. The reader recollects my mention of a young fellow named Edward McArdle—the nephew to our parish priest of the same name. This McArdle, a small, tight, active little fellow, beautifully and symmetrically made, was one of the most celebrated leapers ever known in that part of the country until my appearance. He had leaped a celebrated leap across that portion of the river which ran through Aikins' meadows. This leap of a son of Old David Aikins', named Charley, had shown me a few days before. I need scarcely say that I cleared it with the greatest ease. Charley then told me that McArdle had expressed an intention of leaping the Karry, but had added that on looking at it he had given up the notion—stating as his opinion that the Karry could not be done by any man. He and I then went to the Karry and looked at it.

"He was right," said Charley; "no man could do that."

I looked at it again—and again—and again. It was a dead level, there was not the difference of an inch, I think, between the heights of the banks on either side. Well, I looked and paused—and calculated—went to the brink—walked back to take a view of it from the starting point of the run which I would have taken, and then said:

"Charley, I will leap it; if I fail I can only get a wet coat as I got at the weir, but the weir was no failure, and neither will this, or I am much mistaken."

"I would not recommend you to try it," said he. "I don't think that any man could do it. If anyone could, though, it would surely be yourself. Well," he added, with a smile, "if you had failed in crossing the weir you'd have been dashed to pieces—but if you come short here, all you can get will be a wet jacket."

"Well, Charley," said I, "tell the boys of the neighbourhood that on Friday evening next I will try it at all events—and if I fail it will only be, as you say, a wet jacket."

It was with reference to this intention that my eldest brother spoke, when he alluded with such a bitter sneer to my intention of trying to leap, for it was now very well known throughout the neighbourhood. This dialogue between Charley Aikins and me occurred upon Wednesday, and on the following day a circumstance took place which was very near settling me in obscurity for the remainder of my life. I was living, as I said, with my eldest brother, who certainly made my life miserable. Not that the poor fellow was devoid of brotherly affection towards me—on the contrary, not one of my relations entertained higher or more sanguine hopes of my success. These hopes, however, were in his view altogether disappointed, and he saw nothing for me except a trade or to till the earth as a common labourer. Indeed, to tell the truth, I was much of the same opinion. Lanty Doain, the celebrated stone-cutter, I knew intimately, and I felt that it would be an agreeable thing to learn that trade from a man who was not only my friend, but a warm admirer. I accordingly went to his house the next day, without consulting anyone, and he agreed, but with great reluctance, that I should go to him as an apprentice. He would not have consented to this arrangement if I had not assured him, that if he declined it, I would enlist before twenty-four hours. Lanty knew a little of the classics, and was very proud of what he knew. On that occasion he got down a Justin and translated a portion, of which I can only recollect the words because I thought I had discovered the Latin term for Lord Lieutenant for the first time—*praefectus ipsius*—the Lord Lieutenant—*propositus mediis* —over the Medes; and so on. This bit of Latin told in his favour, and placed him out of the category of common stone-cutters. I accordingly went home with a fixed but somewhat desperate resolution to learn his trade. This was the day before the leap, but I said nothing about having apprenticed myself to Lanty Doain, even to my brother. After I had left Lanty, I felt as if I had accomplished my own ruin and utterly destroyed my hopes for life. For the first time a new indignant feeling took possession of me—a feeling that burned bitterly and hotly into my heart. I became misanthropic. I detested the world. Everything went against me and my family.

The latter, among whom, of course, I was forced to include myself, were almost beggars, and nothing for me, in the shape of any opening in the future, offered itself except the hard shapeless granite—the chisel and the mallet. I could almost have pitched myself down a precipice.

At length Friday evening came, and accompanied by Charley Aikins and about a dozen others, I went to Clogher Karry, the scene of the approaching feat—or failure. Judge my surprise, when, on our arrival there, we found about sixty or seventy persons awaiting us. The reader must perceive that the resolution I had come with to Lanty Doain the day before, and the depressing train of thought—if not absolute despair—under which I laboured, were badly qualified to raise my spirits or prepare me for the exploit I came to perform. After again looking at the leap, with anything but the enthusiastic confidence which I ought to have felt, I appeared cast down, indifferent, and in low spirits. This was observed, and spoken of in side whispers, and I heard one of them saying, "He's hovering." I felt at that moment that the last speaker uttered the truth. My heart was down, and never in my life did such an unaccountable sense of depression sink me. There I stood before them, a fine well-dressed young fellow, in my twenty-first year; an individual from whom great things were expected—yet what would I be in a week? A working-man, no better than one of themselves, with a paper cap on my head and coarse apron before me. The persons assembled, seeing that there was something wrong with me and that my whole bearing evinced marks of hesitation, asked me would I try the leap. I immediately stripped off my coat and waistcoat, my shirt and stockings, and went to the spot from which I had intended to take my run. This was a little blackthorn bush, not two feet high—that blackthorn bush is still there to this day. At that moment I felt in my soul that the spirit of cowardice was upon me and within me. With this impression I took my run from the little blackthorn, towards the part of the bank from which I was to spring. I ran and as I approached the edge my pace became gradually slow, and I concluded the run with a walk that would have done credit to a philosopher. This I repeated half a dozen times under such a sense of shame as I need not attempt to describe.

It fortunately happened that Billy Dickey, who kept the public-house down at Milltown, was one of the spectators; in fact, the ground we stood on was his own.

"Billy," said I, "I am in low spirits; run down—you won't be ten minutes—and bring me up a naggin of whiskey."

"I will," replied honest Billy, "and lose no time about it." Billy returned in about twenty minutes with half a pint, instead of a naggin. I took the bottle and went up to Tom Booth's, already mentioned, whose cottage was not more than a hundred yards above us, on the side of the elevation. I took the bottle—Molly supplied me with a teacup, and a drinking-glass without a bottom. Into this cup I poured a glass of the whiskey, to which I added the proper quantity of water. I drank it, and sat awhile; after this I took another, and sat about ten minutes more. I felt the reaction begin— it proceeded—my spirits became light and were rising rapidly to elevation. I joined the crowd below, I ran about, I gambolled, and in fact seemed almost frantic.

"Now," said I, "stand aside—I feel that I shall do it;" and in order to leave nothing calculated to assist me undone, I tied my pocket handkerchief about my waist. I went again to the little blackthorn— I felt as if I could tread on air—I took my run—I flew to it and in the twinkling of an eye was on the other side safely and triumphantly. I then went down to the river until I came to the steps that were in the mill-race, below the weir, and joined the spectators. The cheers were loud and long, and the honest compliments paid to me most gratifying. I had achieved my greatest feat—I had done that which has never been done from that day to this, although many persons, confident in their own success at leaping, came to the place with an intention of following my example, but after looking at it they shook their heads, and very calmly returned home. This I have been told many times. It is called 'Carleton's Leap' until this day.

4.

'The Lianhan Shee'
from *Traits And Stories Of The Irish Peasantry*, Vol 2 (1833)

ONE SUMMER EVENING Mary Sullivan was sitting at her own well-swept hearth-stone, knitting feet to a pair of sheep's grey stockings for Bartley, her husband. It was one of those serene evenings in the month of June, when the decline of day assumes a calmness and repose, resembling what we might suppose to have irradiated Eden, when our first parents sat in it before their fall. The beams of the sun shone through the windows in clear shafts of amber light, exhibiting millions of those atoms which float to the naked eye within its mild radiance. The dog lay barking in his dream at her feet, and the grey cat sat purring placidly upon his back, from which even his occasional agitation did not dislodge her.

Mrs. Sullivan was the wife of a wealthy farmer, and niece to the Rev. Felix O'Rourke; her kitchen was consequently large, comfortable, and warm. Over where she sat, jutted out the 'brace' well lined with bacon; to the right hung a well-scoured salt-box, and to the left was the jamb, with its little gothic paneless window to admit the light. Within it hung several ash rungs, seasoning for flail-sooples, or boulteens, a dozen of eel-skins, and several stripes of horse-skin, as hangings for them. The dresser was a 'parfit white,' and well furnished with the usual appurtenances. Over the door and on the 'threshel,' were nailed, 'for luck,' two horse-shoes, that had been found by accident. In a little 'hole' in the wall, beneath the salt-box, lay a bottle of holy water to keep the place purified; and against the cope-stone of the gable, on the outside, grew a large lump of house-leek, as a specific for sore eyes, and other maladies. In the corner of the garden were a few stalks of tansy "to kill the theivin' worms in the childhre, the crathurs," together with a little Rosenoble, Solomon's Seal, and Bugloss, each for some medicinal purpose. The 'lime wather' Mrs.

---

* Literally, red water.

Sullivan could make herself, and the 'bog bane' for the *linh roe**, or heart-burn, grew in their own meadow-drain; so that, in fact, she had within her reach a very decent pharmacopoeia, perhaps as harmless as that of the profession itself. Lying on the top of the salt-box was a bunch of fairy flax, and sewed in the folds of her own scapular was the dust of what had once been a four-leaved shamrock, an invaluable specific 'for seein' the good people,' if they happened to come within the bounds of vision. Over the door in the inside, over the beds, and over the cattle in the out-houses, were placed branches of withered palm, that had been consecrated by the priest on Palm Sunday; and when the cows happened to calve, this good woman tied, with her own hands, a woollen thread about their tails, to prevent them from being overlooked by evil eyes, or *elf-shot** by the fairies, who seem to possess a peculiar power over females of every species during the period of parturition. It is unnecessary to mention the variety of charms which she possessed for that obsolete malady the colic, for tooth-ach, head-achs, or for removing warts, and taking motes out of the eyes; let it suffice to inform our readers that she was well stocked with them; and that in addition to this, she, together with her husband, drank a potion made up and administered by an herb-doctor, for preventing for ever the slightest misunderstanding or quarrel between man and wife. Whether it produced this desirable object or not our readers may conjecture, when we add, that the herb-doctor, after having taken a very liberal advantage of their generosity, was immediately compelled to disappear from the neighbourhood, in order to avoid meeting with Bartley, who

* This was, and in remote parts of the country still is, one of the strongest instances of belief in the power of the Fairies. The injury, which, if not counteracted by a charm from the lips of a 'Fairy-man' or 'Fairy-woman', was uniformly inflicted on the animal by what was termed an elf-stone—which was nothing more nor less than a piece of sharp flint, from three to four or five ounces in weight. The cow was supposed to be struck upon the loin with it by these mischievous little beings, and the nature of the wound was said to be very peculiar—that is, it cut the midriff without making any visible or palpable wound on the outward skin. All animals dying of this complaint, were supposed to be carried to the good people, and there are many in the country who would not believe that the dead carcase of the cow was that of the real one at all, but an old log or block of wood made to resemble it. All such frauds, however, and deceptions were inexplicable to every one, but such as happened to possess a four-leaved shamrock, and this enabled its possessor to see the block or log in its real shape, although to others it appeared to be the real carcase.

had a sharp look out for him, not exactly on his own account, but "in regard," he said, "that it had no effect upon *Mary*, at all at all;" whilst Mary, on the other hand, admitted its efficacy upon herself, but maintained, "that Bartley was worse nor ever afther it."

Such was Mary Sullivan, as she sat at her own hearth, quite alone, engaged as we have represented her. What she may have been meditating on we cannot pretend to ascertain; but after some time, she looked sharply into the 'backstone,' or hob, with an air of anxiety and alarm. By and by she suspended her knitting, and listened with much earnestness, leaning her right ear over to the hob, from whence the sounds to which she paid such deep attention proceeded. At length she crossed herself devoutly, and exclaimed, "Queen of saints about us!—is it back ye are? Well sure there's no use in talkin'' bekase they say you know what's said of you, or to you—an' we may as well spake yez fair.—Hem—musha yez are welcome back, crickets, avourneenee! I hope that, not like the last visit ye ped us, yez are comin' for luck now! Moolyeen* died, any way, soon afther your other *kailyee**, ye crathurs ye. Here's the bread, an' the salt, an' the male for yez, an' we wish ye well. Eh?—saints above, if it isn't listenin' they are jist like a Christhien! Wurrah, but ye are the wise an' the quare crathurs all out!"

She then shook a little holy water over the hob, and muttered to herself an Irish charm or prayer against the evils which crickets are often supposed by the peasantry to bring with them, and requested, still in the words of the charm, that their presence might, on that occasion, rather be a presage of good fortune to man and beast belonging to her.

"There now, ye *dhonans** ye, sure ye can't say that ye're ill-thrated here, anyhow, or ever was mocked or made game of in the same family. You have got your hansel, an' full an' plenty of it; hopin' at the same time that you'll have no rason in life to cut our best clothes from revinge. Sure an' I didn't desarve to have my brave stuff *long body** riddled the way it was, the last time ye wor here, an' only bekase little Barny, that has but the sinse of a *gorsoon*, tould yez in a joke to pack off wid yourselves somewhere

---

* Moolyeen = A cow without horns * *Kailyee* = Short visit *
Dhonan = a diminutive delicate little thing
* *long body* = An old-fashioned Irish gown * *caudy* =A little boy.

111

else. Musha, never heed what the likes of him says; sure he's but a *caudy**, that doesn't mane ill, only the bit o' divarsion wid yez."

She then resumed her knitting, occasionally stopping, as she changed her needles, to listen, with her ear set, as if she wished to augur from the nature of their chirping, whether they came for good or evil. This, however, seemed to be beyond her faculty of translating their language; for after sagely shaking her head two or three times, she knit more busily than before.*

At this moment, the shadow of a person passing the house darkened the window opposite which she sat, and immediately a tall female, of a wild dress and aspect, entered the kitchen. "*Gho manby dhea ghud, a ban chohr!* the blessin' o' goodness upon you dacent woman," said Mrs. Sullivan, addressing her in those kindly phrases so peculiar to the Irish language. Instead of making her any reply, however, the woman, whose eye glistened with a wild depth of meaning, exclaimed in low tones, apparently of much anguish, "*Husht, husht, dherum!* husht, husht, I say—let me alone—I will do it—will you husht? I will, I say—I will—there now—that's it—be quiet, an' I will do it—be quiet!" and as she thus spoke, she turned her face back over her left shoulder, as if some invisible being dogged her steps, and stood bending over her.

"*Gho many dhea, a ban chohr, dherhum areesht!* the blessin' o' God on you, honest woman, I say again," said Mrs. Sullivan,

---

* Of the origin of this singular superstition I can find no account whatsoever; it is conceived, however, in a mild, sweet, and hospitable spirit. The visits of these migratory little creatures, which may be termed domestic grasshoppers, are very capricious and uncertain, as are their departures; and it is, I should think, for this reason that they are believed to be cognizant of the ongoings of human life. We can easily suppose, for instance, that the coincidence of their disappearance from a family, and the occurrence of a death in that family, frequently multiplied as such coincidences must be in the country at large, might occasion the people, who are naturally credulous, to associate the one event with the other; and on that slight basis erect the general superstition. Crickets, too, when chirruping, have a habit of suddenly ceasing, so that when any particularly interesting conversation happens to go on about the rustic hearth, this stopping of their little chaunt looks so like listening, that it is scarcely to be wondered at that the country folk think they understand every word that is spoken. They are thought, also, to foresee both good and evil, and are considered vindictive, but yet capable of being conciliated by fair words and kindness. They are also very destructive among wearing-apparel, which they frequently nibble into holes; and this is always looked upon as a piece of revenge, occasioned by some disrespectful language used towards them, or some neglect of their little wants. This note was necessary in order to render the conduct and language of Mary Sullivan perfectly intelligible.

repeating that *sacred* form of salutation with which the peasantry address each other. "'Tis a fine evenin', honest woman, glory be to him that sent the same, and amin! If it was cowld, I'd be axin' your to draw your chair in to the fire; but, any way, won't you sit down?"

As she ceased speaking the piercing eye of the strange woman became rivetted on her with a glare, which, whilst it startled Mrs. Sullivan, seemed full of an agony that almost abstracted her from external life. It was not, however, so wholly absorbing as to prevent it from expressing a marked interest, whether for good or evil, in the woman who addressed her so hospitably. "Husht, now—husht," she said, as if aside—"husht, won't you—sure I may speak *the thing* to her—you said it—there now, husht!" And then fastening her dark eyes on Mrs. Sullivan, she smiled bitterly and mysteriously.

"I know you well," she said, without, however, returning the *blessing* contained in the usual reply to Mrs. Sullivan's salutation—"I know you well, Mary Sullivan—husht, now, husht—yes, I know you well, and the power of all that you carry about you; but you'd be better than you are—and that's well enough now—if you had sense to know—ah, ah, ah!—what's this!" she exclaimed abruptly, with three distinct shrieks, that seemed to be produced by sensations of sharp and piercing agony.

"In the name of goodness, what's over you, honest woman?" inquired Mrs. Sullivan, as she started from her chair, and ran to her in a state of alarm, bordering on terror —"Is it sick you are?"

The woman's face had got haggard, and its features distorted; but in a few minutes they resumed their peculiar expression of settled wildness and mystery. "Sick!" she replied, licking her parched lips, "*awirck, awirck!* look! look!" and she pointed with a shudder that almost convulsed her whole frame, to a lump that rose on her shoulders; this, be it what it might, was covered with a red cloak, closely pinned and tied with great caution about her body—"'tis here! I have it!"

"Blessed mother!" exclaimed Mrs. Sullivan, tottering over to her chair, as finished a picture of horror as the eye could witness, "this day's Friday: the saints stand betwixt me an' all harm! Oh, holy Mary, protect me! *Nhanim an airh*," in the name of the Father, &c., and she forthwith proceeded to bless herself, which she did thirteen times in honour of the blessed virgin and the twelve apostles.

"Ay, it's as you see!" replied the stranger, bitterly. "It is here—husht, now—husht, I say—I will say *the thing* to her, mayn't I? Ay, indeed, Mary Sullivan, 'tis with me always—always. Well, well, no, I won't, I won't—easy. Oh, blessed saints, easy, and I won't!"

In the meantime Mrs. Sullivan had uncorked her bottle of holy water, and plentifully bedewed herself with it, as a preservative against this mysterious woman and her dreadful secret.

"Blessed mother above!" she ejaculated, "*the Lianhan Shee!*" And as she spoke, with the holy water in the palm of her hand, she advanced cautiously, and with great terror, to throw it upon the stranger and the unearthly thing she bore.

"Don't attempt it!" shouted the other, in tones of mingled fierceness and terror; "do you want to give *me* pain without keeping *yourself* anything at all safer? Don't you know *it* doesn't care about your holy water? But I'd suffer for it, an' perhaps so would you."

Mrs. Sullivan, terrified by the agitated looks of the woman, drew back with affright, and threw the holy water with which she intended to purify the other on her own person.

"Why thin, you lost crathur, who or what are you at all?—don't, don't—for the sake of all the saints and angels of heaven, don't come next or near me—keep your distance—but what are you, or how did you come to get that 'good thing' you carry about wid you?"

"Ay, indeed!" replied the woman bitterly, "as if I would or could tell you that! I say, you woman, you're doing what's not right in asking me a question you ought not to let cross your lips—look to yourself, and what's over you."

The simple woman, thinking her meaning literal, almost leaped off her seat with terror, and turned up her eyes to ascertain whether or not any dreadful appearance had approached her, or hung over her where she sat.

"Woman," said she, "I spoke to you kind an' fair, an' I wish you well- but -"

"But what?" replied the other—and her eyes kindled into deep and profound excitement, apparently upon very slight grounds.

"Why—hem—nothin' at all sure, only"—

"Only what?" asked the stranger, with a face of anguish that seemed to torture every feature out of its proper lineaments.

"Dacent woman," said Mrs. Sullivan, whilst the hair began to stand with terror upon her head, "sure it's no wondher in life that I'm in a perplexity, whin a *Lianhan Shee* is undher the one roof wid me. 'Tisn't that I want to know anything at all about it—the dear forbid I should; but I never hard of a person bein' tormented wid it as you are. I always used to hear the people say that it thrated its friends well."

"Husht!" said the woman, looking wildly over her shoulder, "I'll not tell: it's on myself I'll leave the blame! Why, will you never pity me? Am I to be night and day tormented? Oh, you're wicked and cruel for no reason!"

"Thry," said Mrs. Sullivan, "an' bless yourself; call on God."

"Ah!" shouted the other, "are you going to get me killed?" and as she uttered the words, a spasmodic working which must have occasioned great pain, even to torture, became audible in her throat: her bosom heaved up and down, and her head was bent repeatedly on her breast, as if by force.

"Don't mention that name," said she, "in my presence, except you mean to drive me to utter distractions. I mean," she continued, after considerable effort to recover her former tone and manner—"hear me with attention—I mean, woman—you, Mary Sullivan—that if you mention that holy name, you might as well keep plunging sharp knives into my heart! Husht! peace to me for one minute, tormentor! Spare me something, I'm in your power!"

"Will you ate anything?" said Mrs. Sullivan; "poor crathur, you look like hunger an' distress; there's enough in the house, blessed be them that sent it! an' you had bedther thry an' take some nourishment, any way;" and she raised her eyes in a silent prayer of relief and ease for the unhappy woman, whose unhallowed association had, in her opinion, sealed her doom.

"Will I?—will I?—oh!" she replied, "may you never know misery for offering it! Oh, bring me something—some refreshment—some food—for I'm dying with hunger."

Mrs. Sullivan, who, with all her superstition, was remarkable for charity and benevolence, immediately placed food and drink before her, which the stranger absolutely devoured -taking care occasionally to secrete under the protuberance which appeared behind her neck, a portion of what she ate. This, however, she did, not by stealth, but openly; merely taking means to prevent the concealed thing, from being, by any possible accident, discovered. When the craving of hunger was satisfied, she appeared to suffer less from the persecution of her tormentor than before; whether it was, as Mrs. Sullivan thought, that the food with which she plied it, appeased in some degree its irritability, or lessened that of the stranger, it was difficult to say; at all events, she became more composed; her eyes resumed somewhat of a natural expression; each sharp ferocious glare, which shot from them with such intense and rapid flashes, partially disappeared; her knit brows dilated, and part of a forehead, which had once been capacious and handsome, lost the contractions which deformed it by deep wrinkles. Altogether the change was evident, and very much relieved Mrs. Sullivan, who could not avoid observing it.

"It's not that I care much about it, if you'd think it not right o' me, but it's odd enough for you to keep the lower part of your face muffled up in that black cloth, an' then your forehead, too, is covered down on your face a bit? If they're part of the *bargain*,"— and she shuddered at the thought—"between you an' anything that's not good—hem!—I think you'd do well to throw thim off o' you an' turn to thim that can protect you from everything that's bad. Now a scapular would keep all the divils in hell from one; an' if you'd"—

On looking at the stranger she hesitated, for the wild expression of her eyes began to return. "Don't begin my punishment again," replied the woman, "make no allus—don't make mention in my presence of anything that's good. Husht,—husht—it's beginning—easy now—easy! No," said she, "I came to tell you, that only for my breaking a vow I made to this thing upon me, I'd be happy instead of miserable with it. I say, it's a good thing to have, if the person will use this bottle," she added, producing one, "as I will direct them."

"I wouldn't wish, for my part," replied Mrs. Sullivan, "to have anything to do wid it—neither act nor part;" and she crossed herself devoutly, on contemplating such an unholy alliance as that at which her companion hinted.

"Mary Sullivan," replied the other, "I can put good fortune and happiness in the way of you and yours. It is for you the good is intended; if *you* don't get both, *no other* can," and her eyes kindled

116

as she spoke like those of the Pythoness in the moment of inspiration.

Mrs. Sullivan looked at her with awe, fear, and a strong mixture of curiosity; she had often heard that the *Lianhan Shee* had, through means of the person to whom it was bound, conferred wealth upon several, although it could never render this important service to those who exercised direct authority over it. She therefore experienced a conflict between her fears and a love of that wealth, the possession of which was so plainly intimated to her.

"The money," said she, "would be one thing, but to have the *Lianhan Shee* planted over a body's shouldher—och! the saints preserve us!—no, not for oceans of hard goold would I have it in my company one minnit. But in regard to the money—hem! -why, if it could be managed widout havin' act or part wid *that thing*, people would do anything in rason and fairity."

"You have this day been kind to me," replied the woman, "and that's what I can't say of many—dear help me!—husht! Every door is shut in my face! Does not every cheek get pale when I am seen? If I meet a fellow-creature on the road, they turn into the field to avoid me; if I ask for food, it's to a deaf ear I speak; if I am thirsty, they send me to the river. What house would shelter me? In cold, in hunger, in drought, in storm, and in tempest, I am alone and unfriended, hated, feared, an' avoided; starving in the winter's cold, and burning in the summer's heat. All this is my fate here; and—oh! oh! oh!—have mercy, tormentor—have mercy! I will not lift my thoughts there—I'll keep the paction—but spare me *now!*"

She turned round as she spoke, seeming to follow an invisible object, or, perhaps, attempting to get a more complete view of the mysterious being which exercised such a terrible and painful influence over her. Mrs. Sullivan, also, kept her eye fixed upon the lump, and actually believed that she saw it move. Fear of incurring the displeasure of what it contained, and a superstitious reluctance harshly to thrust a person from her door who had eaten of her food, prevented her from desiring the woman to depart.

"In the name of Goodness," she replied, "I will have nothing to do wid your gift. Providence, blessed be his name, has done well for me an' mine; an' it mightn't be right to go beyant what it has pleased *him* to give me."

"A rational sentiment!—I mean there's good sense in what you

117

say," answered the stranger: "but you need not be afraid," and she accompanied the expression by holding up the bottle and kneeling: "now," she added, "listen to me, and judge for yourself, if what I say, when I swear it, can be a lie." She then proceeded to utter oaths of the most solemn nature, the purport of which was to assure Mrs. Sullivan that drinking of the bottle would be attended with no danger.

"You see this little bottle, drink it. Oh, for my sake and your own, drink it; it will give wealth without end, to you, and to all belonging to you. Take one-half of it before sun-rise, and the other half when he goes down. You must stand while drinking it, with your face to the east, in the morning; and at night, to the west. Will you promise to do this?"

"How would drinkin' the bottle get me money?" inquired Mrs. Sullivan, who certainly felt a strong tendency of heart to the wealth.

"That I can't tell you now, nor would you understand it, even if I could; but you will know all when what I say is complied with."

"Keep your bottle, dacent woman. I wash my hands out of it: the saints above guard me from the timptation! I'm sure it's not right, for as I'm a sinner, 'tis getting stronger every minute widin me? Keep it! I'm loth to bid any one that *ett* o' my bread to go from my hearth, but if you go, I'll make it worth your while. Saints above, what's comin' over me. In my whole life I never had such a hankerin' afther money! Well, well, but it's quare entirely!"

"Will you drink it!" asked her companion. "If it does hurt or harm to you or yours, or anything but good, may what is hanging over me be fulfilled!" and she extended a thin, but, considering her years, not ungraceful arm, in the act of holding out the bottle to her kind entertainer. "For the sake of all that's good and gracious take it without scruple—it is not hurtful, a child might drink every drop that's in it. Oh, for the sake of all you love, and all that love you, take it!" and as she urged her, the tears streamed down her cheeks.

"No, no," replied Mrs. Sullivan, "it'll never cross my lips; not if it made me as rich as ould Hendherson, that airs his guineas in the sun, for fraid they'd get light by lyin' past."

"I entreat you to take it?" said the strange woman.

"Never, never!—once for all—I say, I won't; so spare your breath."

The firmness of the good housewife was not, in fact, to be shaken; so, after exhausting all the motives and arguments with which she could urge the accomplishment of her design, the strange woman, having again put the bottle into her bosom, prepared to depart. She had now once more become calm, and resumed her seat with the languid air of one who has suffered much exhaustion and excitement. She put her hand upon her forehead for a few moments, as if collecting her faculties, or endeavouring to remember the purport of their previous conversation. A slight moisture had broken through her skin, and altogether, notwithstanding her avowed criminality in entering into an unholy bond, she appeared an object of deep compassion.

In a moment, her manner changed again, and her eyes blazed out once more, as she asked her alarmed hostess:—

"Again, Mary Sullivan, will you take the gift that I have it in my power to give you? ay or no? speak, poor mortal, if you know what is for your own good?"

Mrs. Sullivan's fears, however, had overcome her love of money, particularly as she thought that wealth obtained in such a manner could not prosper; her only objection being to the means of acquiring it.

"Oh!" said the stranger, "am I doomed never to meet with any one who will take the promise off me by drinking of this bottle. Oh! but I am unhappy! What it is to fear—ah! ah!—and keep *his* commandments. Had *I* done so in my youthful time, I wouldn't now—ah—merciful mother, is there no relief? kill me, tormentor; kill me outright, for surely the pangs of eternity cannot be greater than those you now make me suffer. Woman," said she, and her muscles stood out in extraordinary energy—"woman, Mary Sullivan—ay, if you should kill me—blast me—where I stand, I will say the word—woman—you have daughters—teach them—to fear—" Having got so far, she stopped—her bosom heaved up and down—her frame shook dreadfully—her eyeballs became lurid and fiery—her hands were clenched, and the spasmodic throes of inward convulsion worked the white froth up to her mouth; at length she suddenly became like a white statue, with this wild supernatural expression intense upon her, and with an awful calmness, by far more dreadful than excitement could be, concluded by pronouncing in deep husky tones, the name of God.

Having accomplished this with such a powerful struggle, she turned round with pale despair in her countenance and manner, and with streaming eyes slowly departed, leaving Mrs. Sullivan in a situation not at all to be envied.

In a short time the other members of the family, who had been out at their evening employments, returned. Bartley, her husband, having entered somewhat sooner than his three daughters from milking, was the first to come in; presently the girls followed, and in a few minutes they sat down to supper, together with the servants, who dropped in one by one, after the toil of the day. On placing themselves about the table, Bartley as usual took his seat at the head; but Mrs. Sullivan, instead of occupying hers, sat at the fire in a state of uncommon agitation. Every two or three minutes she would cross herself devoutly, and mutter such prayers against spiritual influences of an evil nature, as she could compose herself to remember.

"Thin, why don't you come to your supper, Mary," said the husband, "while the sowans are warm? Brave and thick they are this night, any way."

His wife was silent, for so strong a hold had the strange woman and her appalling secret upon her mind, that it was not till he repeated his question three or four times—raising his head with surprise, and asking, "Eh, thin Mary, what's come over you—is it unwell you are?"—that she noticed what he said.

"Supper!" she exclaimed, "unwell! 'tis a good right I have to be unwell,—I hope nothin' bad will happen, any way. Feel my face, Nannie," she added, addressing one of her daughters, "it's as cowld an' wet as a lime-stone—ay, an' if you found me a corpse before you, it wouldn't be at all strange."

There was a general pause at the seriousness of this intimation. The husband rose from his supper, and went to the hearth where she sat.

"Turn round to the light," said he; "why, Mary dear, in the name of wondher, what ails you? for you're like a corpse sure enough. Can't you tell us what has happened, or what put you in such a state? Why, childhre, the cowld sweat's teemin' off her!"

The poor woman, unable to sustain the shock produced by her interview with the stranger, found herself getting more weak, and requested a drink of water; but before it could be put to her lips, she laid her head upon the back of the chair and fainted. Grief, and uproar, and confusion, followed this alarming incident. The presence of mind, so necessary on such occasions, was wholly lost; one ran here, and another there, all jostling against each other, without being cool enough to render her proper assistance. The daughters were in tears, and Bartley himself was dreadfully shocked by seeing his wife apparently lifeless before him. She soon recovered, however, and relieved them from the apprehension of her death, which they had thought had actually taken place. "Mary," said the husband, "something quare entirely has happened, or you wouldn't be in this state!"

"Did any of you see a strange woman lavin' the house, a minute or two before ye came in?" she inquired.

"No," they replied, "not a stim of any one did we see."

"Wurrah dheelish! No?—now is it possible ye didn't?" She then described her, but they all declared they had seen no such person.

"Bartley, whisper," said she, and beckoning him over to her, in few words she revealed the secret. The husband grew pale and crossed himself. "Mother of Saints! childhre," said he, "a *Lianhan Shee!*" The words were not sooner uttered, than every countenance assumed the pallidness of death; and every right hand was raised in the act of blessing the person, and crossing the forehead. "*The Lianhan Shee!*" all exclaimed in fear and horror—"This day's Friday, God betwixt us an' harm!"*

It was now after dusk, and the hour had already deepened into the darkness of a calm, moonless, summer night; the hearth, therefore, in a short time, became surrounded by a circle, consisting of every person in the house; the door was closed and securely bolted;—a struggle for the safest seat took place; and to Bartley's shame be it spoken, he lodged himself on the hob within the jamb, as the most distant situation from the fearful being known as the *Lianhan Shee.* The recent terror, however, brooded over them all; their topic of conversation was the mysterious visit, of which Mrs. Sullivan gave a painfully accurate detail; whilst every ear of those who composed her audience was set, and every single hair of their heads bristled up, as if awakened into distinct life by the story. Bartley looked into the fire soberly, except when the cat, in

---

* This short form is supposed to be a safeguard against the Fairies.
The particular day must be always named.

121

prowling about the dresser, electrified him into a start of fear, which sensation went round every link of the living chain about the hearth.

The next day the story spread throughout the whole neighbourhood, accumulating in interest and incident as it went. Where it received the touches, embellishments, and emendations, with which it was amplified, it would be difficult to say; every one told it, forsooth, *exactly* as he heard it from another; but indeed it is not improbable, that those through whom it passed, were unconscious of the additions it had received at their hands. It is not unreasonable to suppose, that imagination in such cases often colours highly without a premeditated design of falsehood. Fear and dread, however, accompanied its progress; such families as had neglected to keep holy water in their houses borrowed some from their neighbours; every old prayer which had become rusty from disuse, was brightened up—charms were hung about the necks of cattle—and gospels about those of children—crosses were placed over the doors and windows;—no unclean water was thrown out before sun-rise or after dusk—

"E'en those prayed now who never prayed before,
And those who always prayed, still prayed the more."

The inscrutable woman who caused such general dismay in the parish, was an object of much pity. Avoided, feared, and detested, she could find no rest for her weary feet, nor any shelter for her unprotected head. If she was seen approaching a house, the door and windows were immediately closed against her; if met on the way she was avoided as a pestilence. How she lived no one could tell, for none would permit themselves to know. It was asserted that she existed without meat or drink, and that she was doomed to remain possessed of life, the prey of hunger and thirst, until she could get some one weak enough to break the spell by drinking her hellish draught, to taste which, they said, would be to change places with herself, and assume her despair and misery.

There had lived in the country about six months before her appearance in it, a man named Stephenson. He was unmarried, and the last of his family. This person led a solitary and secluded life, and exhibited during the last years of his existence strong symptoms of eccentricity, which for some months before his death, assumed a character of unquestionable derangement. He

122

was found one morning hanging by a halter in his own stable, where he had, under the influence of his malady, committed suicide. At this time the public press had not, as now, familiarised the minds of the people to that dreadful crime, and it was consequently looked upon *then* with an intensity of horror, of which we can scarcely entertain any adequate notion.

His farm remained unoccupied, for while an acre of land could be obtained in any other quarter, no man would enter upon such unhallowed premises. The house was locked up, and it was currently reported that Stephenson and the devil each night repeated the hanging scene in the stable; and that when the former was committing the 'hopeless sin', the halter slipped several times from the beam of the stable-loft, when Satan came, in the shape of a dark-complexioned man with a hollow voice, and secured the rope until Stephenson's end was accomplished.

In this stable did the wanderer take up her residence at night; and when we consider the belief of the people in the night-scenes which were supposed to occur in it, we need not be surprised at the new feature of horror which this circumstance superadded to her character. Her presence and appearance in the parish were dreadful; a public outcry was soon raised against her, which, were it not from fear of her power over their lives and cattle, might have ended in her death. None, however, had courage to grapple with her, or to attempt expelling her by violence, lest a signal vengeance might be taken on any who dared to injure a woman that could call in the terrible aid of the *Lianhan Shee*.

In this state of feeling they applied to the parish priest, who, on hearing the marvellous stories related concerning her, and on questioning each man closely upon his authority, could perceive, that, like most other reports, they were to be traced principally to the imagination and fears of the people. He ascertained, however, enough from Bartley Sullivan to justify a belief that there was something certainly uncommon about the woman; and being of a cold, phlegmatic disposition, with some humour, he desired them to go home, if they were wise—he shook his head mysteriously as he spoke—"and do this woman no injury, if they didn't wish"— and with this abrupt hint he sent them about their business.

This, however, did not satisfy them. In the same parish lived a suspended priest, called Father Philip O'Dallaghy, who supported himself, as most of them do, by curing certain diseases of the people—miraculously! He had no other means of subsistence, nor, indeed, did he seem strongly devoted to life, or to the pleasures it afforded. He was not addicted to those intemperate habits which characterise 'Blessed Priests' in general; spirits he never tasted, nor any food that could be termed a luxury, or even a comfort. His communion with the people was brief, and marked by a tone of severe contemptuous misanthropy. He seldom stirred abroad except during morning, or in the evening twilight, when he might be seen gliding amidst the coming darkness, like a dissatisfied spirit. His life was an austere one, and his devotional practices were said to be of the most remorseful character. Such a man, in fact, was calculated to hold a powerful sway over the prejudices and superstitions of the people. This was true. His power was considered almost unlimited, and his life one that would not disgrace the highest saint in the calendar. There were not wanting some persons in the parish who hinted that Father Felix O'Rourke, the parish priest, was himself rather reluctant to incur the displeasure, or challenge the power of the *Lianhan Shee*, by driving its victim out of the parish. The opinion of these persons was, in its distinct unvarnished reality, that Father Felix absolutely showed the white feather on this critical occasion—that he became shy, and begged leave to decline being introduced to this intractable pair—seeming to intimate that he did not at all relish adding them to his stock of acquaintances.

Father Philip they considered a decided contrast to him on this point. His stern and severe manner, rugged, and, when occasion demanded, daring, they believed suitable to the qualities requisite for sustaining such an interview. They accordingly waited on him; and after Bartley and his friends had given as faithful a report of the circumstances as, considering all things, could be expected, he told Bartley he would hear from Mrs. Sullivan's own lips the authentic narrative. This was quite satisfactory, and what was expected from him. As for himself, he appeared to take no particular interest in the matter, further than that of allaying the ferment and alarm which had spread throughout the parish.

"Plase your Reverence," said Bartley, "she came in to Mary, and she alone in the house, and for the matther o' that, I believe she laid hands upon her, and tossed and tumbled the crathur, and she but a sickly woman, through the four corners of the house. Not that Mary let on so much for she's afeard; but I know from her way, when she spakes about her, that it's thruth, your Reverence."

"But didn't the *Lianhan Shee*," said one of them, "put a sharp-pointed knife to her breast, wid a divilish intintion of makin' her give the best of atin' and dhrinkin' the house afforded?"

"She got the victuals, to a sartinty," replied Bartley, "and 'over-looked' my woman for her pains; for she's not the picture of herself since."

Every one now told some magnified and terrible circumstance, illustrating the formidable power of the *Lianhan Shee*.

When they had finished, the sarcastic lip of the priest curled into an expression of irony and contempt; his brow which was naturally black and heavy, darkened; and a keen, but rather a ferocious-looking eye, shot forth a glance, which, while it intimated disdain for those to whom it was directed, spoke also of a dark and troubled spirit in himself. The man seemed to brook with scorn the degrading situation of a religious quack, to which some incontrollable destiny had doomed him.

"I shall see your wife to-morrow," said he to Bartley; "and after hearing the plain account of what happened, I will consider what is best to be done with this dark, perhaps unhappy, perhaps guilty character; but whether dark, or unhappy, or guilty, I for one, should not, and will not, avoid her. Go, and bring me word to-morrow evening, when I can see her on the following day. Begone!"

When they withdrew, Father Philip paced his room for some time in silence and anxiety.

"Ay," said he, "infatuated people! sunk in superstition and ignorance, yet, perhaps, happier in your degradation than those who, in the pride of knowledge, can only look back upon a life of crime and misery. What is a sceptic? What is an infidel? Men who, when they will not submit to moral restraint, harden themselves into scepticism and infidelity, until, in the headlong career of guilt, that which was first adopted to lull the outcry of conscience, is supported by the pretended pride of principle. Principle in a sceptic! Hollow and devilish lie! Would *I* have plunged into scepticism, had I not first violated the moral sanctions of religion? Never. I became an infidel, because I first became a villain!

Writhing under a load of guilt, that which I wished might be true, I soon forced myself to think true: and now"—he here clenched his hands and groaned—"now—ay, now—and hereafter—oh, *that* hereafter! Why can I not shake the thought of it from my conscience? Religion! Christianity! With all the hardness of an infidel's heart, I feel your truth; because, if every man were the villain that infidelity would make him, then indeed might every man curse God for the existence bestowed upon him—as I would, but dare not do. Yet why can I not believe? Alas! why should God accept an unrepentant heart? Am I not a hypocrite, mocking him by a guilty pretension to his power, and leading the dark into thicker darkness? Then these hands—blood!—broken vows!—ha! ha! ha! Well, go—let misery have its laugh, like the light that breaks from the thunder-cloud. Prefer Voltaire to Christ; sow the wind, and reap the whirlwind, as I have done—ha, ha, ha! Swim, world—swim about me! I have lost the ways of Providence, and am dark! *She* awaits me; but I broke that chain that galled us: yet it still rankles—still rankles!"

The unhappy man threw himself into a chair in a paroxysm of frenzied agony. For more than an hour he sat in the same posture, until he became gradually hardened into a stiff, lethargic insensibility, callous and impervious to feeling, reason, or religion—an awful transition from a visitation of conscience so terrible as that which he had just suffered. At length he arose, and by walking moodily about, relapsed into his usual gloomy and restless character. When Bartley went home, he communicated to his wife Father Philip's intention of calling on the following day, to hear a correct account of the *Lianhan Shee*.

"Why, thin," said she, "I'm glad of it, for I intinded myself to go to him, any way, to get my new scapular consecrated. How-an'-ever, as he's to come, I'll get a set of gospels for the boys an' girls, an' he can consecrate all when his hand's in. Aroon, Bartley, they say that man's so holy that he can do anything—ay, melt a body off the face o' the earth, like snow off a ditch. Dear me, but the power they have is strange all out!"

"There's no use in gettin' him anything to ate or dhrink," replied Bartley; "he wouldn't take a glass o' whiskey once in seven years. Throth, myself thinks he's a little too dhry; sure he might be holy enough, an' yet take a sup of an odd time. There's Father Felix, an' though we all know he's far from bein' so blessed a man as him, yet he has friendship and neighbourliness in him, an' never refuses a glass in rason."

"But do you know what I was tould about Father Philip, Bartley?"

"I'll tell you that afther I hear it, Mary, my woman; you won't expect me to tell what I don't know? ha, ha, ha!"

"Behave, Bartley, an' quit yer jokin' now, at all evints; keep it till we're talkin' of somethin' else, an' don't let us be committin' sin, maybe, while we're spakin' of what we're spakin' about; but they say it's as thrue as the sun to the dial:—the Lent afore last it was,—he never tasted meat or dhrink durin' the whole seven weeks! Oh, you needn't stare! it's well known by thim that has as much sinse as you—no, not so much as you'd carry on the point o' this knittin'-needle. Well, sure the housekeeper an' the two sarvants wondhered—faix, they couldn't do less—an' took it into their heads to watch him closely; an' what do you think—blessed be all the saints above!—what do you think they *seen*?"

"The Goodness above knows; for me—I don't"

"Why, thin, whin he was asleep they seen a small silk thread in his mouth, that came down through the ceilin' from heaven, an' he suckin' it, just as a child would his mother's breast whin the crathur 'ud be asleep: so that was the way he was supported by the angels! An' I remember myself, though he's a dark, spare, yellow man at all times, yet he never looked half so fat an' rosy as he did the same Lent!"

"Glory be to Heaven! Well, well—*it is* sthrange the power they have! As for him, I'd as *lee* meet St. Pether, or St. Pathrick himself, as him; for one can't but fear him, somehow."

"Fear him! Och, it 'ud be a pity o' thim that 'ud do anything to vex or anger that man. Why, his very look 'ud wither thim, till there wouldn't be the track * o' thim on the earth; an' as for his curse, why it 'ud scorch thim to ashes!"

As it was generally known that Father Philip was to visit Mrs. Sullivan the next day, in order to hear an account of the mystery which filled the parish with such fear, a very great number of parishioners were assembled in and about Bartley's long before he

---

* Track, foot-mark, put for life.

made his appearance. At length he was seen walking slowly down the road, with an open book in his hand, on the pages of which he looked from time to time. When he approached the house, those who were standing about it assembled in a body, and, with one consent, uncovered their heads, and asked his blessing. His appearance bespoke a mind ill at ease; his face was haggard, and his eyes blood-shot. On seeing the people kneel, he smiled with his usual bitterness, and, shaking his hand with an air of impatience over them, muttered some words, rather in mockery of the ceremony than otherwise. They then rose, and blessing themselves, put on their hats, rubbed the dust off their knees, and appeared to think themselves recruited by a peculiar accession of grace.

On entering the house the same form was repeated; and when it was over, the best chair was placed for him by Mary's own hands, and the fire stirred up, and a line of respect drawn, within which none was to intrude, lest he might feel in any degree incommoded.

"My good neighbour," said he to Mrs. Sullivan, "what strange woman is this, who has thrown the parish into such a ferment? I'm told she paid you a visit? Pray sit down."

"I humbly thank your Reverence," said Mary, curtsying lowly, "but I'd rather not sit, Sir, if you plase. I hope I know what respect manes, your Reverence. Barny Bradagh, I'll thank you to stand up, if you plase, an' his Reverence to the fore, Barny."

"I ax your Reverence's pardon, an' yours, too, Mrs. Sullivan: sure we didn't mane the disrespect, any how, Sir, plase your Reverence."

"About this woman, and the *Lianhan Shee?*" said the priest, without noticing Barney's apology.

"Pray what do you precisely understand by a *Lianhan Shee?*"

"Why, Sir," replied Mary, "some sthrange bein' from the good people, or fairies, that sticks to some persons. There's a bargain, Sir, your Reverence, made atween thim; an' the divil, Sir, that is, the ould boy- the saints about us!—has a hand in it. The *Lianhan Shee*, your Reverence, is never seen only by thim it keeps wid; but— hem!—it always, wid the help of the ould boy, conthrives, Sir, to make the person brake the agreement, an' thin it has *thim* in *its* power; but if they *don't* brake the agreement, thin *it's* in *their* power. If they can get any body to put in their place, they may get

128

out o' the bargain; for they can, of a sartainty, give oceans o' money to people, but can't take any themselves, plase your Reverence. But sure, what's the use of me tellin' your Reverence what you know betther nor myself? an' why shouldn't you, or any one that has the power you have?"

He smiled again at this in his own peculiar manner, and was proceeding to inquire more particularly into the nature of the interview between them, when the noise of feet, and sounds of general alarm, accompanied by a rush of people into the house, arrested his attention, and he hastily inquired into the cause of the commotion. Before he could receive a reply, however, the house was almost crowded; and it was not without considerable difficulty that, by the exertions of Mrs. Sullivan and Bartley, sufficient order and quiet were obtained to hear distinctly what was said.

"Plase your Reverence," said several voices at once, "they're comin' hot-foot, into the very house to us! Was ever the likes seen! an' they must know right well, Sir, that you're widin in it."

"Who are coming?" he inquired.

"Why the woman, Sir, an' her *good pet*, the *Lianhan Shee*, your Reverence."

"Well," said he, "but why should you all appear so blanched with terror? Let her come in, and we shall see how far she is capable of injuring her fellow-creatures: some maniac," he muttered, in a low soliloquy, "whom the villainy of the world has driven into derangement -some victim to a hand like m——. Well, they say there *is* a Providence, yet such things are permitted!"

"He's sayin' a prayer now," observed one of them; "haven't we a good right to be thankful that he's in the place wid us while she's in it, or dear knows what harm she might do us—maybe *rise* the wind!" *

As the latter speaker concluded, there was a dead silence. The persons about the door crushed each other backwards, their feet set out before them, and their shoulders laid with violent pressure against those who stood behind, for each felt anxious to avoid all danger of contact with a being against whose power even a blessed priest found it necessary to guard himself by a prayer.

---

* It is generally supposed by the people, that persons who have entered into a compact with Satan can raise the wind by calling him up, and that it cannot be laid unless by the death of a black cock, a black dog, or an unchristened child.

At length a low murmur ran among the people—"Father O'Rourke!—here's Father O'Rourke!—he has turned the corner after her, an' they're both comin' in." Immediately they entered, but it was quite evident from the manner of the worthy priest, that he was unacquainted with the person of this singular being. When they crossed the threshold, the priest advanced, and expressed his surprise at the throng of people assembled.

"Plase your Reverence," said Bartley, "*that's* the woman," nodding significantly towards her as he spoke, but without looking at her person, lest the evil eye he dreaded so much might meet his, and give him 'the blast'.

The dreaded female, on seeing the house in such a crowded state, started, paused, and glanced with some terror at the persons assembled. Her dress was not altered since her last visit; but her countenance, though more meagre and emaciated, expressed but little of the unsettled energy which then flashed from her eyes, and distorted her features by the depth of that mysterious excitement by which she had been agitated. Her countenance was still muffled as before, the awful protuberance rose from her shoulders, and the same band which Mrs. Sullivan had alluded to during their interview, was bound about the upper part of her forehead.

She had already stood upwards of two minutes, during which the fall of a feather might be heard, yet none bade God bless her— no kind hand was extended to greet her—no heart warmed in affection towards her; on the contrary, every eye glanced at her, as a being marked with enmity towards God. Blanched faces and knit brows, the signs of fear and hatred, were turned upon her; her breath was considered pestilential, and her touch paralysis. There she stood, proscribed, avoided, and hunted like a tigress, all fearing to encounter, yet wishing to exterminate her! Who could she be?—or what had she done, that the finger of the Almighty marked her out for such a fearful weight of vengeance?"

Father Philip rose and advanced a few steps, until he stood confronting her. His person was tall, his features dark, severe, and solemn: and when the nature of the investigation about to take place is considered, it need not be wondered at, that the moment was, to those present, one of deep and impressive interest—such a visible conflict between a supposed champion of God and a supernatural being was calculated to excite.

"Woman," said he, in his deep stern voice, "tell me who and what you are, and why you assume a character of such a repulsive and mysterious nature, when it can entail only misery, shame, and persecution on yourself? I conjure you, in the name of Him after whose image you are created, to speak truly?"

He paused, and the tall figure stood mute before him. The silence was dead as death—every breath was hushed—and the persons assembled stood immoveable as statues! Still she spoke not; but the violent heaving of her breast evinced the internal working of some dreadful struggle. Her face before was pale—it was now ghastly; her lips became blue, and her eyes vacant.

"Speak!" said he, "I conjure you in the name of the power by whom you live!"

It is probable that the agitation under which she laboured was produced by the severe effort made to sustain the unexpected trial she had to undergo.

For some minutes her struggle subsided until it settled in a calmness which appeared fixed and awful as the resolution of despair. With breathless composure she turned round, and put back that part of her dress which concealed her face, except the band on her forehead, which she did not remove; having done this, she turned again, and walked calmly towards Father Philip, with a deadly smile upon her lips. When within a step of where he stood, she paused, and rivetting her eyes upon him, exclaimed-

"Who and what am I? The victim of infidelity and you, the bearer of a cursed existence, the scoff and scorn of the world, the monument of a broken vow and a guilty life, a being scourged by the scorpion lash of conscience, blasted by periodical insanity, pelted by the winter's storm, scorched by the summer's heat, withered by starvation, hated by man, and touched into my inmost spirit by the anticipated tortures of future misery. I have no rest for the sole of my foot, no repose for a head distracted by the contemplation of a guilty life; I am the unclean spirit which walketh to seek rest and findeth none; I am—*what you have made me.* Behold," she added, holding up the bottle, "this failed, and I live to accuse you. But no, you are my husband—though our union was but a guilty form, and I will bury that in silence. You thought me dead, and you flew to avoid punishment—did you avoid it? No; the finger of God has written pain and punishment upon your brow. I have been in all characters, in all shapes, have spoken with the tongue of a peasant, moved in my natural sphere; but my knees were smitten, my brain stricken, and the wild malady which banishes me from society has been upon me for years. Such I am, and such I say, have you made me. As for you, kind-hearted woman, there was nothing in this bottle but pure water. The interval of reason returned this day, and having remembered glimpses of our conversation, I came to apologise to you, and to explain the nature of my unhappy distemper, and to beg a little bread, which I have not tasted for two days. I at times conceive myself attended by an evil spirit, shaped by a guilty conscience, and this is the only familiar which attends me, and by it I have been dogged into madness through every turning of life. Whilst it lasts I am subject to spasms and convulsive starts which are exceedingly painful. The lump on my back is the robe I wore when innocent in my peaceful convent."

The intensity of general interest was now transferred to Father Philip; every face was turned towards him, but he cared not. A solemn stillness yet prevailed among all present. From the moment she spoke, her eye drew his with the power of a basilisk. His pale face became like marble, not a muscle moved; and when she ceased speaking, his blood-shot eyes were still fixed upon her countenance with a gloomy calmness like that which precedes a tempest. They stood before each other, dreadful counterparts in guilt, for truly his spirit was as dark as hers.

At length he glanced angrily around him:—"Well," said he, "what is it now, ye poor infatuated wretches, to trust in the sanctity *of man?* Learn from me to place the same confidence in God which you place in his *guilty creatures*, and you will not lean on a broken reed. Father O'Rourke, you, too, witness my disgrace, but not my punishment. It is pleasant, no doubt, to have a topic of conversation at your Conferences; enjoy it. As for you, Margaret, if society lessens misery, we may be less miserable. But the band of your order, and the remembrance of your vow is on your forehead, like the mark of Cain—tear it off, and let it not blast a man who is the victim of prejudice still, nay of superstition, as well as of guilt, tear it from my sight." His eyes kindled fearfully as he attempted to pull it away by force.

She calmly took it off, and he immediately tore it into pieces, and stamped upon the fragments as he flung them on the ground.

"Come," said the despairing man—"come—there is shelter for you, *but no peace!*—food, and drink, and raiment, *but no peace!*—NO PEACE!" As he uttered these words, in a voice that sank to its deepest pitch, he took her hand, and they both departed to his own residence.

The amazement and horror of those who were assembled in Bartley's house cannot be described. Our readers may be assured that they deepened in character as they spread throughout the parish. An undefined fear of this mysterious pair seized upon the people, for their images were associated in their minds with darkness and crime, and supernatural communion. The departing words of Father Philip rang in their ears: they trembled, and devoutly crossed themselves, as fancy again repeated the awful exclamation of the priest—"No peace! no peace!"

When Father Philip and his unhappy associate went home, he instantly made her a surrender of his small property; but with difficulty did he command sufficient calmness to accomplish even this. He was distracted—his blood seemed to have been turned to fire—he clenched his hands, and he gnashed his teeth, and exhibited the wildest symptoms of madness. About ten o'clock he desired fuel for a large fire to be brought into the kitchen, and got a strong cord, which he coiled, and threw carelessly on the table. The family were then ordered to bed. About eleven they were all asleep; and at the solemn hour of twelve he heaped additional fuel upon the living turf, until the blaze shone with scorching light upon everything around. Dark and desolating was the tempest within him, as he paced, with agitated steps, before the crackling fire.

"She is risen!" he exclaimed—"the spectre of all my crimes is risen to haunt me through life! I *am* a murderer—yet she lives, and my guilt is not the less! The stamp of eternal infamy is upon me—the finger of scorn will mark me out—the tongue of reproach will sting me like that of the serpent—the deadly touch of shame will cover me like a leper—the laws of society will crush the murderer, not the less that his wickedness in blood has miscarried: after that comes the black and terrible tribunal of the Almighty's vengeance—of his fiery indignation! Hush!—What sounds are those? They deepen—they deepen! Is it thunder? It cannot be the crackling of the blaze! *It is* thunder!—but it speaks only to *my* ear! Hush—Great God, there is a change in my voice! It is hollow and supernatural! Could a change have come over me? Am I living? Could I have— Hah!—Could I have departed? and am I now at length given over to the worm that never dies? If it be at my heart, I may feel it. God!— I am damned! Here is a viper twined about my limbs, trying to dart its fangs into my heart! Hah!—there are feet pacing in the room, too, and I hear voices! I am surrounded by evil spirits! Who's there?—What are you?—Speak! They are silent!—There is no answer! Again comes the thunder! But perchance this is not my place of punishment, and I will try to leave these horrible spirits!"

He opened the door, and passed out into a small green field that lay behind the house. The night was calm, and the silence profound as death. Not a cloud obscured the heavens;—the light of the moon fell upon the stillness of the scene around him, with all the touching beauty of a moonlit midnight in summer. Here he paused a moment, felt his brow, then his heart, the palpitations of which fell audibly upon his ear. He became somewhat cooler; the images of madness which had swept through his stormy brain disappeared, and were succeeded by a lethargic vacancy of thought, which almost deprived him of the consciousness of his own identity. From the green field he descended mechanically to a little glen which opened beside it. It was one of those delightful spots to which the heart clingeth. Its sloping sides were clothed with patches of wood, on the leaves of which the moonlight glanced with a soft lustre, rendered more beautiful by their stillness. That side on which the light could not fall, lay in deep shadow, which occasionally gave to the rocks and small projecting precipices an appearance of monstrous and unnatural life. Having passed through the tangled mazes of the glen, he at length reached its bottom, along which ran a brook, such as in the description of the poet,—

"In the leafy month of June,
Unto the sleeping woods all night,
Singeth a quiet tune."

Here he stood, and looked upon the green winding margin of the streamlet—but its song he heard not. With the workings of a guilty conscience, the beautiful in nature can have no association.

He looked up the glen, but its picturesque windings, soft vistas, and wild underwood mingling with gray rocks and taller trees, all mellowed by the moon-beams, had no charms for him. He maintained a profound silence—but it was not the silence of peace or reflection. He endeavoured to recall the scenes of the past day, but could not bring them back to his memory. Even the fiery tide of thought, which, like burning lava, seared his brain a few moments before, was now cold and hardened. He could remember nothing. The convulsion of his mind was over, and his faculties were impotent and collapsed.

In this state he unconsciously retraced his steps, and had again reached the paddock adjoining his house, when, as he thought, the figure of his paramour stood before him. In a moment his former paroxysm returned, and with it the gloomy images of a guilty mind, charged with the extravagant horrors of brain-struck madness.

"What!" he exclaimed, "the band is still on your forehead! Tear it off!"

He caught at the form as he spoke, but there was no resistance to his grasp. On looking again towards the spot it had ceased to be visible. The storm within him arose once more; he rushed into the kitchen, where the fire blazed out with fiercer heat; again he imagined that the thunder came to his ears, but the thunderings which he heard were only the voice of conscience. Again his own footsteps and his voice sounded in his fancy as the footsteps and voices of fiends, with which his imagination peopled the room. His state and his existence seemed to him a confused and troubled dream; he tore his hair—threw it on the table—and immediately started back with a hollow groan; for his locks, which but a few hours before had been as black as the raven's wing, were now as white as snow!

On discovering this, he gave a low but frantic laugh. "Ha, ha, ha!" he exclaimed; "here is another mark—here is food for despair. Silently, but surely, did the hand of God work this, as a proof that I am hopeless! But I will bear it; I will bear the sight! I now feel myself a man blasted by the eye of God himself! Ha, ha, ha! Food for despair! Food for despair!"

Immediately he passed into his own room, and approaching the looking glass beheld a sight calculated to move a statue. His hair had become literally white, but the shades of his dark complexion, now distorted by terror and madness, flitted, as his features worked under the influence of his tremendous passions, into an expression so frightful, that deep fear came over himself. He snatched one of his razors, and fled from the glass to the kitchen. He looked upon the fire, and saw the white ashes lying around its edge.

"Ha!" said he, "the light is come! I see the sign. I am directed, and I will follow it. There is yet ONE hope. The immolation! I shall be saved, yet so as by fire. It is for this my hair has become white;— the sublime warning for my self-sacrifice! The colour of ashes!— white -white! It is so!—I will sacrifice my body in material fire, to save my soul from that which is eternal! But I had anticipated the SIGN! The self-sacrifice is accepted!" *

We must draw a veil over that which ensued, as the description of it would be both unnatural and revolting. Let it be sufficient to say, that the next morning he was found burned to a cinder, with the exception of his feet and legs, which remained as monuments of, perhaps, the most dreadful suicide that ever was committed by man. His razor, too, was found bloody, and several clots of gore were discovered about the hearth; from which circumstances it was plain the he had reduced his strength so much by loss of blood, that when he committed himself to the flames, he was unable, even had he been willing, to avoid the fiery and awful sacrifice of which he made himself the victim. If anything could deepen the impression of fear and awe, already so general among the people, it was the unparalleled nature of his death. Its circumstances are yet remembered in the parish and county wherein it occurred—*for it is no fiction*, gentle reader! and the titular bishop who then presided over the diocese, declared, that while he lived, no person bearing the unhappy man's name should ever be admitted to the clerical order.

The shock produced by his death struck the miserable woman into the utter darkness of settled derangement. She survived him some years, but wandered about the province, still, according to the superstitious belief of the people, tormented by the terrible enmity of the *Lianban Shee*.

---

* As the reader may be disposed to consider the nature of the priest's death an unjustifiable stretch of fiction, I have only to say in my reply, that it is no fiction at all.

It is not, I believe, more than forty, or perhaps fifty years, since a priest committed his body to the flames for the purpose of saving his soul by an incrementary sacrifice. The object of the suicide being founded on the superstitious belief, that a priest guilty of great crimes possessed the privilege of securing salvation by self-sacrifice. We have heard two or three legends among the people in which this principle predominated. The outline of one of these, called "The Young Priest and Brian Braar", was as follows:-

A young priest on his way to the College of Valladolid, in Spain, was benighted; but found a lodging in a small inn on the road side. Here he was tempted by a young maiden of great beauty, who, in the moment of his weakness, extorted from him a bond signed with his blood, binding him to her for ever. She turned out to be an evil spirit: and the young priest proceeded to Valladolid with a heavy heart, confessed his crime to the Superior, who sent him to the Pope, who sent him to a Friar in the County of Armagh, called Brian Braar, who sent him to the devil. The devil, on the strength of Brian Braar's letter, gave him a warm reception, held a cabinet council immediately, and laid the despatch before his colleagues, who agreed that the claimant should get back his bond from the brimstone lady who had inveigled him. She, however, obstinately refused to surrender it, and stood upon her bond, until threatened with being thrown three times into Brian Braar's furnace. This tamed her: the man got his bond, and returned to Brian Braar on earth. Now Brian Braar had for three years past abandoned God, and taken to the study of magic with the devil; a circumstance which accounts for his influence below. The young priest, having possessed himself of his bond, went to Lough Derg to wash away his sins; and Brian Braar, having also become penitent, the two worthies accompanied each other to the lake. On entering the boat, however, to cross over to the island, such a storm arose as drove them back. Brian assured his companion that he himself was the cause of it.

"There is now," said he, "but one more chance for *me*; and we must have recourse to it."

He then returned homewards, and both had reached a hill-side near Brian's house, when the latter desired the young priest to remain there a few minutes, and he would return to him; which he did with a hatchet in his hand.

"Now," said he, "you must cut me into four quarters, and mince my body into small bits, then cast them into the air, and let them go with the wind."

The priest, after much entreaty, complied with his wishes, and returned to Lough Derg, where he afterwards lived twelve years upon one meal of bread and water *per diem*. Having thus purified himself, he returned home; but on passing the hill where he had minced the Friar, he was astonished to see the same man celebrating mass, attended by a very penitential-looking congregation of spirits.

"Ah," said Brian Braar, when mass was over, "you are now a happy man. With regard to my state, *for the voluntary sacrifice I have made of myself, I am to be saved*; but I must remain on this mountain until the Day of Judgement." So saying he disappeared.

There is little to be said about the superstition of the *Lianhan Shee*, except that it existed as we have drawn it, and that it is now fading away fast. There is also something appropriate in associating the heroine of this little story with the being called the *Lianhan Shee*, because, setting the superstition aside, any female who fell into her crime was called *Lianhan Shee*. *Lianhan Shee an Sogarth* signifies a priest's paramour, or, as the country people say, "Miss." Both terms have now nearly become obsolete.

5.

The Castle Of Aughentain
from the *Irish Penny Journal* (1841)

WHEN TOM HAD expressed an intention of relating an old story, the hum of general conversation gradually subsided into silence, and every face assumed an expression of curiosity and interest, with the exception of Jemsy Baccagh, who was rather deaf, and blind George M'Givor, so called because he wanted an eye; both of whom, in high and piercing tones, carried on an angry discussion touching a small law-suit that had gone against Jemsy in the Court Leet, of which George was a kind of rustic attorney. An outburst of impatient rebuke was immediately poured upon them from fifty voices. "Whist with yez, ye pair of devils' limbs, an' Tom goin' to tell us a story. Jemsy, your sowl's as crooked as your lame leg, you sinner; an' as for blind George, if roguery would save a man, he'd escape the devil yet. Tarenation to yez, an' be quiet till we hear the story!"

"Ay," said Tom, "Scripthur says that when the blind leads the blind, both will fall into the ditch; but God help the lame that have blind George to lead them; we might aisily guess where he'd guide them to, especially such a poor innocent as Jemsy there." This banter, as it was not intended to give offence, so was it received by the parties to whom it was addressed with laughter and good humour.

"Silence, boys," said Tom; "I'll jist take a draw of the pipe till I put my mind in a proper state of transmigration for what I'm going to narrate."

He smoked on for a few minutes, his eyes complacently but meditatively closed, and his whole face composed into the philosophic spirit of a man who knew and felt his own superiority, as well as what was expected from him. When he had sufficiently arranged the materials in his mind, he took the pipe out of his mouth, rubbed the shank-end of it against the cuff of his coat, then handed it to his next neighbour, and having given a short preparatory cough, thus commenced his legend:—

"You must know that afther Charles the First happened to miss his head one day, havin' lost while playing a game of 'Heads an' Points' with the Scotch, that a man called Nolly Rednose, or Oliver Crummle, was sent over to Ireland with a parcel of breekless Highlanders an' English Bodaghs to subduvate the Irish, an' as many of the Prodestans as had been friends to the late king, who were called Royalists. Now, it appears that by many larned transfigurations that Nolly Rednose had in his army a man named Balgruntie, or the Hog of Cupar; a fellow who was as coorse as sackin', as cunnin' as a fox, an' as gross as the swine he was named afther. Rednose, there is no doubt of it, was as nate a hand at takin' a town or a castle as ever went about it; but then, any town that didn't surrendher at discretion was sure to experience little mitigation at his hands; an' whenever he was bent on wickedness, he was sure to say his prayers at the commencement of every siege or battle; that is, he intended to show no marcy in, for he'd get a book, an' openin' it at the head of his army, he'd cry, 'Ahem, my brethren, let us praise God by endeavourin' till sing sich or sich a psalm;' an' God help the man, woman, or child, that came before him after that.

Well an' good: it so happened that a squadron of his psalm-singers were dispatched by him from Enniskillen, where he stopped to rendher assistance to a part of his army that O'Neill was leatherin' down near Dungannon, an' on their way they happened to take up their quarthers for the night at the Mill of Aughentain. Now, above all men in the creation, who should be appointed to lead this same squadron but the Hog of Cupar. 'Balgruntie, go off wid you,' said Crummle, when administering his instructions to him; 'but be sure that whenever you meet a fat royalist on the way, to pay your respects to him as a Christian ought,' says he; 'an', above all things, my dear brother Balgruntie, don't neglect your devotions, otherwise our arms can't prosper; and be sure,' says he, with a pious smile, 'that if they promulgate opposition, you will make them bleed anyhow, either in purse or person; or if they provoke the grace o' God, take a little from them in both; an' so the Lord's name be praised, yeamen!'

Balgruntie sang a psalm of thanksgivin' for bein' elected by his commander to sich a holy office, set out on his march, an' the next

139

night he an' his choir slep in the mill of Aughentaín, as I said. Now, Balgruntie had in this same congregation of his a long-legged Scotchman named Sandy Saveall, which name he got by way of etymology, for his charity; for it appears by the historical elucidations that Sandy was perpetually rantinizin' about sistherly affection an' brotherly love: an' what showed more taciturnity than any thing else was, that while this same Sandy had the persuasion to make every one believe that he thought of nothing else, he shot more people than any ten men in the squadron. He was indeed what they call a dead shot, for no one ever knew him to miss any thing he fired at. He had a musket that could throw point blank an English mile, an' if he only saw a man's nose at that distance, he used to say that with aid from above he could blow it for him with a musket bullet; and so by all associations he could, for indeed the faits he performed were very insiniuating an' problematical.

Now, it so happened that at this period there lived in the castle a fine wealthy ould royalist, named Graham or Grimes, as they are often denominated, who had but one child, a daughter, whose beauty and perfections were mellifluous far an' near over the country, an' who had her health drunk, as the toast of Ireland, by the Lord Lieutenant in the Castle of Dublin, undher the sympathetic appellation of 'the Rose of Aughentain'. It was her son that afterwards ran through the estate, and was forced to part with the castle; an' it's to him the proverb colludes, which mentions 'ould John Grame, that swallowed the castle of Aughentain.'

Howsomever, that bears no prodigality to the story I'm narratin'. So what would you have of it, but Balgruntie, who had heard of the father's wealth and the daughter's beauty, took a holy hankerin' afther both; an' havin' as usual said his prayers an' sung a psalm, he determined for to clap his thumb upon the father's money, thinkin' that the daughter would be the more aisily superinduced to folly it. In other words, he made up his mind to sack the castle, carry off the daughter and marry her righteously, rather, he said, through a sincere wish to bring her into a state of grace, by a union with a God-fearin' man, whose walk he trusted was Zionward, than from any cardinal detachment for her wealth or beauty. He accordingly sent up a file of the most pious men he had, picked fellows, with good psalm-singin' voices and strong noses, to request that John Graham would give them possession of the castle for a time, an' afterwards join them at prayers, as a proof that he was no royalist, but a friend to Crummle an' the Commonwealth. Now, you see, the best of it was, that the very man they demanded this from was commonly denominated by the people as 'Gunpowdher Jack,' in consequence of the great signification of his courage; an', besides, he was known to be a member of the Hell-fire Club, that no person could join that hadn't fought three duels, and killed at least one man; and in ordher to show that they regarded neither God nor hell, they were obligated to dip one hand in blood an' the other in fire, before they could be made members of the club. It's aisy to see, then, that Graham was not likely to quail before a handful of the very men he hated wid all the vociferation in his power, an' he accordingly put his head out of the windy, an' axed them their tergiversation for bein' there.

'Begone about your business,' said he; 'I owe you no regard. What brings you before the castle of a man who despises you? Don't think to determinate me, you canting rascals, for you can't. My castle's well provided wid men, an' ammunition, an' food; an' if you don't be off, I'll make you sing a different tune from a psalm one.' Begad he did, plump to them, out of the windy.

When Crummle's men returned to Balgruntie in the mill, they related what had tuck place, an' he said that afther prayers he'd send a second message in writin', an' if it wasn't attended to, they'd put their trust in God an' storm the castle. The squadron he commanded was not a numerous one; an' as they had no artillery, an' were surrounded by enemies, the takin' of the castle, which was a strong one, might cost them some snufflication. At all events, Balgruntie was bent on makin' the attempt, especially afther he heard that the castle was well vittled, an' indeed he was meritoriously joined by his men, who piously licked their lips on hearin' of such glad tidings. Graham was a hot-headed man, without much ambidexterity or deliberation, otherwise he might have known that the bare mintion of the beef an' mutton in his castle was only fit to make such a hungry pack desperate. But be that as it may, in a short time Balgruntie wrote him a letter, demandin' of him, in the name of Nolly Rednose an' the Commonwealth, to surrendher the castle, or if not, that, ould as he was, he would make him as soople as a two-year-ould. Graham, after readin' it, threw the letther back to the messengers wid a certain recommendation to Balgruntie regardin' it; but whether the same recommendation was followed up an' acted on so soon as he wished, historical relatiations do not inform.

On their return the military narrated to their commander the reception they resaved a second time from Graham, an' he then resolved to lay regular siege to the castle; but as he knew they could not readily take it by violence, he determined, as they say, to starve the garrison leisurely an' by degrees. But, first an' foremost, a thought struck him, an' he immediately called Sandy Saveall behind the mill-hopper, which he had now turned into a pulpit for the purpose of expoundin' the word, an' givin' exhortations to his men.

'Sandy,' said he, 'are you in a state of justification today?"

'Towards noon,' replied Sandy, 'I had some strong wristlings with the enemy; but I am able, undher praise, to say that I defated him in three attacks, and I consequently feel my righteousness much recruited. I had some wholesome communings with the miller's daughter, a comely lass, who may yet be recovered from the world, an' led out of the darkness of Aigyp, by a word in saison.'

'Well, Sandy,' replied the other, 'I lave her to your own instructions; there is another poor benighted maiden, who is also comely, up in the castle of that godless sinner, who belongeth to the Perdition Club; an', indeed, Sandy, until he is somehow removed, I think there is little hope of plucking her like a brand out of the burning.'

He serenaded Sandy in the face as he spoke, an' then cast an extemporary glance at the musket, which was as much as to say 'can you translate an insinivation?' Sandy concocted a smilin' reply; and takin' up the gun, rubbed the barrel, an' pattin' it as a sportsman would pat the neck of his horse or dog, wid reverence for comparin' the villain to either one or the other.

'If it was known, Sandy,' said Balgruntie, 'it would harden her heart against me; an' as he is hopeless at all events, bein' a member of that Perdition Club'-

'True,' said Sandy, 'but you lave the miller's daughter to me?'

'I said so.' 'Well, if his removal will give you any consolation in the matther, you may say no more.'

'I could not, Sandy, justify it to myself to take him away by open

142

violence, for you know that I bear a conscience if any thing too tendher and dissolute. Also I wish, Sandy, to presarve an ondeniable reputation for humanity; an', besides, the daughter might become as reprobate as the father if she suspected me to be personally concarned in it. I have heard a good deal about him, an' am sensibly informed that he has been shot at twice before, by the sons, it is thought, of an enemy that he himself killed rather significantly in a duel.'

'Very well,' replied Sandy; 'I would myself feel scruples; but as both our conscience is touched in the business, I think I am justified. Indeed, captain, it is very likely that afther all that we are but the mere instruments in it, an' that it is through us that this ould unrighteous sinner is to be removed by a more transplendant judgment.'

Begad, neighbours, when a rascal is bent on wickedness, it is aisy to find cogitations enough to back him in his villainy. An' so was it with Sandy Saveall and Balgruntie. That evenin' ould Graham was shot through the head standin' in the windy of his own castle, an' to extenuate the suspicion of sich an act from Crummle's men, Balgruntie himself went up the next day, beggin' very politely to have a friendly explanation with the Squire Graham, sayin' that he had harsh ordhers, but that if the castle was peaceably delivered to him, he would, for the sake of the young lady, see that no injury should be offered either to her or her father.

The young lady, however, had the high drop in her, and becoorse the only answer he got was a flag of defiance. This nettled the villain, an' he found there was nothin' else for it but to plant a strong guard about the castle to keep all that was in, in— and all that was out, out.

In the mean time, the very appearance of the Crumwellians in the neighbourhood struck such terror into the people, that the country, which was then only very thinly inhabited, became quite desarted, an' for miles about the face of a human bein' could not be seen, barrin' their own, sich as they were. Crummle's track was always a bloody one, an' the people knew that they were wise in puttin' the hills an' mountain passes between him an' them. The miller an' his daughter bein' encouraged by Sandy, stayed principally for the sake of Miss Graham; but except them, there was not a man or woman in the barony to bid good-morrow to, or say

Salvey Dominey. On the beginnin' of the third day, Balgruntie, who knew his officialities extremely well, an' had sent down a messenger to Dungannon to see whether matters were so bad as they had been reported, was delighted to hear that O'Neill had disappeared from the neighbourhood. He immediately informed Crummle of this, and tould him that he had laid siege to one of the leadin' passes of the north, an' that, by gettin' possession of the two castles of Aughentain and Augher, he could keep O'Neill in check, and command that part of the country. Nolly approved of this, an' ordhered him to proceed, but was sorry that he could send him no assistance at present; 'however,' said he, 'with a good cause, sharp swords, an' aid from above, there is no fear of us.'

They now set themselves to take the castle in airnest. Balgruntie an' Sandy undherstood one another, an' not a day passed that some one wasn't dropped in it. As soon as ever a face appeared, pop went the deadly musket, an' down fell the corpse of whoever it was aimed at. Miss Graham herself was spared for good reasons, but in the coorse of ten or twelve days she was nearly alone. Ould Graham, though a man that feared nothing, was only guilty of a profound swagger when he reported the strength of the castle and the state of the provisions to Balgruntie an' his crew. But above all things, that which eclipsed their distresses was the want of wather. There was none in the castle, an' although there is a beautiful well beside it, yet, *fareer gair*, it was of small responsibility to them. Here, then, was the poor young lady placed at the marcy of her father's murdherer; for however she might have doubted in the beginnin' that he was shot by the Crumwellians, yet the death of nearly all the servants of the house in the same way was a sufficient proof that it was like masther like man in this case. What, however, was to be done? The whole garrison now consisted only of Miss Graham herself, a fat man cook advanced in years, who danced in his distress in ordher that he might suck his own perspiration, and a little orphan boy that she tuck undher her purtection. It was a hard case, an' yet, God bless her, she held out like a man.

It is an ould sayin' that there's no tyin' up the tongue of Fame, an' it's also a true one. The account of the siege had gone far an' near in the counthry, an' none of the Irish, no matter what they were who ever heard it, but wor sorry. Sandy Saveall was now the devil an' all. As there was no more in the castle to shoot, he should

144

find something to regenerate his hand upon: for instance, he practised upon three or four of Graham's friends, who undher one pretence or other were seen skulkin' about the castle, an' none of their relations durst come to take away the bodies in ordher to bury them. At length things came to pass, that poor Miss Graham was at the last gasp for something to drink; she had ferreted out as well as she could a drop of moisture here an' there in the damp corners of the castle, but now all that was gone; the fat cook had sucked himself to death, and the little orphan boy died calmly away a few hours afther him, lavin' the helpless lady with a tongue swelled an' furred, and a mouth parched and burned, for want of drink. Still the blood of the Grahams was in her, and yield she would not do to the villain that left her as she was. Sich then was the transparency of her situation, when, happening to be on the battlements to catch, if possible, a little of the dew of heaven, she was surprised to see something flung up, which rolled down towards her feet: she lifted it, an' on examinin' the contents, found it to be a stone covered with a piece of brown paper, inside which was a slip of white, containing the words, 'Endure—relief is near you!' But, poor young lady, of what retrospection could these tidings be to one in her situation?—she could scarcely see to read them; her brain was dizzy, her mouth felt like a cindher, her tongue swelled an' black, an' her breath felt as hot as a furnace. She could barely breathe, an' was in the very act of lyin' down undher the triumphant air of heaven to die, when she heard the shrill voice of a young kid in the castle yard, and immediately remembered that a brown goat which her lover, a gentleman named Simpson, had, when it was a kid, made her a present of, remained in the castle about the stable during the whole siege. She instantly made her way slowly down stairs, got a bowl, and havin' milked the goat, she took a little of the milk, which I need not asseverate at once relieved her. By this means she recovered, an' findin' no further anticipation from druth, she resolved like a hairo to keep the Crumwellians out, an' to wait till either God or man might lend her a helpin' hand.

Now, you must know that the miller's purty daughter had also a sweetheart called Suil Gair Maguire, or sharp-eye'd Maguire, an humble branch of the great Maguires of Enniskillen; an' this same Suil Gair was servant an' foster-brother to Simpson, who was the intended husband of Miss Graham. Simpson, who lived some miles off, on hearin' the condition of the castle, gathered together all the royalists far an' near; an' as Crummle was honestly hated by both Romans an' Prodestans, faith, you see, Maguire himself promised to send a few of his followers to the rescue. In the mean time, Suil Gair dressed himself up like a fool or idiot, an' undher the purtection of the miller's daughter, who blarnied Saveall in great style, was allowed to wandher about an' joke wid the sogers; but especially he took a fancy to Sandy, and challenged him to put one stone out of five in one of the port-holes of the castle, at a match of finger-stone. Sandy, who was nearly as famous at that as the musket, was rather relaxed when he saw that Suil Gair could at least put in every second stone, an' that he himself could hardly put in one out of twenty. Well, at all events it was durin' their sport that fool Paddy, as they called him, contrived to fling the scrap of writin' I spoke of across the battlements at all chances; for when he undhertook to go to the castle, he gave up his life as lost; but he didn't care about that, set in case he was able to save either his foster-brother or Miss Graham. But this is not at all indispensable, for it is well known that many a foster-brother sacrificed his life the same way, and in cases of great danger, when the real brother would beg to decline the compliment.

Things were now in a very connubial state entirely. Balgruntie heard that relief was comin' to the castle, an' what to do he did not know; there was little time to be lost, however, an' something must be done. He praiched flowery discourses twice a-day from the mill-hopper, an' sang psalms for grace to be directed in his righteous intentions; but as yet he derived no particular predilection from either. Sandy appeared to have got a more bountiful modelum of grace than his captain, for he succeeded at last in bringin' the miller's daughter to sit undher the word at her father's hopper. Fool Paddy, as they called Maguire, had now become a great favourite wid the sogers, an' as he proved to be quite harmless and inoffensive, they let him run about the place widout opposition. The castle, to be sure, was still guarded, but Miss Graham kept her heart up in consequence of the note, for she hoped every day to get relief from her friends. Balgruntie, now seein' that the miller's daughter was becomin' more serious undher the taichin' of Saveall, formed a plan that he thought might enable him to penetrate the castle, an' bear off the lady an' the money. This was to strive wid very delicate meditation to prevail on the miller's daughter, through the renown that he thought Sandy had over her, to open a correspondency wid Miss Graham; for he knew that if one of the gates was unlocked, and the unsuspectin' girl let in, the whole squadron would soon be in afther her. Now, this plan was the more dangerous to Miss Graham, because the miller's daughter had intended to bring about the very same denouncement for a different purpose. Between her friend an' her enemies it was clear the poor lady had little chance; an' it was Balgruntie's intention, the moment he had sequestrated her and the money, to make his escape, an' lave the castle to whomsoever might choose to take it. Things, however, were ordhered to take a different bereavement: the Hog of Cupar was to be trapped in the hydrostatics of his own hypocrisy, an' Saveall to be overmatched in his own premises. Well, the plot was mentioned to Sandy, who was promised a good sketch of the prog; an' as it was jist the very thing he dreamt about night an' day, he snapped at it as a hungry dog would at a sheep's trotter. That night the miller's daughter—whose name I may as well say was Nannie Duffy, the purtiest girl an' the sweetest singer that ever was in the country—was to go to the castle an' tell Miss Graham that the sogers wor all gone, Crummle killed, an' his whole army massacrayed to atoms. This was a different plan from poor Nannie's, who now saw clearly what they were at. But never heed a woman for bein' witty when hard pushed.

'I don't like to do it,' said she, 'for it looks like thrachery, espishilly as my father has left the neighbourhood, and I don't know where he is gone to; an' you know thrachery's ondacent in either man or woman. Still, Sandy, it goes hard for me to refuse one that I—I—well, I wish I knew where my father is—I would like to know what he'd think of it.'

'Hut,' said Sandy, 'where's the use of such scruples in a good cause?—when we get the money, we'll fly. It is principally for the sake of waining you an' her from the darkness of idolatry that we do it. Indeed, my conscience would not rest well if I let a soul an' body like yours remain a prey to Sathan, my darlin'.'

'Well,' says she, 'doesn't the captain exhort this evenin'?'

'He does, my beloved, an' with a blessin' will expound a few verses from the Song of Solomon.'

'It's betther then,' said she, 'to sit under the word, an' perhaps some light may be given to us.'

This delighted Saveall's heart, who now looked upon pretty Nannie as his own; indeed, he was obliged to go gradually and cautiously to his work, for cruel though Nolly Rednose was, Sandy knew that if any violent act of that kind should raich him, the guilty party would sup sorrow. Well, accordin' to this pious arrangement, Balgruntie assembled all his men who were not on duty about the hopper, in which he stood as usual, an' had commenced a powerful exhortation, the sub-stratum of which was devoted to Nannie; he dwelt upon the happiness of religious love; said that scruples were often suggested by Satan, an' that a heavenly duty was but terrestrial when put in comparishment wid an earthly one. He also made collusion to the old Squire that was popped by Sandy; said it was often a judgment for the wicked man to die in his sins; an' was gettin' on wid great eloquence an' emulation, when a low rumblin' noise was heard, an' Balgruntie, throwin' up his clenched hands an' grinding his teeth, shouted out, 'Hell and d—n, I'll be ground to death! The mill's goin' on! Murdher! murdher! I'm gone! 'Faith, it was true enough she had been wickedly set a-goin' by some one; an' before they had time to stop her, the Hog of Cupar had the feet and legs twisted off him before their eyes—a fair illustration of his own doctrine, that it is often a judgment for the wicked man to die in his sins.

When the mill was stopped, he was pulled out, but didn't live twenty minutes, in consequence of the loss of blood. Time was pressin', so they ran up a shell of a coffin, and tumbled it into a pit that was hastily dug for it on the mill-common. This, however, by no manner of manes relieved poor Nannie from the difficulty, for Saveall, finding himself now first in command, determined not to lose a moment in tolerating his plan upon the castle.

'You see,' said he, ' that a way is opened for us that we didn't expect; an' let us not close our eyes to the light that has been given, lest it might be suddenly taken from us again. In this instance I suspect that Paddy has been made the chosen instrument; for it appears upon inquiry that he too has disappeared. However, heaven's will be done! we will have the more to ourselves, my beloved—ehem! It is now dark,' he proceeded, 'so I shall go an' take my usual smoke at the mill window, an' in about a quarther of an hour I'll be ready.'

'But I'm all in a tremor after sich a frightful accident,' replied Nannie: 'an' I want to get a few minutes' quiet before we engage upon our undhertakin'.'

This was very natural, and Saveall accordingly took his usual seat at a little windy in the gable of the mill, that faced the miller's house; an' from the way the bench was fixed, he was obliged to sit with his face exactly towards the same direction. There we leave him meditatin' upon his own righteous approximations, till we folly Suil Gair Maguire, or fool Paddy, as they called him, who practicated all that was done. Maguire and Nannie, findin' that no time was to be lost, gave all over as ruined, unless somethin' could be acted on quickly. Suil Gair at once thought of settin' the mill a-goin', but kept the plan to himself, any further than tellin' her not to be surprised at any thing she might see. He then told her to steal him a gun, but if possible to let it be Saveall's, as he knew it could be depended on. 'But I hope you won't shed any blood if you can avoid it,' said she; 'that I don't like.' 'Tut,' replied Suil Gair, makin' evasion to the question, 'it's good to have it about me for my own defence.'

He could often have shot either Balgruntie or Saveall in day-light, but not without certain death himself, as he knew escape was impossible. Besides, time was not before so pressin' upon them, an' every day relief was expected. Now, royalists an' Maguire's men must be within a couple of hours journey—it would be too intrinsic entirely to see the castle plundhered, and the lady carried off by such a long-legged skyhill as Saveall. Nannie consequently, at great risk, took an opportunity of slipping his gun to Suil Gair, who was the best shot of the day in that or any other part of the country; and it was in consequence of this that he was called Suil Gair, or Sharp Eye.

But, indeed, all the Maguires were famous shots; an' I'm tould there's one of them now in Dublin that could hit a pigeon's egg or a silver sixpence at the distance of a hundred yards. Suil Gair did not merely raise the sluice when he set the mill a-goin', but he whipped it out altogether an' threw it in the dam, so that the possibility of saving the Hog of Cupar was irretrievable. He made off, however, an' threw himself among the tall ragweeds that grew

149

upon the common, till it got dark, when Saveall, as was his custom, should take his evenin' smoke at the windy. Here he sat for some period, thinkin' over many ruminations, before he lit his cutty pipe, as he called it.

'Now,' said he to himself, 'what is there to hindher me from takin' away, or rather from makin' sure of the grand lassie, instead of the miller's daughter? If I get intil the castle, it can soon be effected; for if she has any regard for her reputation, she will be quiet. I'm a braw handsome lad enough, a wee thought high in the cheek bones, scaly in the skin, an' knock-knee'd a trifle, but stout an' lathy, an' tough as a withy. But, again, what is to be done wi Nannie? Hut, she's but a miller's daughter, an' may be disposed of if she is troublesome. I know she's fond of me, but I dinna blame her for that. However, it wadna become me now to entertain scruples, seein' that the way is made so plain for me. But, save us! eh, sirs, that was an awful death, an' very like a judgment on the Hog of Cupar! It is often a judgment for the wicked to die in their sins! Balgruntie wasna that'—Whatever he intended to say further, cannot be analogized by man, for, just as he had uttered the last word, which he did while holding the candle to his pipe, the bullet of his own gun entered between his eyes, and the next moment he was a corpse.

Suil Gair desarved the name he got, for truer did never bullet go to the mark from Saveall's aim than it did from his. There is now little more to be superadded to my story. Before daybreak the next mornin', Simpson came to the relief of his intended wife; Crummle's party was surprised, taken, an' cut to pieces; an' it so happened that from that day to this the face of a soger belongin' to him was never seen near the mill or the castle of Aughentain, with one exception only, and that was this—You all know that the mill is often heard to go at night when nobody sets her a-goin', an' that the most sevendable screams of torture come out of the hopper, an' that when any one has the courage to look in, they're sure to see a man dressed like a soger, with a white mealy face, in the act, so to say, of havin' his legs ground off him. Many a guess was made about who the spirit could be, but all to no purpose. There, however, is the truth for yez; the spirit that shrieks in the hopper is Balgruntie's ghost, an' he's to be ground that way till the day of judgment.

Be coorse, Simpson and Miss Graham were married, as was Nannie Duffy an' Suil Gair; an' if they all lived long an' happy, I wish we may all live ten times longer an' happier; an' so we will, but in a betther world than this, plaise God."

"Well, but, Tom," said Gordon, "how does that account for my name, which you said you'd tell me?"

"Right," said Tom; "begad I was near forgettin' it. Why, you see, sich was their veneration for the goat that was the manes, undher God, of savin' Miss Graham's life, that they changed the name of Simpson to Gordon, which signifies in Irish *gor dhun*, or a brown goat, that all their posterity might know the great obligations they lay undher to that reverend animal."

"An' do you mane to tell me," said Gordon, "that my name was never heard of until Oliver Crummle's time?"

"I do. Never in the wide an' subterraneous earth was sich a name known till afther the prognostication I tould you; an' it never would either, only for the goat, sure. I can prove it by the pathepathetics. Denny Mullin, will you give us another draw o' the pipe?"

Tom's authority in these matters was unquestionable, and, besides, there was no one present learned enough to contradict him, with any chance of success, before such an audience. The argument was consequently, without further discussion, decided in his favour, and Gordon was silenced touching the origin and etymology of his own name.

This legend we have related as nearly as we can remember in Tom's words. We may as well, however, state at once that many of his legends were wofully deficient in authenticity, as indeed those of most countries are. Nearly half the Irish legends are *ex post facto* or *postliminious*. There is no record, for instance, that Oliver Cromwell ever saw the castle of Aughentain, or that any such event as that narrated by Tom ever happened in or about it. It is much more likely that the story, if ever there was any truth in it, is of Scotch origin, as indeed the names would seem to import. There is no doubt, however, that the castle of Aughentain, which is now in the possession of a gentleman named Browne we think, was once the property of a family named Graham. In our boyhood there was a respectable family of that name living in its immediate vicinity, but we know not whether they are the descendants of those who owned the castle or not.

6.

'Lyrical Touches'
from *Rody The Rover; Or, The Ribbonman* (1845)

IT WAS ONE of those breathless and serene evenings towards the close of May; the sun wanted somewhat less than an hour of setting, but from the cloudless aspect of the sky, and the faint hues of purple which began gradually to deepen as he approached the west, it was evident that he would go down to his evening rest in that calm and majestic splendour, which makes our early fancy imagine that the beautiful clouds he leaves behind him are the golden gates of heaven, through which the souls of the just pass into peace and happiness. The fields were green, and the evening light lay upon them with a hue which blended its radiance with their verdure, so as to produce that charm of almost indescribable beauty, which infuses, without our being conscious of its origin, a sense of hope and pure delight into the heart. The trees and green hedges were vocal with the melody of a thousand warblers; the cuckoo's happy note was still heard, as was the hum of a truant or over industrious bee that hurried home, as if apprehensive of being belated. Up at the other end of the green, where it shelved into the smooth sandy edge of the calm river, were the village children at play amongst themselves; whilst their shouting and laughter, as they were dispersed into little busy groups, came upon the ear in touching accordance with the simple harmonies that breathed from surrounding nature. The labours of the day had for some time closed, and the young men of the village of Ballybracken were amusing themselves in those harmless, but healthful feats, which constitute a considerable portion of simple and primitive happiness. Some were wrestling, some throwing the stone; whilst others again were engaged in the active and manly sport of leaping;—for we should have informed our readers, that from the lower end of Ballybracken a tolerably sized green stretched down to the river that flowed past, on the banks of which, about fifty yards above the ford where it was crossed, the inhabitants bleached their yarn and household linen. Standing neatly dressed in small groups were many of the village maidens, some sewing and others knitting, and all interested in the success of a brother, cousin, or a sweetheart, as the case happened; whilst removed at a little distance, might be observed a couple of either sex, here and there engaged in apparently deep and serious conversation; or indulging in that light-hearted mirth which is only to be found in the buoyancy of spirits that are yet simple and not depressed by crime. Tempted by the smoothness of the green sward, one of the crack dancers of the neighbourhood, Ned Moynagh, now calls upon Nannie Duffy to sing him the College Hornpipe, or Shaun Buie, or Jackson's Morning Brush, a call which immediately puts an end to the other sports, and brings the youngsters of the whole village, male and female about him. Then indeed commences the performance of the jig, reel, or hornpipe— and to such living melody as has seldom been heard to proceed from female lips. How could any one, however, look upon these lips and expect anything except music and sweetness from them? But now the shades of this peaceful evening are deepening; the crows seek their ancient rookery at Corick for the night; the cows are assembled in the village, and by their gentle and moan-like lowings, call upon the well-known maidens to ease them of their fragrant stores; and lastly, sure sign of approaching twilight, the hum of the snipe, as he rises and sinks above the mist covered meadow, reminds them, as does the fast falling honey-dew, that it is time to close their innocent pastimes for the day.

This was a happy group, composed as it was of young persons of both sexes, each remarkable for that freshness of heart and purity of morals, which are to be found in their most touching simplicity, among those who people the more distant recesses of rustic life—far away among the green vales and pastoral retreats of our beloved country.

7.

'The Native Doric' from
The Evil Eye; Or, The Black Spectre (1860)

THE FIRST HOUSE he went into was a small country cabin, such as a petty farmer of five or six acres at that time occupied. The door was not of wood, but of wicker-work woven across long wattles and plastered over with clay mortar. The house had two small holes in the front side-walls to admit the light; but during severe weather these were filled up with straw or rags to keep out the storm. On one side of the door stood a large curra, or, "ould man," for it was occasionally termed both—composed of brambles and wattles tied up lengthwise together—about the height of a man and as thick as an ordinary sack. This was used, as they termed it, "to keep the wind from the door." If the blast came from the right, it was placed on that side, and if from the left, it was changed to the opposite. Chimneys, at that period, were to be found only upon the houses of extensive and wealthy farmers, the only substitute for them being a simple hole in the roof over the fireplace. The small farmer in question cultivated his acres with a spade: and after sowing his grain he harrowed it in with a large thorn bush, which he himself, or one of his sons, dragged over it with a heavy stone on the top to keep it close to the surface. When Barney entered this cabin he found the vanithee, or woman of the house, engaged in the act of grinding oats into meal for their dinner with a quern, consisting of two diminutive millstones turned by the hand; this was placed upon a *praskeen*, or coarse apron, spread under it on the floor to receive the meal. An old woman, her mother, sat spinning flax with the distaff—for as yet flax wheels were scarcely known—and a lubberly young fellow about sixteen, with able, well shaped limbs and great promise of bodily strength, sat before the fire managing a double task, to wit, roasting, first, a lot of potatoes in the greeshaugh, which consisted of half embers and half ashes, glowing hot; and, secondly, at a little distance from the larger lighted turf, two ducks eggs, which, as well as the potatoes, he turned from time to time, that they might be equally done. All this he conducted by the aid of what was termed a *muddha ristha,* or rustic tongs, which was nothing more than a wattle, or stick, broken in the middle, between the ends of which he held both his potatoes and his eggs whilst turning them. Two good-looking, fresh-coloured girls were squatted on their hunkers (hams), cutting potatoes for seed—late as the season was—with two case knives, which had been borrowed from a neighbouring farmer of some wealth. The dress of the women was similar and simple. It consisted of a long-bodied gown that had only half skirts; that is to say, instead of encompassing the whole person, the lower part of it came forward only as far as the hip bones, on each side, leaving the front of the petticoat exposed. This posterior part of the gown would, if left to fall its full length, have formed a train behind them of at least two feet in length. It was pinned up, however, to a convenient length, and was not at all an ungraceful garment, if we except the sleeves, which went no farther than the elbows— a fashion in dress which is always unbecoming, especially when the arms are thin. The hair of the elder woman was covered by a *dowd cap,* the most primitive of all female headdresses, being a plain shell, or skull-cap, as it were, for the head, pointed behind, and without any fringe whatsoever. This turning up of the hair was peculiar only to married life, of which condition it was universally a badge.

8.

'A Bite and a Sup'
from *Parra Sastha, Or The History of Paddy Go-easy And His Wife Nancy* (1845)

DINNER WAS READY to be dished, as the saying is, but Nancy had yet to witness an instance of ingenuity and skill that had never come within her experience before. There stood beside the fire, fixed upon three large stones, placed in a triangle, an immense pot—one of those huge ones, in which it was customary, formerly, to distil illicit spirits—and for this very reason it is called poteen. Under this pot was a large turf fire, and in it three geese, two turkeys, an immense flitch of bacon, together with another commodity or two, which we shall soon describe. Each of the three Misses Go-easy got about this pot, which somewhat resembled that of the witches in Macbeth, only that here the fair witches took out instead of putting in. First out came the three fine fat geese; next appeared the two turkeys, after these, the bacon we spoke of, and, though last not least, something which sadly puzzled Mrs. Go-easy to understand. Whatever it may have been, it lay close to the bottom of the pot as if reluctant to give up its position, or, as one might not inappropriately imagine, from a strong apprehension of falling into unfriendly hands. Various were the attempts they made to get it up, and sometimes they did succeed in forcing it to raise its head, but no sooner had it seen the array of eager-looking faces, each with a ravenous spirit glaring out of his eyes, than down it popped once more to the bottom, as if determined to escape the impending onslaught. Pot-stick and churn-staff were tried in vain; it was too agile, and slipped and turned about in every direction, but refused point blank to come up.

"Begad, girls," said Paddy, "I believe it's goin' to be too many for yez—you'll never get it out at that rate."

"Bad scran to it," said Madge, whose perspiration as well as that of her large plump sisters was fast enriching the pot, "it's the sorrow of a pudden. What's to be done, Paddy?"

"Why then," said Paddy, scratching his head, "if I know, that I may never sup sorrow."

"Aisey," said Peggy, wiping the large beads of perspiration from her forehead with her greasy palm—"Aisy, be d—d but I'll bring it out or lose a fall for it."

In an instant she disappeared, and almost as quickly returned with a horse's halter in her hand.

"Here," said she, "we'll put a loop on this, and when we get the pudden into it, never fear but we'll make it skip."

"Upon my conscience, Peggy, achora"—(Peggy by the way was the genius of the family) said Paddy, "you'd flog Europe for invintion—Isn't that cute, Nancy darlin'?" he added, turning to his wife—"now only jist watch how she'll manage it."

"Come now, " proceeded Peggy, who felt her pride gratified, and her genius sharpened by this compliment, "come now, you two—let one o' you get the churn-staff, and the other the big pot-stick—then hoise its head up a' bit, I'll slip the loop about it, and then let it refuse to come if it dare."

These instructions were complied with, the loop was got about it, then drawn tight, and by a long pull, a strong pull, and a pull altogether, up came the bolster at full length, surcharged with the materials that had been previously determined on in conclave, the garlick included, as every nose present could now very decidedly determine.

The process of removing it was irresistible. Paddy held the halter, and the three sisters, aided by a female relative who was present, clapped the pot-stick and churn-staff under it, precisely as they carry coffins upon handspikes in the North, so that it had somewhat the appearance of a funeral procession, as they bore it from the fire to the table.

The dinner was now ready, but not yet set out in order, when the female relative alluded to, said to Madge, in a whisper, "My goodness, Madge, have you a table-cloth?"

"Oh, devil a stitch was undher the roof wid us for years."

"Throth, thin, it's a shame not to have a table-cloth," observed the girl, whose name was Sally Farrell.

"What's that," said Peggy, also in a whisper—"what is it, Sally?" Sally repeated her observation to Peggy. "Throth you're right," said the latter, "but wait a minute," continued the genius, "we won't be widout a table-cloth aither—the sorra bit;" and again she disappeared.

"Take these things off o' the table," she said, on her return; "we can very well do widout a sheet for a night or two, as we often did afore."

This was to Sally, but still in a whisper. The dishes being removed, she spread a sheet of very questionable pretensions to cleanliness upon the table, her slow but lucid eye brightening as she looked at Paddy, from whom she expected the usual meed of approbation; nor was she disappointed. Paddy, with a smile, clapped her on the back, exclaiming as he did it, "Augh, Peggy, begad you *are* the girl at a pinch."

Poor Nancy, ever since her arrival, felt herself alternating between smiles and tears, on looking at every thing about her, on witnessing their system of cooking, and on feeling through her olfactory organs the atmosphere she was coming to breathe; then, on comparing all this with the spotless and fragrant cleanliness of every thing she had left behind her, and been accustomed to, we need not feel surprised if she sometimes experienced much difficulty in restraining her tears; but again, there was mingled through all this such comic originality, such an unconsciousness of every thing that was offensive, and such wonderful simplicity and kindness of heart; all, too, so ludicrously displayed, that, allowing for her own strong perception of the humorous, we can easily understand the alternations just mentioned.

It is not for us to describe the dinner at any great length; but when we inform our readers that Paddy carved the fowl, and did the other honours of the table, they may form a tolerably accurate conception of the taste and tact with which he acquitted himself. As his mode of carving was one very prevalent in the remoter districts of the country, and still is so, though in a lesser degree, we feel it necessary to mention that he disparted the geese and turkeys on the old Adamic principle that existed before knives and forks were made. For instance, he took the goose or turkey, as the case might be, by the two legs, and pulled until one of them came off, which he handed to the person for whom it was designed. That person received it, and eat it out of his or her hand. The other leg and wings were separated in the same way; but it sometimes happened that the fowl was old and tough, in which case two persons stepped to the floor in order to have a clear stage and no favour, where each pulled, until after much hard tugging the joint gave way.

Upon this system it was that Paddy *carved* the fowls, and as they had but one knife in the house, and no fork, so it was necessary that the bacon should be cut into thin slices, which were eaten with the fingers. It may be observed here that after dinner had commenced, as Paddy's family always ate their meals with the door most hospitably open, the invited guests were joined by a very unexpected accession of those to whom no invitations had been given. Three or four pigs entered the kitchen, and approaching the table with a very knowing and privileged air, appeared to demand a portion of the good things that were so abundant. These again were followed by hens, ducks, turkeys, geese, all of which seemed as well acquainted, from habit and indulgence, with the hour of meals as did any of the family. It was in vain to try to drive them out. When repulsed directly from the table, they roved through the kitchen, poking their heads or noses experimentally into the vessels about the dresser, overturning some and shivering others, if they happened to meet with crockery, and uttering at the same time such a variety of noises as constituted but a very indifferent orchestra for the amusement of those who were at dinner. Habit, however, appeared to have rendered this a second nature to the family, who, provided they kept them immediately from the table, hindered them no further.

Chapter Four:
ROMANCE

Carleton's accounts of what we might term 'gentry romances' are not a great success. The ladies are paragons of virtue, the men are either dashing though weighed down by dark secrets or are heroes of perilous missions. They are frankly artificial confections whose register is limited to fatuous betrothals and tragic embraces. As in The Black Baronet *and* Willy Reilly, *it is all rather dreary stuff. But Carleton comes into his own in the portrayal of romance among the ordinary people. Here he relies on real speech, gestures and comic exaggeration. The characters are earthy, convincing and amusing. Neal Malone, "blue moulded for the want of a beatin'", finds romance more than meets his pugilistic aspirations in a story reminiscent of Flann O'Brien at his comic best. Perhaps Neal might have fared better through the ministrations of 'Mary Murray, the Irish Matchmaker'.*

1.

'Neal Malone' from *University Review and Quarterly Magazine* (1833)

THERE NEVER WAS a greater souled or doughtier tailor than little Neal Malone. Though but four feet four in height, he paced the earth with the courage and confidence of a giant; nay, one would have imagined that he walked as if he feared the world itself was about to give way under him. Let none dare to say in future that a tailor is but the ninth part of a man. That reproach has been gloriously taken away from the character of the cross-legged corporation by Neal Malone. He has wiped it off like a stain from the collar of a second-hand coat; he has pressed this wrinkle out of the lying front of antiquity; he has drawn together this rent in the respectability of his profession. No. By him who was the breeches-maker to the gods—that is, except, like Highlanders, they eschewed inexpressibles—by him who cut Jupiter's frieze jocks for winter, and eke by the bottom of his thimble, we swear, that Neal Malone was *more* than the ninth part of a man!

Setting aside the Patagonians, we maintain that two-thirds of mortal humanity were comprised in Neal; and, perhaps, we might venture to assert, that two-thirds of Neal's humanity were equal to six-thirds of another man's. It is right well known that Alexander the Great was a little man, and we doubt whether, had Alexander the Great been bred to the tailoring business, he would have exhibited so much of the hero as Neal Malone. Neal was descended from a fighting family, who had signalised themselves in as many battles as ever any single hero of antiquity fought. His father, his grandfather, and his great grandfather, were all fighting men, and his ancestors in general, up, probably, to Con of the Hundred Battles himself. No wonder, therefore, that Neal's blood should cry out against the cowardice of his calling; no wonder that he should be an epitome of all that was valorous and heroic in a peaceable man, for we neglected to inform the reader that Neal, though 'bearing no base mind,' never fought any man in his own person. That, however, deducted nothing from his courage. If he did not fight, it was simply because he found cowardice universal. No man would engage him; his spirit blazed in vain: his thirst for battle was doomed to remain unquenched, except by whiskey, and this only increased it. In short, he could find no foe. He has often been known to challenge the first cudgel-players and pugilists of the parish; to provoke men of fourteen stone weight; and to bid mortal defiance to faction heroes of all grades—but in vain. There was that in him which told them that an encounter with Neal would strip them of their laurels. Neal saw all this with a lofty indignation; he deplored the degeneracy of the times, and thought it hard that the descendant of such a fighting family should be doomed to pass through life peaceably, while so many excellent rows and riots took place around him. It was a calamity to see every man's head broken but his own; a dismal thing to observe his neighbours go about with their bones in bandages, yet his untouched; and his friends beat black and blue, whilst his own cuticle remained undiscoloured.

"Blur-an'-agers!" exclaimed Neal one day, when half-tipsy in the fair, "am I never to get a bit of fightin'? Is there no cowardly spalpeen to stand afore Neal Malone? Be this an' be that, *I'm blue-*

mowlded for want of a batin'! I'm disgracin' my relations by the life I'm ladin'! Will none o' ye fight me aither for love, money, or whiskey—frind or inimy, an' bad luck to ye? I don't care a *traneen* which, only out o' pure frindship, let us have a morsel o' the rale kick-up, 'tany rate. Frind or inimy, I say agin, if you regard me; sure *that* makes no differ, only let us have a fight."

This excellent heroism was all wasted; Neal could not find a single adversary. Except he divided himself like Hotspur, and went to buffets one hand against the other, there was no chance of a fight; no person to be found sufficiently magnanimous to encounter the tailor. On the contrary, every one of his friends—or, in other words, every man in the parish—was ready to support him. He was clapped on the back, until his bones were nearly dislocated in his body; and his hand shaken, until his arm lost its cunning at the needle for half a week afterwards. This, to be sure, was a bitter business—a state of being past endurance. Every man was his friend—no man was his enemy. A desperate position for any person to find himself in, but doubly calamitous to a martial tailor.

Many a dolorous complaint did Neal make upon the misfortune of having none to wish him ill; and what rendered this hardship doubly oppressive, was the unlucky fact that no exertions of his, however offensive, could procure him a single foe. In vain did he insult, abuse, and malign all his acquaintances. In vain did he father upon them all the rascality and villainy he could think of; he lied against them with a force and originality that would have made many a modern novelist blush for want of invention—but all to no purpose. The world for once became astonishingly Christian; it paid back all his efforts to excite its resentment with the purest of charity; when Neal struck it on the one cheek, it meekly turned the other. It could scarcely be expected that Neal would bear this. To have the whole world in friendship with a man is beyond doubt rather an affliction. Not to have the face of a single enemy to look upon, would decidedly be considered a deprivation of many agreeable sensations by most people, as well as by Neal Malone. Let who might sustain a loss, or experience a calamity, it was a matter of indifference to Neal. They were *only* his friends, and he troubled neither his head nor his heart about them.

Heaven help us! There is no man without his trials; and Neal, the reader perceives, was not exempt from his. What did it avail him that he carried a cudgel ready for all hostile contingencies? or knit his brows and shook his *kippeen* at the fiercest of his fighting friends? The moment he appeared, they softened into downright cordiality. His presence was the signal of peace; for, notwithstanding his unconquerable propensity to warfare, he went abroad as the genius of unanimity, though carrying in his bosom the redoubtable disposition of a warrior; just as the sun, though the source of light himself, is said to be dark enough at bottom.

It could not be expected that Neal, with whatever fortitude he might bear his other afflictions, could bear such tranquillity like a hero. To say that he bore it as one, would be to basely surrender his character; for what hero ever bore a state of tranquillity with courage? It affected his cutting out! It produced what Burton calls 'a windie melancholie,' which was nothing else than an accumulation of courage that had no means of escaping, if courage can without indignity ever be said to escape. He sat uneasily on his lapboard. Instead of cutting out soberly, he flourished his scissors as if he were heading a faction; he wasted much chalk by scoring his cloth in wrong places, and even caught his hot goose without a holder. These symptoms alarmed his friends, who persuaded him to go to a doctor. Neal went, to satisfy them; but he knew that no prescription could drive the courage out of him—that he was too far gone in heroism to be made a coward of by apothecary stuff. Nothing in the pharmacopoeia could physic him into a pacific state. His disease was simply the want of an enemy, and an unaccountable superabundance of friendship on the part of his acquaintances. How could a doctor remedy this by a prescription? Impossible. The doctor, indeed, recommended bloodletting; but to lose blood in a peaceable manner was not only cowardly, but a bad cure for courage. Neal declined it: he would lose no blood for any man until he could not help it; which was giving the character of a hero at a single touch. *His* blood was not to be thrown away in this manner; the only lancet ever applied to his relations was the cudgel, and Neal scorned to abandon the principles of his family.

His friends finding that he reserved his blood for more heroic purposes than dastardly phlebotomy, knew not what to do with him. His perpetual exclamation was, as we have already stated,

"I'm blue-mowlded for want of a batin'!" They did everything in their power to cheer him up with the hope of a drubbing; told him he lived in an excellent country for a man afflicted with his malady; and promised, if it were at all possible, to create him a private enemy or two, who, they hoped in heaven, might trounce him to some purpose.

This sustained him for a while; but as day after day passed, and no appearance of action presented itself, he could not choose but increase in courage. His soul, like a sword-blade too long in the scabbard, was beginning to get fuliginous by inactivity. He looked upon the point of his own needle, with a bitter pang, when he thought of the spirit rusting within him: he meditated fresh insults, studied new plans, and hunted out cunning devices for provoking his acquaintances to battle, until by degrees he began to confound his own brain, and to commit more grievous oversights in his business than ever. Sometimes he sent home to one person a coat, with the legs of a pair of trousers attached to it for sleeves, and despatched to another the arms of the aforesaid coat tacked together as a pair of trousers. Sometimes the coat was made to button behind instead of before, and he frequently placed the pockets in the lower part of the skirts, as if he had been in league with cut-purses.

This was a melancholy situation, and his friends pitied him accordingly.

"Don't be cast down, Neal," said they, "your friends feel for you, poor fellow."

"Divil carry my frinds," replied Neal, "sure there's not one o' yez frindly enough to be my inimy. Tare-an'-ounze! what'll I do? *I'm blue-mowlded for want of a batin'!"*

Seeing that their consolation was thrown away on him, they resolved to leave him to his fate; which they had no sooner done than Neal had thoughts of taking to the *Skiomachia* as a last remedy. In this mood he looked with considerable antipathy at his own shadow for several nights; and it is not to be questioned, but that some hard battles would have taken place between them, were it not for the cunning of the shadow, which declined to fight him in any other position than with its back to the wall. This occasioned him to pause, for the wall was a fearful antagonist, inasmuch that it knew not when it was beaten; but there was still an alternative left. He went to the garden one clear day about noon, and hoped to have a bout with the shade, free from interruption. Both approached, apparently eager for the combat, and resolved to conquer or die, when a villainous cloud happening to intercept the light, gave the shadow an opportunity of disappearing; and Neal found himself once more without an opponent.

"It's aisy known," said Neal, "you haven't the *blood* in you, or you'd come up to the scratch like a man."

He now saw that fate was against him, and that any further hostility towards the shadow was only a tempting of Providence. He lost his health, spirits, and everything but his courage. His countenance became pale and peaceful looking; the bluster departed from him; his body shrunk up like a withered parsnip. Thrice he was compelled to take in his clothes, and thrice did he ascertain that much of his time would be necessarily spent in pursuing his retreating person through the solitude of his almost deserted garments.

God knows it is difficult to form a correct opinion upon a situation so paradoxical as Neal's was. To be reduced to skin and bone by the downright friendship of the world, was, as the sagacious reader will admit, next to a miracle. We appeal to the conscience of any man who finds himself without an enemy, whether he be not a greater skeleton than the tailor; we will give him fifty guineas provided he can show a calf to his leg. We know he could not; for the tailor had none, and that was because he had not an enemy. No man in friendship with the world ever has calves to his legs. To sum up all in a paradox of our own invention, for which we can claim the full credit of originality, we now assert, that *more men have risen in the world by the injury of their enemies, than have risen by the kindness of their friends*. You may take this, reader, in any sense; apply it to hanging if you like, it is still immutably and immovably true.

One day Neal sat cross-legged, as tailors usually sit, in the act of pressing a pair of breeches; his hands were placed, backs up, upon the handle of his goose, and his chin rested upon the back of his hands. To judge from his sorrowful complexion one would suppose that he sat rather to be sketched as a picture of misery, or of heroism in distress, than for the industrious purpose of pressing the seams of a garment. There was a great deal of New Burlington-street pathos in his countenance; his face, like the times, was rather out of joint; "the sun was just setting, and his golden beams fell, with a saddened splendour, athwart the tailor's"—the reader may fill up the picture.

In this position sat Neal, when Mr. O'Connor, the schoolmaster, whose inexpressibles he was turning for the third time, entered the workshop. Mr. O'Connor, himself, was as finished a picture of misery as the tailor. There was a patient, subdued kind of expression in his face, which indicated a very fair portion of calamity; his eye seemed charged with affliction of the first water; upon each side of his nose might be traced two dry channels which, no doubt, were full enough while the tropical rains of his countenance lasted. Altogether, to conclude from appearances, it was a dead match in affliction between him and the tailor; both seemed sad, fleshless, and unthriving.

"Misther O'Connor," said the tailor, when the schoolmaster entered, "won't you be pleased to sit down?"

Mr. O'Connor sat; and, after wiping his forehead, laid his hat upon the lap-board, put his half handkerchief in his pocket, and looked upon the tailor. The tailor, in return, looked upon Mr. O'Connor; but neither of them spoke for some minutes. Neal, in fact, appeared to be wrapped up in his own misery, and Mr. O'Connor in his; or, as we often have much gratuitous sympathy for the distresses of our friends, we question but the tailor was wrapped up in Mr. O'Connor's misery, and Mr. O'Connor in the tailor's.

Mr. O'Connor at length said—"Neal, are my inexpressibles finished?"

"I am now pressin' your inexpressibles," replied Neal; "but, be my sowl, Mr. O'Connor, it's not your inexpressibles I'm thinkin' of. I'm not the ninth part of what I was. I'd hardly make paddin' for a collar now."

"Are you able to carry a staff still, Neal?"

"I've a light hazel one that's handy," said the tailor; "but where's the use of carryin' it, whin I can get no one to fight wid. Sure I'm disgracing my relations by the life I'm leadin'. I'll go to my grave widout ever batin' a man, or bein' bate myself; that's the vexation. Divil the row ever I was able to kick up in my life; *so that I'm fairly*

166

blue-mowlded for want of a batin'. But if you have patience—"

"Patience!" said Mr. O'Connor, with a shake of the head, that was perfectly disastrous even to look at; "patience, did you say, Neal?"

"Ay," said Neal, "an', be my sowl, if you deny that I said patience, I'll break your head!"

"Ah, Neal," said the other, "I don't deny it—for though I am teaching philosophy, knowledge, and mathematics, every day in my life, yet I'm learning patience myself both night and day. No, Neal; I have forgotten to deny any thing. I have not been guilty of a contradiction, out of my own school, for the last fourteen years. I once expressed the shadow of a doubt about twelve years ago, but ever since have abandoned even doubting. That doubt was the last expiring effort at maintaining my domestic authority—but I suffered for it."

"Well," said Neal, "if you have the patience, I'll tell you what afflicts me from beginnin' to endin'."

"I *will* have patience," said Mr. O'Connor, and he accordingly heard a dismal and indignant tale from the tailor.

"You have told me that fifty times over," said Mr. O'Connor, after hearing the story. "Your spirit is too martial for a pacific life. If you follow my advice, I will teach you how to ripple the calm current of your existence to some purpose. *Marry a wife*. For twenty-five years I have given instructions in three branches, viz.—philosophy, knowledge, and mathematics—I am also well versed in matrimony, and I declare that, upon my misery, it is my solemn and melancholy opinion, that, if you marry a wife, you will, before three months pass over your concatenated state, not have a single complaint to make touching a superabundance of peace and tranquillity, or a love of fighting."

"Do you mean to say that any woman would make me afeard?" said the tailor, deliberately rising up and getting his cudgel. "I'll thank you merely to go over the words agin, till I thrash you widin an inch o' your life. That's all."

"Neal," said the schoolmaster, meekly, "I won't fight; I have been too often subdued ever to presume on the hope of a single victory. My spirit is long since evaporated; I am like one of your own shreds, a mere selvage. Do you not know how much my habilaments have shrunk in, even within the last five years? Hear

167

me, Neal; and venerate my words as if they proceeded from the lips of a prophet. If you wish to taste the luxury of being subdued—if you are, as you say, *blue-moulded for want of a beating*, and sick at heart of a peaceful existence—why, MARRY A WIFE. Neal, send my breeches home with all haste, *for they are wanted*, you understand. Farewell!"

Mr. O'Connor, having thus expressed himself, departed, and Neal stood, with the cudgel in his hand, looking at the door out of which he passed, with an expression of fierceness, contempt, and reflection, strongly blended on the ruins of his once heroic visage.

Many a man has happiness within his reach if he but knew it. The tailor had been, hitherto, miserable because he pursued the wrong object. The schoolmaster, however, suggested a train of thought upon which Neal now fastened with all the ardour of a chivalrous temperament. Nay, he wondered that the family spirit should have so completely seized upon the fighting side of his heart, as to preclude all thoughts of matrimony; for he could not but remember that his relations were as ready for marriage as for fighting. To doubt this, would have been to throw a blot on his own escutcheon. He, therefore, very prudently asked himself, to whom, if he did not marry, should he transmit his courage. He was a single man, and, dying as such, he would be the sole depository of his own valour, which, like Junius's secret, must perish with him. If he could have left it, as a legacy, to such of his friends as were most remarkable for cowardice, why the case would be altered; but this was impossible—and he had now no other means of preserving it to posterity than by creating a posterity to inherit it. He saw, too, that the world was likely to become convulsed. Wars, as everybody knew, were certainly to break out; and would it not be an excellent opportunity for being father to a colonel, or, perhaps, a general, that might astonish the world.

The change visible in Neal, after the schoolmaster's last visit, absolutely thunderstruck all who knew him. The clothes, which he had rashly taken in to fit his shrivelled limbs, were once more let out. The tailor expanded with a new spirit; his joints ceased to be supple, as in the days of his valour; his eye became less fiery, but more brilliant. From being martial, he got desperately gallant; but, somehow, he could not afford to act the hero and lover both at the same time. This, perhaps, would be too much to expect from

168

a tailor. His policy was better. He resolved to bring all his available energy to bear upon the charms of whatever fair nymph he should select for the honour of matrimony; to waste his spirit in fighting would, therefore, be a deduction from the single purpose in view.

The transition from war to love is by no means so remarkable as we might at first imagine. We quote Jack Falstaff in proof of this, or, if the reader be disposed to reject our authority, then we quote Ancient Pistol himself—both of whom we consider as the most finished specimens of heroism that ever carried a safe skin. Acres would have been a hero had he worn gloves to prevent the courage from oozing out at his palms, or not felt such an unlucky antipathy to the "snug lying in the Abbey;" and as for Captain Bobadil, he never had an opportunity of putting his plan, for vanquishing an army, into practice. We fear, indeed, that neither his character, nor Ben Jonson's knowledge of human nature, is properly understood; for it certainly could not be expected that a man, whose spirit glowed to encounter a whole host, could, without tarnishing his dignity, if closely pressed, condescend to fight an individual. But as these remarks on courage may be felt by the reader as an invidious introduction of a subject disagreeable to him, we beg to hush it for the present and return to the tailor.

No sooner had Neal begun to feel an inclination to matrimony, than his friends knew that his principles had veered, by the change now visible in his person and deportment. They saw that he had *ratted* from courage, and joined love. Heretofore his life had been all winter, darkened by storm and hurricane. The fiercer virtues had played the devil with him; every word was thunder, every look lightning; but now all that had passed away;—before, he was the *fortiter in re*, at present he was the *suaviter in modo*. His existence was perfect spring—beautifully vernal. All the amiable and softer qualities began to bud about his heart; a genial warmth was diffused over him; his soul got green within him; every day was serene, and if a cloud happened to become visible, there was a roguish rainbow astride it, on which sat a beautiful Iris that laughed down at him, and seemed to say, "why the dickens, Neal, don't you marry a wife?"

Neal could not resist the afflatus which descended on him; an ethereal light dwelled, he thought, upon the face of nature; the colour of the cloth, which he cut out from day to day, was, to his enraptured eye, like the colour of cupid's wings—all purple; his visions were worth their weight in gold; his dreams, a credit to the bed he slept on; and his feelings, like blind puppies, young and alive to the milk of love and kindness which they drew from his heart. Most of this delight escaped the observation of the world, for Neal, like your true lover, became shy and mysterious. It is difficult to say what he resembled; no dark lantern ever had more light shut up within itself, than Neal had in his soul, although his friends were not aware of it. They knew, indeed, that he had turned his back upon valour; but beyond this their knowledge did not extend.

Neal was shrewd enough to know that what he felt must be love;—nothing else could distend him with happiness, until his soul felt light and bladder-like, but love. As an oyster opens, when expecting the tide, so did his soul expand at the contemplation of matrimony. Labour ceased to be a trouble to him; he sang and sewed from morning to night; his hot goose no longer burned him, for his heart was as hot as his goose; the vibrations of his head, at each successive stitch, were no longer sad and melancholy. There was a buoyant shake of exultation in them which showed that his soul was placid and happy within him.

Endless honour be to Neal Malone for the originality with which he managed the tender sentiment! He did not, like your common-place lovers, first discover a pretty girl, and afterwards become enamoured of her. No such thing, he had the passion prepared beforehand—cut out and made-up as it were ready for any girl whom it might fit. This was falling in love in the abstract, and let no man condemn it without a trial; for many a long-winded argument could be urged in its defence. It is always wrong to commence a business without capital, and Neal had a good stock to begin with. All we beg is, that the reader will not confound it with Platonism, which never marries; but he is at full liberty to call it Socratism, which takes unto itself a wife, and suffers accordingly.

Let no one suppose that Neal forgot the schoolmaster's kindness, or failed to be duly grateful for it. Mr. O'Connor was the first person whom he consulted touching his passion. With a cheerful soul he waited on that melancholy and gentleman-like man, and in the very luxury of his heart told him that he was in love.

"In love, Neal!" said the schoolmaster. "May I inquire with whom?"

"Wid nobody in particular, yet," replied Neal; "but of late I'm got divilish fond o' the girls in general."

"And do you call that being in love, Neal?" said Mr. O'Connor.

"Why, what else would I call it?" returned the tailor. "Amn't I fond of them?"

"Then it must be what is termed the Universal Passion, Neal," observed Mr. O'Connor, "although it is the first time I have seen such an illustration of it as you present in your own person."

"I wish you would advise me how to act," said Neal; "I'm as happy as a prince since I began to get fond o' them, an' to think of marriage."

The schoolmaster shook his head again, and looked rather miserable. Neal rubbed his hands with glee, and looked perfectly happy. The schoolmaster shook his head again, and looked more miserable than before. Neal's happiness also increased on the second rubbing.

Now, to tell the secret at once, Mr. O'Connor would not have appeared so miserable, were it not for Neal's happiness; nor Neal so happy, were it not for Mr. O'Connor's misery. It was all the result of *contrast*; but this you will not understand unless you be deeply read in modern novels.

Mr. O'Connor, however, was a man of sense, who knew, upon this principle, that the longer he continued to shake his head, the more miserable he must become, and the more also would he increase Neal's happiness; but he had no intention of increasing Neal's happiness at his own expense—for, upon the same hypothesis, it would have been for Neal's interest had he remained shaking his head there, and getting miserable until the day of judgment. He consequently declined giving the third shake, for he thought that plain conversation was, after all, more significant and forcible than the most eloquent nod, however ably translated.

"Neal," said he, "could you, by stretching your imagination, contrive to rest contented with nursing your passion in solitude, and love the sex at a distance?"

"How could I nurse and mind my business?" replied the tailor. "I'll never nurse so long as I'll have the wife; and as for 'magination it depends upon the grain of it, whether I can stretch it or not. I don't know that I ever made a coat of it in my life."

"You don't understand me, Neal," said the schoolmaster. "In

recommending marriage, I was only driving one evil out of you by introducing another. Do you think that, if you abandoned all thoughts of a wife, you would get heroic again?—that is, would you take once more to the love of fighting?"

"There's no doubt but I would," said the tailor: "if I miss the wife, I'll kick up such a dust as never was seen in the parish, an' you're the first man that I'll lick. But now that I'm in love," he continued, "sure, I ought to look out for the wife."

"Ah! Neal," said the schoolmaster, "you are tempting destiny: your temerity be, with all its melancholy consequences, upon your own head."

"Come," said the tailor, "it wasn't to hear you groaning to the tune of 'Dhrimmindhoo,' or 'The ould woman rockin' her cradle,' that I came; but to know if you could help me in makin' out the wife. That's the discoorse."

"Look at me, Neal," said the schoolmaster, solemnly; "I am at this moment, and have been any time for the last fifteen years, a living *caveto* against matrimony. I do not think that earth possesses such a luxury as a single solitary life. Neal, the monks of old were happy men: they were all fat and had double chins and, Neal, I tell you, that all fat men are in general happy. Care cannot come at them so readily as at a thin man; before it gets through the strong outworks of flesh and blood with which they are surrounded, it becomes treacherous to its original purpose, joins the cheerful spirits it meets in the system, and dances about the heart in all the madness of mirth; just like a sincere ecclesiastic, who comes to lecture a good fellow against drinking, but who forgets his lecture over his cups, and is laid out under the table with such success, that he either never comes to finish his lecture, or comes often to be laid under the table. Look at me, Neal, how wasted, fleshless, and miserable, I stand before you. You know how my garments have shrunk in, and what a solid man I was before marriage. Neal, pause, I beseech you: otherwise you stand a strong chance of becoming a nonentity like myself."

"I don't care what I become," said the tailor; "I can't think that you'd be so unrasonable as to expect that any of the Malones should pass out of the world widout either bein' bate or marrid. Have reason, Mr. O'Connor, an' if you can help me to the wife, I promise to take in your coat the next time for nothin'."

172

"Well, then," said Mr. O'Connor, "what would you think of the butcher's daughter, Biddy Neil? You have always had a thirst for blood, and here you may have it gratified in an innocent manner, should you ever become sanguinary again. 'Tis true, Neal, she is twice your size, and possesses three times your strength; but for that very reason, Neal, marry her if you can. Large animals are placid; and heaven preserve those bachelors, whom I wish well, from a small wife: 'tis such who always wield the sceptre of domestic life, and rule their husbands with a rod of iron."

"Say no more, Mr. O'Connor," replied the tailor, "she's the very girl I'm in love wid, an' never fear, but I'll overcome her heart if it can be done by man. Now, step over the way to my house, an' we'll have a sup on the head of it. Who's that calling?"

"Ah! Neal, I know the tones—there's a shrillness in them not to be mistaken. Farewell! I must depart; you have heard the proverb, 'those who are bound must obey.' Young Jack, I presume is squalling, and I must either nurse him, rock the cradle, or sing comic tunes for him, though heaven knows with what a disastrous heart I often sing 'Begone dull care,' the 'Rakes of Newcastle,' or, 'Peas upon a trencher.' Neal, I say again, pause before you take this leap in the dark. Pause, Neal, I entreat you. Farewell!"

Neal, however, was gifted with the heart of an Irishman, and scorned caution as the characteristic of a coward; he had, as it appeared, abandoned all design of fighting, but the courage still adhered to him even in making love. He consequently conducted the siege of Biddy Neil's heart with a degree of skill and valour which would not have come amiss to Marshal Gerald at the siege of Antwerp. Locke or Dugald Stewart, indeed, had they been cognizant of the tailor's triumph, might have illustrated the principle on which he succeeded—as to ourselves, we can only conjecture it. Our own opinion is, that they were both animated with a congenial spirit. Biddy was the very pink of pugnacity, and could throw in a body blow, or plant a facer, with singular energy and science. Her prowess hitherto had, we confess, been displayed only within the limited range of domestic life; but should she ever find it necessary to exercise it upon a larger scale, there was no doubt whatsoever, in the opinion of her mother, brothers, and sisters, every one of whom she had successively subdued, that she must undoubtedly distinguish herself. There was certainly one difficulty which the tailor had *not* to encounter in the progress of his courtship; the field was his own; he had not a rival to dispute his claim. Neither was there any opposition given by her friends; they were, on the contrary, all anxious for the match; and when the arrangements were concluded, Neal felt his hand squeezed by them in succession, with an expression more resembling condolence than joy. Neal, however, had been bred to tailoring, and not to metaphysics; he could cut out a coat very well, but we do not say that he could trace a principle—as what tailor, except Jeremy Taylor, could?

There was nothing particular in the wedding. Mr. O'Connor was asked by Neal to be present at it: but he shook his head, and told him that he had not the courage to attend it, or inclination to witness any man's sorrows but his own. He met the wedding party by accident, and was heard to exclaim with a sigh, as they flaunted past him in gay exuberance of spirits—"Ah, poor Neal! He is going like one of her father's cattle to the shambles! Woe is me for having suggested matrimony to the tailor! He will not long be under the necessity of saying that he 'is blue-moulded for want of a beating.' The butcheress will fell him like a Kerry ox, and I may have his blood to answer for, and his discomfiture to feel for, in addition to my own miseries."

On the evening of the wedding-day, about the hour of ten o'clock, Neal—whose spirits were uncommonly exalted, for his heart luxuriated within him—danced with his bride's maid; after the dance he sat beside her, and got eloquent in praise of her beauty; and it is said too, that he whispered to her, and chucked her chin with considerable gallantry.

The *tête-à-tête* continued for some time without exciting particular attention, with one exception; but *that* exception was worth a whole chapter of general rules. Mrs. Malone rose up, then sat down again, and took off a glass of the native; she got up a second time—all the wife rushed upon her heart—she approached them, and in a fit of the most exquisite sensibility, knocked the bride's maid down, and gave the tailor a kick of affecting pathos upon the inexpressibles. The whole scene was a touching one on both sides. The tailor was sent on all-fours to the floor; but Mrs. Malone took him quietly up, put him under her arm, as one would a lap dog, and with stately step marched away to the connubial apartment, in which everything remained very quiet for the rest of the night.

The next morning Mr. O'Connor presented himself to congratulate the tailor on his happiness. Neal, as his friend shook hands with him, gave the schoolmaster's fingers a slight squeeze, such as a man gives who would gently intreat your sympathy. The schoolmaster looked at him, and thought he shook his head. Of this, however, he could not be certain; for, as he shook his own during the moment of observation, he concluded that it might be a mere mistake of the eye, or, perhaps, the result of a mind predisposed to be credulous on the subject of shaking heads.

We wish it were in our power to draw a veil, or curtain, or blind of some description, over the remnant of the tailor's narrative that is to follow; but as it is the duty of every faithful historian to give the secret causes of appearances which the world in general do not understand, so we think it but honest to go on, impartially and faithfully, without shrinking from the responsibility that is frequently annexed to truth.

For the first three days after matrimony, Neal felt like a man who had been translated to a new and more lively state of existence. He had expected, and flattered himself, that, the moment this event should take place, he would once more resume his heroism, and experience the pleasure of a drubbing. This determination he kept a profound secret—nor was it known until a future period, when he disclosed it to Mr. O'Connor. He intended, therefore, that marriage should be nothing more than a mere parenthesis in his life—a kind of asterisk, pointing, in a note at the bottom, to this single exception in his general conduct—a *nota bene* to the spirit of a martial man, intimating that he had been peaceful only for a while. In truth, he was, during the influence of love over him, and up to the very day of his marriage, secretly as blue-moulded as ever for want of a beating. The heroic *penchant* lay snugly latent in his heart, unchecked and unmodified. He flattered himself that he was achieving a capital imposition upon the world at large—that he was actually hoaxing mankind in general—and that such an excellent piece of knavish tranquillity had never been perpetrated before his time.

On the first week after his marriage, there chanced to be a fair in the next market-town. Neal, after breakfast, brought forward a bunch of *shillelahs*, in order to select the best; the wife inquired the purpose of the selection, and Neal declared that he was resolved to have a fight that day, if it were to be had, he said for "love or money." "The thruth is," he exclaimed, strutting with fortitude about the house, "the thruth is, that I've *done* the whole of yez— *I'm as blue-mowlded as ever for want of a batin'*."

"Don't go," said the wife.

"I *will* go," said Neal, with vehemence; "I'll go if the whole parish was to go to prevint me."

In about another half-hour Neal sat down quietly to his business, instead of going to the fair!

Much ingenious speculation might be indulged in, upon this abrupt termination to the tailor's most formidable resolution; but, for our own part, we will prefer going on with the narrative, leaving the reader at liberty to solve the mystery as he pleases. In the mean time, we say this much—let those who cannot make it out, carry it to their tailor; it is a tailor's mystery, and no one has so good a right to understand it—except perhaps, a tailor's wife.

At the period of his matrimony, Neal had become as plump and as stout as he ever was known to be in his plumpest and stoutest days. He and the schoolmaster had been very intimate about this time; but we know not how it happened that soon afterwards he felt a modest bridelike reluctance in meeting with that afflicted gentleman. As the eve of his union approached, he was in the habit, during the schoolmaster's visits to his workshop, of alluding, in rather a sarcastic tone, considering the unthriving appearance of his friend, to the increasing lustiness of his person. Nay, he has often leaped up from his lap-board, and, in the strong spirit of exultation, thrust out his leg in attestation of his assertion, slapping it, moreover, with a loud laugh of triumph, that sounded like a knell to the happiness of his emaciated acquaintance. The schoolmaster's philosophy, was, however, unlike his flesh, never departed from him; his usual observation was, "Neal, we are both receding from the same point; you increase in flesh, whilst I, heaven help me, am fast diminishing."

The tailor received these remarks with very boisterous mirth, whilst Mr. O'Connor simply shook his head, and looked sadly upon his limbs, now shrouded in a superfluity of garments, somewhat resembling a slender thread of water in a shallow summer stream, nearly wasted away, and surrounded by an unproportionate extent of channel.

The fourth month after the marriage arrived. Neal, one day, near its close, began to dress himself in his best apparel. Even then, when buttoning his waistcoat, he shook his head after the manner of Mr. O'Connor, and made observations upon the great extent to which it over-folded him.

Well, thought he, with a sigh—this waistcoat certainly *did* fit me to a T; but it's wondherful to think how—cloth stretches!

"Neal," said the wife, on perceiving him drest, "where are you bound for?"

"Faith, *for life*," replied Neal, with a mitigated swagger; "and I'd as soon, if it had been the will of Provid—"

He paused.

"Where are you going?" asked the wife, a second time.

"Why," he answered, "only to the dance at Jemmy Connolly's; I'll be back early."

"Don't go," said the wife.

"I'll go," said Neal, "if the whole counthry was to prevent me. Thunder an' lightnin', woman, who am I?" he exclaimed, in a loud but rather infirm voice; "amn't I Neal Malone, that never met a *man* who'd fight him! Neal Malone, that was never beat by *man*! Why, tare-an-ounze, woman! Whoo! I'll get enraged some time, an' play the divil? Who's afeard, I say?"

"Don't go," added the wife, a third time, giving Neal a significant look in the face.

In about another half-hour, Neal sat down quietly to his business, instead of going to the dance!

Neal now turned himself, like many a sage in similar circumstances, to philosophy; that is to say—he began to shake his head upon principle, after the manner of the schoolmaster. He would, indeed, have preferred the bottle upon principle; but there was no getting at the bottle, except through the wife; and it so happened that by the time it reached him, there was little consolation left in it. Neal bore all in silence; for silence, his friend had often told him, was a proof of wisdom.

Soon after this, Neal, one evening, met Mr. O'Connor by chance upon a plank which crossed a river. This plank was only a foot in breadth, so that no two individuals could pass each other upon it.

We cannot find words in which to express the dismay of both, on finding that they absolutely glided past one another without collision.

Both paused, and surveyed each other solemnly; but the astonishment was all on the side of Mr. O'Connor.

"Neal," said the schoolmaster, "by all the household gods, I conjure you to speak, that I may be assured you live!"

The ghost of a blush crossed the church-yard visage of the tailor.

"Oh!" he exclaimed, "why the devil did you tempt me to marry a wife."

"Neal," said his friend, "answer me in the most solemn manner possible—throw into your countenance all the gravity you can assume; speak as if you were under the hands of the hangman, with the rope about your neck, for the question is, indeed, a trying one which I am about to put. Are you still 'blue-moulded for want of beating?'"

The tailor collected himself to make a reply; he put one leg out—the very leg which he used to show in triumph to his friend; but, alas, how dwindled! He opened his waistcoat, and lapped it round him, until he looked like a weasel on its hind legs. He then raised himself up on his tip toes, and, in an awful whisper, replied, "No!!! the devil a bit I'm *blue-moulded* for want of a batin'."

The schoolmaster shook his head in his own miserable manner; but, alas! he soon perceived that the tailor was as great an adept at shaking his head as himself. Nay, he saw that there was a calamitous refinement—a delicacy of shake in the tailor's vibrations, which gave to his nod a very commonplace character.

The next day the tailor took in his clothes; and from time to time continued to adjust them to the dimensions of his shrinking person. The schoolmaster and he, whenever they could steal a moment, met and sympathised together. Mr. O'Connor, however, bore up somewhat better than Neal. The latter was subdued in heart and in spirit; thoroughly, completely, and intensely vanquished. His features became sharpened by misery, for a termagant wife is the whetstone on which all the calamities of a henpecked husband are painted by the devil. He no longer strutted as he was wont to do; he no longer carried a cudgel as if he wished to wage a universal battle with mankind. He was now a married man.—Sneakingly, and with a cowardly crawl did he creep along as if every step brought him nearer to the gallows. The school-master's march of misery was far slower than Neal's: the latter distanced him. Before three years passed, he had shrunk so much, that he could not walk abroad on a windy day without carrying weights in his pockets to keep him firm on the earth, which he once trod with the step of a giant. He again sought the school-master, with whom indeed he associated as much as possible. Here he felt certain of receiving sympathy; nor was he disappointed. That worthy, but miserable man, and Neal, often retired beyond the hearing of their respective wives, and supported each other by every argument in their power. Often have they been heard, in the dusk of evening, singing behind a remote hedge that melancholy ditty, "Let us *both* be unhappy together;" which rose upon the twilight breeze with a cautious quaver of sorrow truly heart-rending and lugubrious.

"Neal," said Mr. O'Connor, on one of those occasions, "here is a book which I recommend to your perusal; it is called 'The Afflicted Man's Companion;' try, if you cannot glean some consolation out of it."

"Faith," said Neal, "I'm for ever oblaged to you, but I don't want it. I've had 'The Afflicted Man's Companion' too long, and divil an atom of consolation I can get out of it. I have *one* o' them I tell you; but, be me sowl, I'll not undhertake *a pair* o' them. The very name's enough for me." They then separated.

The tailor's *vis vitae* must have been powerful, or he would have died. In two years more his friends could not distinguish him from his own shadow; a circumstance which was of great inconvenience to him. Several grasped at the hand of the shadow instead of his; and one man was near paying it five and sixpence for making a pair of small-clothes. Neal, it is true, undeceived him with some trouble; but candidly admitted that he was not able to carry home the money. It was difficult, indeed, for the poor tailor to bear what he felt; it is true he bore it as long as he could: but at length he became suicidal, and often had thoughts of "making his own *quietus* with his bare bodkin." After many deliberations and afflictions, he ultimately made the attempt; but, alas! he found that the blood of the Malones refused to flow upon so ignominious an occasion. So *he* solved the phenomenon; although the truth was, that his blood was not "i' the vein" for it; none was to be had. What then was to be done? He resolved to get rid of life by some process; and the next that occurred to him was hanging. In a solemn spirit he prepared a selvage, and suspended himself from the rafter of his workshop; but here another disappointment awaited him—he would not hang. Such was his want of gravity, that his own weight proved insufficient to occasion his death by mere suspension. His third attempt was at drowning, but he was too light to sink; all the elements—all his own energies joined themselves, he thought, in a wicked conspiracy to save his life. Having thus tried every avenue to destruction, and failed in all, he felt like a man doomed to live for ever. Henceforward he shrunk and shrivelled by slow degrees, until in the course of time he became so attenuated, that the grossness of human vision could no longer reach him.

This, however, could not last always. Though still alive, he was to all intents and purposes imperceptible. He could now only be heard; he was reduced to a mere essence—the very echo of human existence, *vox et præterea nihil*. It is true the schoolmaster asserted that he occasionally caught passing glimpses of him; but that was because he had been himself nearly spiritualised by affliction, and his visual ray purged in the furnace of domestic tribulation. By and by Neal's voice lessened, got fainter and more indistinct, until at length nothing but a doubtful murmur could be heard, which ultimately could scarcely be distinguished from a ringing in the ears.

Such was the awful and mysterious fate of the tailor, who, as a hero, could not of course die; he merely dissolved like an icicle, wasted into immateriality, and finally melted away beyond the perception of mortal sense. Mr. O'Connor is still living, and once more in the fulness of perfect health and strength. His wife, however, we may as well hint, has been dead more than two years.

2.

'First Love' from *Fardorougha, The Miser* (1839)

OH THAT FIRST meeting of pure and youthful love! With what a glory is it ever encircled in the memory of the human heart! No matter how long or how melancholy the lapse of time since its past existence may be, still, still, is it remembered by our feelings when the recollection of every tie but itself has departed.

The charm, however, that murmured its many-toned music through the soul of Una O'Brien was not, upon the evening in question, wholly free from a shade of melancholy for which she could not account; and this impression did not result from any previous examination of her love for Connor O'Donovan, though many such she had. She knew that in this the utmost opposition from both her parents must be expected; nor was it the consequence of a consciousness on her part, that in promising him a clandestine meeting, she had taken a step which could not be justified. Of this, too, she had been aware before; but, until the hour of appointment drew near, the heaviness which pressed her down was such as caused her to admit that the sensation, however painful and gloomy, was new to her, and bore a character distinct from anything that could proceed from the various lights in which she had previously considered her attachment. This was, moreover, heightened by the boding aspect of the heavens and the dread repose of the evening, so unlike anything she had ever witnessed before. Notwithstanding all this, she was sustained by the eager and impatient buoyancy of first affection; which, when imagination pictured the handsome form of her young and manly lover, predominated for the time over every reflection and feeling that was opposed to itself. Her mind, indeed, resembled a fair autumn landscape, over which the cloud-shadows may be seen sweeping for a moment, whilst again the sun comes out and turns all into serenity and light.

The place appointed for their interview was a small paddock shaded by alders, behind her father's garden, and thither, with trembling limbs and palpitating heart, did the young and graceful daughter of Bodagh Buie proceed.

For a considerable time, that is to say, for three long years before this delicious appointment, had Connor O'Donovan and Una been wrapped in the elysium of mutual love. At mass, at fair, and at market, had they often and often met, and as frequently did their eyes search each other out, and reveal in long blushing glances the state of their respective hearts. Many a time did he seek an opportunity to disclose what he felt, and as often, with confusion, and fear, and delight, did she afford him what he sought. Thus did one opportunity after another pass away, and as often did he form the towering resolution to reveal his affection if he were ever favored with another. Still would some disheartening reflection, arising from the uncommon gentleness and extreme modesty of his character, throw a damp upon his spirit. He questioned his own penetration; perhaps she was in the habit of glancing as much at others as she glanced at him. Could it be possible that the beautiful daughter of Bodagh Buie, the wealthiest man, and of his wife, the proudest woman, within a large circle of the country, would love the son of Fardorougha Donovan, whose name had, alas, become so odious and unpopular? But then the blushing face, and dark lucid eyes, and the long earnest glance, rose before his imagination, and told him that, let the difference in the character and the station of their parents be what it might, the fair dark daughter of O'Brien was not insensible to him, nor to the anxieties he felt ...

3.

'A Cynical Perspective' from *The Black Baronet* (1852)

"LOVE BEFORE MARRIAGE, in my opinion, is exceedingly dangerous to future happiness; and I will tell you why I think so. In the first place, a great deal of that fuel which feeds the post-matrimonial flame is burned away and wasted unnecessarily; the imagination, too, is raised to a ridiculous and most enthusiastic expectation of perpetual bliss and ecstasy; then comes disappointment, coolness, indifference, and the lights go out for want of the fuel I mentioned; and altogether the domestic life becomes rather a dull and tedious affair. The wife wonders that the husband is no longer a lover; and the husband cannot for the soul of him see all the—the—the—ahem!—I scarcely know what to call them—that enchanted him before marriage. Then, you perceive, that when love is necessary, the fact comes out that it was most injudiciously expended before the day of necessity. Both parties feel, in fact, that the property has been prematurely squandered—like many another property—and when it is wanted, there is nothing to fall back upon. I wish to God affection could be funded, so that when a married couple found themselves low in pocket in that commodity they could draw the interest or sell out at once."

"And what can you expect, my lord, from those who marry without affection?" asked Lucy.

"Ten chances for happiness," replied his lordship, "for one that results from love. When such persons meet, mark you, Miss Gourlay, they are not enveloped in an artificial veil of splendor, which the cares of life, and occasionally a better knowledge of each other, cause to dissolve from about them, leaving them stripped of those imaginary qualities of mind and person which never had any existence at all, except in their hypochondriac brains, when love-stricken; whereas, your honest, matter-of-fact people come together—first with indifference, and, as there is nothing angelic to be expected on either side, there is consequently no disappointment. There has, in fact, been no sentimental fraud committed—no swindle of the heart—for love, too, like its relation, knavery, has its black-legs, and very frequently raises credit upon false pretences; the consequence is, that plain honesty begins to produce its natural effects."

"Can this man," thought Lucy, "have been taking lessons from papa? And pray, my lord," she proceeded, "what are those effects which marriage without love produces?"

"Why, a good honest indifference, in the first place, which keeps the heart easy and somewhat indolent withal. There is none of that sharp jealousy which is perpetually on the spy for offence. None of that pulling and pouting—falling out and falling in—which are ever the accessories of love. On the contrary, honest indifference minds the family—mark, buys the beef and mutton, reckons the household linen—eschews parties and all places of fashionable resort, attends to the children—sees them educated, bled, blistered, et cetera, when necessary; and ... looks to their religion, hears them their catechism, brings them, in their clean bibs and tuckers, to church, and rewards that one who carries home most of the sermon with a large lump of sugar-candy."

"These are very original views of marriage, my lord."

"Aha!" thought his lordship, "I knew the originality would catch her."

"Why, the fact is, Miss Gourlay, that I believe—at least I think I may say—that originality is my *forte*. I have a horror against everything common."

"I thought so, my lord," replied Lucy; "your sense, for instance, is anything but common sense."

"You are pleased to flatter me, Miss Gourlay, but you speak very truly; and that is because I always think for myself—I do not wish to be measured by a common standard."

"You are very right, my lord; it would be difficult, I fear, to find a common standard to measure you by. One would imagine, for instance, that you have been on this principle absolutely studying the subject of matrimony. At least, you are the first person I have ever met who has succeeded in completely stripping it of common sense, and there I must admit your originality."

"Gad!" thought his lordship, "I have her with me—I am getting on famously."

"They would imagine right, Miss Gourlay; these principles are the result of a deep and laborious investigation into that mysterious and awful topic. Honest indifference has no intrigues, no elopements, no disgraceful trials for criminal conversation, no divorces. No; your lovers in the yoke of matrimony, when they tilt with each other, do it sharply, with naked weapons; whereas, the worthy indifferents, in the same circumstances, have a wholesome regard for each other, and rattle away only with the scabbards. Upon my honor, Miss Gourlay, I am quite delighted to hear that you are not attached to me. I can now marry upon my own principles. It is not my intention to coax, and fondle, and tease you after marriage; not at all. I shall interfere as little as possible with your habits, and you, I trust, as little with mine. We shall see each other only occasionally, say at church, for instance, for I hope you will have no objection to accompany me there."

4.

'Mary Murray, the Irish Match-Maker' from the *Irish Penny Journal* (1840)

OUR READERS ARE not to understand that in Ireland there exists, like the fiddler or dancing-master, a distinct character openly known by the appellation of match-maker. No such thing. On the contrary, the negotiations they undertake are all performed under false colours. The business, in fact, is close and secret, and always carried on with the profoundest mystery, veiled by the sanction of some other ostensible occupation.

One of the best specimens of the kind we ever met was old Mary Murray. Mary was a tidy creature of middle size, who always went dressed in a short crimson cloak, much faded, a striped red and blue drugget petticoat, and a heather-coloured gown of the same fabric. When walking, which she did with the aid of a light hazel staff hooked at the top, she generally kept the hood of the cloak over her head, which gave to her whole figure a picturesque effect; and when she threw it back, one could not help admiring how well her small but symmetrical features agreed with the dowd cap of white linen, with a plain muslin border, which she wore. A pair of blue stockings and sharp-pointed shoes, high in the heels, completed her dress. Her features were good-natured and Irish, but over the whole countenance there lay an expression of quickness and sagacity, contracted no doubt by an habitual exercise of penetration and circumspection. At the time I saw her she was very old, and I believe had the reputation of being the last in that part of the country who was known to go about from house to house spinning on the distaff, an instrument which has now passed away, being more conveniently replaced by the spinning wheel.

The manner and style of Mary's visits were different from those of any other who could come to a farmer's house, or even to an humble cottage, for to the inmates of both were her services equally rendered. Let us suppose, for instance, the whole female part of a farmer's family assembled of a summer evening about five o'clock, each engaged in some domestic employment: in runs a lad who has been sporting about, breathlessly exclaiming, whilst his eyes are lit up with delight, "Mother, mother, here's Mary Murray comin' down the boreen!" "Get out, avick: no, she's not." "Bad cess to me but she is; that I may never stir if she isn't now!" The whole family are instantly at the door to see if it be she, with the exception of the prettiest of them all, Kitty, who sits at her wheel, and immediately begins to croon over an old Irish air, which is sadly out of tune; and well do we know, notwithstanding the mellow tones of that sweet voice, why it is so, and also why that youthful cheek, in which health and beauty meet, is the colour of crimson.

"*Oh, Vara, acushula, cead millia failte ghud?* (Mary, darling, a hundred thousand welcomes to you!) Och, musha, what kep' you away so long, Mary? Sure you won't have us this month o' Sundays, Mary!" are only a few of the cordial expressions of hospitality and kindness with which she is received. But Kitty, whose cheek but a moment ago was carmine, why is it now pale as the lily?

"An' what news, Mary," asks one of her sisters: "sure you'll tell us everything: won't you?"

"Throth, avilish, *I have no bad news*, any how—an' as to tellin' you *all*—Biddy, *lhig dumh*, let me alone. No, I have no bad news, God be praised, *but good news.*"

Kitty's cheek is again crimson, and her lips, ripe and red as cherries, expand with the sweet soft smile of her country, exhibiting a set of teeth for which many a countess would barter thousands, and giving out a breath more delicious than the fragrance of a summer meadow. Oh, no wonder, indeed, that the kind heart of Mary contains in its recesses a message to her as tender as ever was transmitted from man to woman.

"An', Kitty acushla, where's the welcome from *you*, that's my favourite? Now don't be jealous, childre; sure you all know she is, an' ever an' always was."

"If it's not upon my lips, it's in my heart, Mary, an' from that heart you're welcome."

She rises up and kisses Mary, who gives her one glance of meaning, accompanied by the slightest imaginable smile, and a gentle but significant pressure of the hand, which thrills to her heart, and diffuses a sense of ecstasy through her whole spirit.

Nothing now remains but the opportunity, which is equally sought for by Mary and her to hear without interruption the purport of her lover's communication, and this we leave to lovers to imagine.

In Ireland, however odd it may seem, there occur among the very poorest classes some of the hardest and most penurious bargains in match-making than ever were heard of or known. Now, strangers might imagine that all this close higgling proceeds from a spirit naturally near and sordid, but it is not so. The real secret of it lies in the poverty and necessity of the parties, and chiefly in the bitter experience of their parents, who, having come together in a state of destitution, are anxious, each as much at the expense of the other as possible, to prevent their children from experiencing the same privation and misery which they themselves felt. Many a time have matches been suspended, or altogether broken off, because one party refuses to give his son "*a slip of a pig*," or another his daughter "a pair of blankets;" and it was no unusual thing for a match-maker to say, "Never mind; I have it all settled *but the slip*." One might naturally wonder why those who are so shrewd and provident upon this subject do not strive to prevent early marriages where the poverty is so great. So unquestionably they ought, but it is a settled usage of the country, and one, too, which Irishmen have never been in the habit of considering as an evil. We have no doubt that if they once began to reason upon it as such, they would be very strongly disposed to check a custom which has been the means of involving themselves and their unhappy offspring in misery, penury, and not unfrequently in guilt itself.

Mary, like many others in this world who are not conscious of the same failing, smelt strongly of the shop; in other words her conversation had a strong matrimonial tendency. No two beings ever lived so decidedly antithetical to each other in this point of view as the match-maker and the *Keener*. Mention the name of an individual or a family to the keener, and the medium through which her memory passes back to them is that of her professed employment—a mourner at wakes and funerals.

"Don't you know young Kelly of Tamlaght?"

"I do, avick," replies the keener, "and what about him?"

"Why he was married to-day mornin' to ould Jack M'Cluskey's daughter."

187

"Well, God grant them luck an' happiness, poor things! I do indeed remember his father's wake an' funeral well—ould Risthard Kelly of Tamlaght—a dacent corpse he made for his years, an' well he looked. But indeed I *knewn* by the colour that sted in his cheeks, and the limbs remaining soople for the twenty-four hours afther his departure, that some of the family 'ud follow him afore the year was out, an' so she did. The youngest daughter, poor thing, by raison of a could she got, over-heatin' herself at a dance, was stretched beside him that very day was eleven months; an' God knows it was from the heart my grief kem for *her*—to see the poor han'some colleen laid low so soon. But whin a gallopin' consumption sets in, avouneen, sure we all know what's to happen. In Crockaniska churchyard they sleep—the Lord make both their beds in heaven this day."

The very reverse of this, but at the same time as inveterately professional, was Mary Murray.

"God save you, Mary."

"God save you kindly, avick. Eh, let me look at you. Aren't you red Billy M'Guirk's son from Ballagh?"

"I am, Mary. An', Mary, how is yourself and the world gettin' an?"

"Can't complain, dear, in such times. How are yez all at home, alanna?" "Faix middlin' well, Mary, thank God an' you. You hard of my grand-uncle's death, big Ned M'Coul?"

"I did, avick, God rest him. Sure it's well I remember his weddin', poor man, by the same atoken that I know one that helped him an wid it a thrifle. He was married in a blue coat an' buskins, an' wore a scarlet waistcoat that you'd see three miles off. Oh, well I remember it. An' whin he was settin' out that mornin' to the priest's house, 'Ned', says I, an' I fwhishpered him, 'dhrop a button on the right knee afore you get the words said." '*Thighum*,' said he, wid a smile, an' he slipped ten thirteens into my hand as he spoke. 'I'll do it,' said he, 'and thin a fig for the fairies!—because, you see if there's a button of the right knee left unbuttoned, the fairies—this day's Friday, God stand betune us and harm!—can do neither hurt nor harm to sowl or body, an' sure that's a great blessin', avick. He left two fine slips o' girls behind him."

"He did so—as good-lookin' girls as there's in the parish."

"Faix, an' kind mother for them, avick. She'll be marryin' agin, I'm judgin', she bein' sich a fresh good-lookin' woman."

"Why, it's very likely, Mary."

"Throth it's natural, achora. What can a lone woman do wid such a large family on her hands, widout having some one to manage it for her, an' prevint her from bein' imposed on? But indeed the first thing she ought to do is to marry off her two girls widout 'oss of time, in regard that it's hard to say how a stepfather an' thim might agree; and I've often known the mother herself, when she had a fresh family comin' an her, to be as unnatural to her fatherless childre as if she was a stranger to thim, and that the same blood didn't run in their veins. Not saying that Mary M'Coul will or would act that way by her own; for indeed she's come of a kind ould stock, an' ought to have a good heart. Tell her, avick, when you see her, that I'll spind a day or two wid her—let me see— the day after to-morrow will be Palm Sunday—why, about the Aisther holidays."

"Indeed I will, Mary, with great pleasure."

"An' fwhishsper, dear, just tell her that I've a thing to say to her— that I had a long dish o' discoorse about her wid *a friend o' mine*. You won't forget, now?"

"Oh, the dickens a forget!"

"Thank you, dear: God mark you to grace, avourneen! When you're a little oulder, maybe I'll be a friend to you yet."

This last intimation was given with a kind of mysterious be-nevolence, very visible in the complacent shrewdness of her face, and with a twinkle in the eye, full of grave humour and consider-able self-importance, leaving the mind of the person she spoke to in such an agreeable uncertainty as rendered it a matter of great difficulty to determine whether she was serious or only in jest, but at all events throwing the onus of inquiry upon him.

The ease and tact with which Mary could involve two young persons of opposite sexes in a mutual attachment, were very remarkable. In truth, she was a kind of matrimonial incendiary, who went through the country holding her torch now to this heart and again to that—first to one and then to another, until she had the parish more or less in a flame. And when we consider the combustible materials of which the Irish heart is composed, it is no wonder indeed that the labour of taking the census in Ireland increases at such a rapid rate, during the time that elapses between the period of its being made out. If Mary, for instance, met a young

189

woman of her acquaintance accidentally—and it was wonderful to think how regularly these accidental meetings took place—she would address her probably somewhat as follows:—

"Arra, Biddy Sullivan, how are you, a-colleen?"

"Faix, bravely, thank you, Mary. How is yourself?" "Indeed, thin' sorra a bit o' the health we can complain of, Bhried, barrin' whin this pain in the back comes upon us. The last time I seen your mother, Biddy, she was complainin' of a *weid*.* I hope she's betther, poor woman?"

"Hut! bad scran to the thing ails her! She has as light a foot as e'er a one of us, an' can dance 'Jackson's mornin' brush' as well as ever she could."

"Throth, an' I'm proud to hear it. Och! och! 'Jackson's mornin' brush' ! and it was *she* that could do it. Sure I remimber her wedding-day like yestherday. Ay, far an' near her fame wint as a dancer, an' the clanest-made girl that ever came from Lisbuie. Like yestherday do I remimber it, an' how the squire himself an' the ladies from the Big House came down to see herself an' your father, the bride and groom—an' it wasn't on every hill head you'd get sich a couple—dancin' the same 'Jackson's mornin' brush.' Oh! it was far and near her fame wint for dancin' that,—An' is there no news wid you, Bhried, at all at all?"

"The sorra word, Mary: where 'ud I get news? Sure it's yourself that's always on the fut that ought to have the news for *us*, woman alive."

"An' maybe I have too. I was spaikin' to a friend o' mine about you the other day."

"A friend o' yours, Mary! Why, what friend could it be?"

"A friend o' mine—ay, an' of yours too. Maybe you have more friends than you think, Biddy—and kind ones too, as far as wishin' you well goes, 't any rate. Ay have you faix, an' friends that e'er a girl in the parish might be proud to hear named in the one day wid her. Awouh!"

"Bedad we're in luck, thin, for that's more than I knew of. An' who may these great friends of ours be, Mary?"

"Awouh! Faix, as dacent a boy as ever broke bread the same boy is, 'and,' says he, 'if I had goold in bushelfuls, I'd think it too little

---

* A feverish cold

190

for that girl;' but poor lad, he's not aisy or happy in his mind in regard o' that. 'I'm afeared,' says he, 'that she'd put scorn upon me, an' not think me her aiquals. An' no more I am,' says he again, 'for where, afther all, would you get the likes o' Biddy Sullivan?'—Poor boy! throth my heart aches for him!"

"Well, can't you fall in love wid him yourself, Mary, whoever he is?"

"Indeed, an' if I was at your age, it would be no shame to me to do so; but, to tell you the thruth, the sorra often ever the likes of Paul Heffernan came acrass me."

"Paul Heffernan! Why, Mary," replied Biddy, smiling with the assumed lightness of indifference, "is that your beauty? If it is, why, keep him, an' make much of him."

"Oh, wurrah! the differ there is between the hearts an' tongues of some people—one from another—an' the way they spaik behind others' backs! Well, well, I'm sure that wasn't the way he spoke of you, Biddy, an' God forgive you for runnin' down the poor boy as you're doin'. Trogs! I believe you're the only girl would do it."

"Who, me! I'm not runnin' him down. I am neither runnin' him up nor down. I have neither good nor bad to say about him—the boy's a black stranger to me, barrin' to know this face."

"Faix, an' he's in consate wid you these three months past, an' intends to be at the dance on Friday next, in Jack Gormly's new house. Now, good-bye, alanna; keep your own counsel till the time comes, an' mind what I said to you. It's not behind every ditch the likes of Paul Heffernan grows. *Bannaght lhath!* My blessin' be wid you!"

Thus would Mary depart just at the critical moment, for well she knew that by husbanding her information and leaving the heart something to find out, she took the most effectual steps to excite and sustain that kind of interest which is apt ultimately to ripen, even from its own agitation, into the attachment she is anxious to promote.

The next day, by a meeting similarly accidental, she comes in contact with Paul Heffernan, who, honest lad, had never probably bestowed a thought on Biddy Sullivan in his life.

"*Morrow ghud*, Paul!—how is your father's son, ahager?"

"*Morrow ghutcha*, Mary!—my father's son wants nothin' but a good wife, Mary."

"An' it's not every set day or bonfire night that a good wife is to be had, Paul—that is, a *good* one, as you say; for, throth, there's many o' them in the market, sich as they are. I was talkin' about you to a friend of mine the other day—an' trogs, I'm afeard you're not worth all the abuse we gave you."

"More power to you, Mary! I'm oblaged to you. But who is the friend in the manetime?"

"Poor girl! Throth, when your name slipped out an her, the point of a rush 'ud take a drop of blood out o' her cheek, the way she crimsoned up. 'Ah, Mary,' says she, "if ever I know you to braith it to man or mortual, my lips I'll never open to you to my dyin' day.' Trogs, when I looked at her, an' the tears standin' in her purty black eyes, I thought I didn't see a betther favoured girl, for both face and figure, this many a day, than the same Biddy Sullivan."

"Biddy Sullivan! Is that long Jack's daughter of Carga?"

"The same. But, Paul avick, if a syllable o' what I tould you—"

"Hut, Mary! honour bright! Do you think me a *stag*, that I'd go and inform on you."

"Fwhishsper, Paul: she'll be at the dance on Friday next in Jack Gormly's new house. So *bannagh lhath*, an' think o' what I bethrayed to you."

Thus did Mary very quietly and sagaciously bind two young hearts together, who probably might otherwise have never for a moment even thought of each other. Of course, when Paul and Biddy met at the dance on the following Friday, the one was the object of the closest attention to the other; and each being prepared to witness strong proofs of attachment from the opposite party, everything fell out exactly according to their expectations.

Sometimes it happens that a booby of a fellow, during his calf love, will employ a male friend to plead his suit with a pretty girl, who, if the principal party had spunk, might be very willing to marry him. To the credit of our fair country-women, however, be it said, that in scarcely one instance out of twenty does it happen, or has it ever happened, that any of them ever fails to punish the faint heart by bestowing the fair lady upon what is called the blackfoot or spokesman whom he selects to make love for him. In such a case it is very naturally supposed that the latter will speak

192

two words for himself and one for his friend, and indeed the result bears out the supposition. Now, nothing on earth gratifies the heart of the established matchmaker so much as to hear of such a disaster befalling a spoony. She exults over his misfortune for months, and publishes his shame to the uttermost bounds of her own little world, branding him "as a poor pitiful creature, who had not the courage to spaik up for himself, or—to employ them that could." In fact, she entertains much the same feeling against him that a regular physician would towards some weak-minded patient, who prefers the knavish ignorance of a quack to the skill and services of an able and educated practitioner.

Characters like Mary are fast disappearing in Ireland; and indeed in a country where the means of life were generally inadequate to the wants of the population, they were calculated, however warmly the heart may look back upon the memory of their services, to do more harm than good, by inducing young folks to enter into early and improvident marriages. They certainly sprang up from a state of society not thoroughly formed by proper education and knowledge—where the language of a people, too, was in many extensive districts in such a state of transition as in the interchange of affection to render an interpreter absolutely necessary. We have ourselves witnessed marriages where the husband and wife spoke the one English and the other Irish, each being able with difficulty to understand the other. In all such cases Mary was invaluable. She spoke Irish and English fluently, and indeed was acquainted with every thing in the slightest or most remote degree necessary to the conduct of a love affair, from the first glance up until the priest had pronounced the last words—or, to speak more correctly, until "the throwing of the stocking."

Mary was invariably placed upon the *bob*, which is the seat of comfort and honour at a farmer's fireside, and there she sat neat and tidy, detailing all the news of the parish, telling them how such a marriage was one unbroken honeymoon—a sure proof, by the way, that she herself had a hand in it—and again, how another one didn't turn out well, and she said so; "there was always a bad dhrop in the Haggarties; but, my dear, the girl herself was *for* him; so as she made her own bed, she must lie in it, poor thing. Any way, thanks be to goodness, I had nothing to do wid it."

Mary was to be found in every fair and market, and always at a

193

particular place at a certain hour of the day, where the parties engaged in a courtship were sure to meet her on these occasions. She took a chirping glass, but never so as to become unsteady. Great deference was paid to everything she said; and if not conceded to her, she extorted it with a high hand. Nobody living could drink a health with half the comic significance that Mary threw into her eyes when saying, "Well, young couple, here's everything as you wish it."

Mary's motions from place to place usually were very slow, and for the best reason in the world—she was frequently interrupted. For instance, if she met a young man on her way, ten to one but he stood and held a long and earnest conversation with her; and that it was both important and confidential, might easily be gathered from the fact, that whenever a stranger passed, it was either suspended altogether, or carried on in so low a tone as to be inaudible. This held equally good with the girls. Many a time have I seen them retracing their steps, and probably walking back a mile or two, all the time engaged in discussing some topic evidently of more than ordinary interest to themselves. And when they shook hands and bade each other good-bye, heavens! at what a pace did the latter scamper homewards across fields and ditches, in order to make up for the time she had lost!

Chapter Five:
LITTLE WORLDS
IN STRANGE PLACES

*While Carleton was strongly disposed to write of physical territories
that were familiar and even homely, he was also, from early days,
attracted to the exotic and the outré. His satirical bent often led
him to describe particular places as microcosmic worlds revealing
in some phantasmagoric way the panoply of human depravity.
The eye may be jaundiced, but it is not without a certain keenness.*

1.

'The Madhouse' from *The Black Baronet* (1852)

IT IS NOT our intention to place before our readers any lengthened
description of this gloomy temple of departed reason. Every one
who enters a lunatic asylum for the first time, must feel a wild and
indescribable emotion, such as he has never before experienced,
and which amounts to an extraordinary sense of solemnity and
fear. Nor do the sensations of the stranger rest here. He feels as if
he were surrounded by something sacred as well as melancholy,
something that creates at once pity, reverence, and awe. Indeed,
so strongly antithetical to each other are his first impressions, that
a kind of confusion arises in his mind, and he begins to fear that
his senses have been affected by the atmosphere of the place. That
a shock takes place which slightly disarranges the faculty of
thought, and generates strong but erroneous impressions, is still
more clearly established by the fact that the visitor, for a considerable time after leaving an asylum, can scarcely rid himself of the

belief that every person he meets is insane.

The stranger, on entering the long room in which the convalescents were assembled, felt, in the silence of the patients, and in their vague and fantastic movements, that he was in a position where novelty, in general the source of pleasure, was here associated only with pain. Their startling looks, the absence of interest in some instances, and its intensity in others, at the appearance of strangers, without any intelligent motive in either case, produced a feeling that seemed to bear the character of a disagreeable dream.

"All the patients here," said his conductor, "are not absolutely in a state of convalescence. A great number of them are; but we also allow such confirmed lunatics as are harmless to mingle with them. There is scarcely a profession, or a passion, or a vanity in life, which has not here its representative. Law, religion, physic, the arts, the sciences, all contribute their share to this melancholy picture gallery. Avarice, love, ambition, pride, jealousy, having overgrown the force of reason, are here, as its ideal skeletons, wild and gigantic—fretting, gambolling, moping, grinning, raving, and vapouring—each wrapped in its own VISION, and indifferent to all the influence of the collateral faculties. There, now, is a man, moping about, the very picture of stolidity; observe how his chin rests upon his breastbone, his mouth open and almost dribbling. That man, sir, so unpoetical and idiotic in appearance, imagines himself the author of Beattie's 'Minstrel'. He is a Scotchman, and I will call him over."

"Come here, Sandy, speak to this gentleman." Sandy, without raising his lack-lustre eye, came over and replied, "Aw—ay—'Am the author o' Betty's Menstrel;" and having uttered this piece of intelligence, he shuffled across the room, dragging one foot after the other, at about a quarter of a minute per step. Never was poor Beattie so libellously represented.

"Do you see that round-faced, good-humoured looking man, with a decent frieze coat on?" said their conductor. "He's a wealthy and respectable farmer from the county of Kilkenny, who imagines that he is Christ. His name is Rody Rafferty."

"Come here, Rody."

Rody came over, and looking at the stranger, said, "Arra, now, do you know who I am? Troth, I go bail you don't."

"No," replied the stranger, "I do not; but I hope you will tell me."

"I'm Christ," replied Rody; "and, upon my word, if you don't get me out o' this, I'll work a miracle on you."

"Why," asked the stranger, "what will you do?"

"Troth, I'll turn you into a blackin' brush, and polish my shoes wid you. You were at Barney's death, too."

The poor man had gone deranged, it seemed, by the violent death of his only child—a son.

"There's another man," said the conductor; "that little fellow with the angry face. He is a shoemaker, who went mad on the score of humanity. He took a strong feeling of resentment against all who had flat feet, and refused to make shoes for them."

"How was that?" inquired the stranger.

"Why, sir," said the other, smiling, "he said that they murdered the clocks (beetles) and he looked upon every man with flat feet as an inhuman villain, who deserves, he says, to have his feet chopped off, and to be compelled to dance a hornpipe three times a day on his stumps."

"Who is that broad-shouldered man," asked the stranger, "dressed in rusty black, with the red head?"

"He went mad," replied the conductor, "on a principle of religious charity. He is a priest from the county of Wexford, who had been called in to baptize the child of a Protestant mother, which, having done, he seized a tub, and placing it on the child's neck, killed it; exclaiming, 'I am now sure of having sent one soul to heaven.'"

"You are not without poets here, of course?" said the stranger.

"We have, unfortunately," replied the other, "more individuals of that class than we can well manage. They ought to have an asylum for themselves. There's a fellow, now, he in the tattered jacket and nightcap, who has written a heroic poem, of eighty-six thousand verses, which he entitles 'Balaam's Ass, or the Great Unsaddled'. Shall I call him over?"

"Oh, for heaven's sake, no," replied the stranger; "keep me from the poets."

"There is one of the other species," replied the gentleman, "the thin, red-eyed fellow, who grinds his teeth. He fancies himself as a wit and a satirist, and is the author of an unpublished poem, called 'The Smoking Dunghill, Or Parnassus In A Fume'. He published several things, which were justly attacked on account of their dullness, and he is now in an awful fury against all the poets of the day, to every one of whom he has given an appropriate position on the sublime pedestal, which he has, as it were, with his own hands, erected for them. He certainly ought to be the best constructor of a dunghill in the world, for he deals in nothing but dirt. He refuses to wash his hands, because, he says, it would disqualify him from giving the last touch to his poem and his characters."

"Have you philosophers as well as poets here?" asked the stranger.

"Oh dear, yes, sir. We have poetical philosophers, and philosophical poets; but, I protest to heaven, the wisdom of Solomon, or of an archangel, could not decide the difference between their folly. There's a man now, with the old stocking in his hand, it is one of his own, for you may observe that he has one leg bare—who is pacing up and down in a deep thinking mood. That man, sir, was set mad by a definition of his own making."

"Well, let us hear it," said the stranger.

"Why, sir, he imagines that he had discovered a definition for 'NOTHING'. The definition, however, will make you smile."

"And what, pray, is it?"

"Nothing, he says, is—A FOOTLESS STOCKING WITHOUT A LEG; and maintains that he ought to hold the first rank as a philosopher for having invented the definition, and deserves a pension from the crown."

"Who are these two men dressed in black, walking arm in arm?" asked the stranger, "They appear to be clergymen."

"Yes, sir," replied his conductor, "so they are; two celebrated polemical controversialists, who, when they were at large, created by their attacks, each upon the religion of the other, more ill-will, rancour and religious animosity, than either of their religions, with all their virtues, could remove. It is impossible to describe the evil they did. Ever since they came here, however, they are like brothers. They were placed in the same room, each in a strong strait-waistcoat, for the space of three months; but on being allowed to walk about, they became sworn friends, and now amuse themselves more than any other two in the establishment. They indulge in immoderate fits of laughter, look each other knowingly in the face, wink, and run the forefinger up the nose, after which their mirth bursts out afresh, and they laugh until the tears come down their cheeks." ...

As they sauntered up and down the room, other symptoms reached them besides those that were then subjected to their sight. As a door opened, a peal of wild laughter might be heard—sometimes groaning—and occasionally the most awful blasphemies. Ambition contributed a large number to its dreary cells. In fact, one would imagine that the house had been converted into a temple of justice, and contained within its walls most of the crowned heads and generals of Europe, both living and dead, together with a fair sample of the saints. The Emperor of Russia was strapped down to a chair that had been screwed into the floor, with the additional security of a strait-waistcoat to keep his majesty quiet. The Pope challenged Henry the Eighth to box, and St. Peter, as the cell door opened, asked Anthony Corbet for a glass of whiskey. Napoleon Bonaparte, in the person of a heroic tailor, was singing "Bob and Joan"; and the Archbishop of Dublin said he would pledge his mitre for a good cigar and a pot of porter. Sometimes a frightful yell would reach their ears; then a furious set of howlings, followed again by peals of maniac laughter, as before.

2.

'The Lodging House' from *Autobiography* (1896)

THE CELLAR WAS very spacious: I should think that the entrance into Dante's Inferno was paradise compared with it. I know and have known Dublin now for about half a century, better probably than any other man in it. I have lived in the Liberty and in every

199

close and outlet in the City of the Panniers*, driven by poverty to the most wretched of its localities, and I must confess that the scene which burst upon me that night stands beyond anything the highest flight of my imagination could have conceived without my having an opportunity of seeing it. Burns must have witnessed something of the sort, or he could never have written the most graphic and animated of all his productions—'The Jolly Beggars'.

The inhabitants of Dublin, and even strangers, are in the habit of listening to the importunities of those irreclaimable beggars whom no law can keep from the streets, of ballad-singers, strolling fiddlers, pipers, flute-players, and the very considerable variety of that class which even now, when we have to pay poor-rates, continue to infest our thoroughfares. What must not the city have been, however, before the enactment of the poor-laws? Why, at that period, there existed in Dublin two distinct worlds, each as ignorant of the other—at least, in a particular point of view, and during certain portions of the day—as if they did not inhabit the same country. I have heard many a man of sense and intellect ask, before the establishment of the poor-laws, where the vast crowds of paupers passed the night; I never heard the question satisfactorily answered. On that night, however, I found a solution of it, and ever since it has been no mystery to me.

When I got down to the cellar, and looked about me, I was struck, but only for an instant, by the blazing fire which glowed in the grate. My eyes then ran over the scene about me, but how to describe it is the difficulty. It resembled nothing I ever saw either before or since. The inmates were mostly in bed, both men and women, but still a good number of them were up, and indulging in liquors of every description, from strong whiskey downwards. The beds were mostly what are called 'shakedowns'—that is, simple straw, sometimes with a rag of sheet, and sometimes with none. There were there the lame, the blind, the dumb, and all who suffered from actual and natural infirmity; but in addition to these, there was every variety of impostor about me—most of them stripped of their mechanical accessories of deceit, but by no means all. If not seen, the character of those assembled and their conduct could not possibly be believed. This was half a century ago*, when

---

* Carleton has mistaken *cliath* for *cliabh* in the word Ath-cliath (Dublin), which signifies 'The Ford of Hurdles'. *Cliabh* signifies a basket or pannier. * About 1818.

Dublin was swarming with beggars and street impostors of every possible description. This, I understood afterwards, was one of the cellars to which these persons resorted at night, and there they flung off all the restraints imposed on them during the course of the day. I learned afterwards that there were upwards of two dozen such nightly haunts in the suburban parts of the city. Crutches, wooden legs, artificial cancers, scrofulous necks, artificial wens, sore legs, and a vast variety of similar complaints, were hung up on the walls of the cellars, and made me reflect upon the degree of perverted talent and ingenuity that must have been necessary to sustain such a mighty mass of imposture. Had the same amount of intellect, thought I, been devoted to the exercise of honest and virtuous industry, how much advantage in the shape of energy and example might not society have derived from it. The songs and the gestures were infamous, but if one thing puzzled me more than another, it was the fluency and originality of blackguardism as expressed in language. In fact these people possessed an indecent slang, which constituted a kind of language known only to themselves, and was never spoken except at such orgies as I am describing. Several offered me seats, and were very respectful; but I preferred standing, at least for a time, that I might have a better view of them. While I was in this position a couple of young vagabonds—pickpockets, of course—came and stood beside me. Instinct told me their object, but as I knew the amount in my purse—one penny—I felt little apprehension in having my pockets picked. On entering the cellar, I had to pay twopence for my bed, so I had just one penny left.

How the night passed I need not say. Of course I never closed my eyes; but so soon as the first glimpse of anything like light appeared, I left the place, and went out on my solitary rambles through the city.

3.

'The Watch-House' from *The Black Baronet* (1852)

◆

ON ENTERING THE watch-house, the heart of the humane priest was painfully oppressed at the scenes of uproar, confusion, debauchery, and shameless profligacy, of which he saw either the present exhibition or the unquestionable evidences. There was the lost and hardened female, uttering the wild screams of intoxication, or pouring forth from her dark, filthy place of confinement torrents of polluted mirth; the juvenile pickpocket, ripe in all the ribald wit and traditional slang of his profession; the ruffian burglar, with strong animal frame, dark eyebrows, low forehead, and face full of coarseness and brutality; the open robber, reckless and jocular, indifferent to consequences, and holding his life only in trust for the hangman, or for some determined opponent who may treat him to cold lead instead of pure gold; the sneaking thief, cool and cowardly, ready-witted at the extricating falsehood—for it is well known that the thief and liar are convertible terms—his eye feeble, cunning, and circumspective, and his whole appearance redolent of duplicity and fraud; the receiver of stolen goods, affecting much honest simplicity; the good creature, whether man or woman, apparently in great distress, and wondering that industrious and unsuspecting people, struggling to bring up their families in honesty and decency, should be imposed upon and taken in by people that one couldn't think of suspecting. There, too, was the servant out of place, who first a forger of discharges, next became a thief, and heroically adventuring to the dignity of a burglar for which he had neither skill nor daring, was made prisoner in the act; and there he sits, half drunk, in that corner, repenting his failure instead of his crime, forgetting his cowardice, and making moral resolutions with himself, that, should he escape now, he will execute the next burglary in a safe and virtuous state of sobriety. But we need not proceed: there was the idle and drunken mechanic, or, perhaps, the wife, whose Saturday night visits to the tap-room in order to fetch him home, or to rescue the wages of his industry from the publican, had at length corrupted herself.

Two other characters were there which we cannot overlook, both of whom had passed through the world with a strong but holy scorn for the errors and failings of their fellow-creatures. One of them was a man of gross, carnal-looking features, trained, as it seemed to the uninitiated, into a severe and sanctified expression by the sheer force of religion. His face was full of godly intolerance against everything at variance with the one thing needful, whatever that was, and against all who did not, like himself, travel on fearlessly and zealously Zionward. He did not feel himself justified in the use of common and profane language; and, consequently, his vocabulary was taken principally from the Bible, which he called "the Lord's word." Sunday was not Sunday with him, but "the Lord's day;" and he never went to church in his life, but always to "service." Like most of his class, however, he seemed to be influenced by that extraordinary anomaly which characterizes the saints—that is to say, as great a reverence for the name of the devil as for that of God himself; for in his whole life and conversation he was never known to pronounce it as we have written it. Satan— the enemy—the destroyer, were the names he applied to him: and this, we presume, lest the world might suspect that there subsisted any private familiarity between them. His great ruling principle, however, originated in what he termed a godless system of religious liberality; in other words, he attributed all the calamities and scourges of the land to the influence of Popery, and its toleration by the powers that be. He was a big-boned, coarse man, with black, greasy hair, cut short; projecting cheek-bones, that argued great cruelty; dull, but lascivious eyes; and an upper lip like a dropsical sausage. We forget now the locality in which he had committed the offence that had caused him to be brought there. But it does not much matter; it is enough to say that he was caught, about three o'clock, perambulating the streets, considerably the worse for liquor and not in the best society. Even as it was, and in the very face of those who had detected him so circumstanced, he was railing against the ungodliness of our "rulers," the degeneracy of human nature, and the awful scourges that the existence of Popery was bringing on the land.

As it happened, however, this worthy representative of his class was not without a counterpart among the moral inmates of the watch-house. Another man, who was known among his friends as a Catholic voteen, or devotee, happened to have been brought to the same establishment, much in the same circumstances, and for some similar offence. When compared together, it was really curious to observe the extraordinary resemblance which these two men bore to each other. Each was dressed in sober clothes, for your puritan of every creed must, like his progenitors the Pharisees of old, have some peculiarity in his dress that will gain him credit for religion. Their features were marked by the same dark, sullen shade which betokens intolerance. The devotee was thinner, and not so large a man as the other; but he made up in the cunning energy which glistened from his eyes for the want of physical strength, as compared with the Protestant saint; not at all that he was deficient in it *per se*, for though a smaller man, he was better built and more compact than his brother. Indeed, so nearly identical was the expression of their features—the sensual Milesian mouth, and naturally amorous temperament, hypocrisized into formality, and darkened into bitterness by bigotry—that on discovering each other in the watch-house, neither could for his life determine whether the man before him belonged to idolatrous Rome on the one hand, or the arch heresy on the other.

There they stood, exact counterparts, each a thousand times more anxious to damn the other than to save himself. They were not long, however, in discovering each other, and in a moment the jargon of controversy rang loud and high amidst the uproar and confusion of the place. The Protestant saint attributed all the iniquity by which the land, he said, was overflowed, and the judgments under which it was righteously suffering, to the guilt of our rulers, who forgot God, and connived at Popery.

The Popish saint, on the other hand, asserted that so long as a fat and oppressive heresy was permitted to trample upon the people, the country could never prosper. The other one said, that idolatry—Popish idolatry—was the cause of all; and that it was the scourge by which "the Lord" was inflicting judicial punishment upon the country at large. If it were not for that he would not be in such a sink of iniquity at that moment. Popish idolatry it was that brought him there; and the abominations of the Romish harlot were desolating the land.

The other replied, that perhaps she was the only harlot of the kind he would run away from; and maintained, that until all heresy was abolished, and rooted out of the country, the curse of God would sit upon them, as the corrupt law church does now in the shape of an overgrown nightmare. What brought him, who was ready to die for his persecuted church, here? He could tell the heretic;—it was Protestant ascendancy, and he could prove it;—yes, Protestant ascendancy, and nothing else, was it that brought him to that house, its representative, in which he now stood. He maintained that it resembled a watch-house; was it not full of wickedness, noise, and blasphemy; and were there any two creeds in it that agreed together, and did not fight like devils?

How much longer this fiery discussion might have proceeded it is difficult to say. The constable of the night, finding that the two hypocritical vagabonds were a nuisance to the whole place, had them handcuffed together, and both placed in the black hole to finish their argument.

In short, there was around the good man—vice, with all her discordant sounds and hideous aspects, clanging in his ear the multitudinous din that arose from the loud and noisy tumult of her brutal, drunken, and debauched votaries.

Select Bibliography

'An Irish Election in the Forties', *Dublin University Magazine*, Vol. XXI, No.176, August 1847, pp. 176-192.

Autobiography of William Carleton: The Life of William Carleton, Being his Biography and Letters, and an Account of his Life and Writings, from the Point at which the Autobiography Breaks Off. ed. David J. O'Donoghue. London: Downey, 1896; rpt. with preface by Patrick Kavanagh, London: Macgibbon and Kee, 1968; rpt. New York and London: Garland, 1979.

The Black Baronet, originally titled *Red Hall or the Baronet's Daughter* London: Saunders & Otley, 1852; retitled *The Black Baronet or The Chronicles of Ballytrain*. Dublin: Duffy, 1858.

The Black Prophet, A Tale of the Irish Famine, Dublin University Magazine, Vol. XXVII, No. 161, May 1846—Vol. XVIII, No. 168, December 1846. rpt. Belfast: Simms & McIntyre, 1847.

'The Castle of Aughentain; or A Legend of the Brown Goat, A Tale of Tom Grassiey [sic], the Shanahus.' *Irish Penny Journal*, Vol. I, No. 49, 5 June 1841, pp. 386-389; rpt. *Tales and Sketches of the Irish Peasantry*. Dublin: Duffy, 1845

The Emigrants of Ahadarra.
London and Belfast: Simms & McIntyre, 1848

'Fin M'Coul, the Knockmanny Giant', *Tales and Sketches Illustrating the Character, Usages, Traditions, Sports and Pastimes of the Irish Peasantry*. Dublin: Duffy, 1845

'The Lianhan Shee, An Irish Superstition' *Christian Examiner*, Vol. X, No. 68, November 1830, pp. 845-861; rpt. in *Traits and Stories of the Irish Peasantry*, second series. Dublin: Wakeman, 1833.

'Neal Malone' *University Review and Quarterly Magazine*, Vol. I, No.1, January 1833, pp. 151-170; rpt. in *Tales of Ireland*. Dublin: Curry, 1834.

'Mary Murray, the Irish Match-Maker' *Irish Penny Journal*, Vol. I, No. 14, 3 October 1840, pp. 116-120; rpt. *Tales and Sketches*. Dublin: Duffy, 1845.

Parra Sastha or the History of Paddy Go-Easy and His Wife Nancy. Dublin: Duffy, 1845.

The Evil Eye or the Black Spectre. Dublin: Duffy, 1860.

Fardorougha the Miser or the Convicts of Lisnamona. Dublin University Magazine, Vol.1X, No. 50. February 1837—Vol. XI, No. 62, February 1838; rpt. Dublin: Curry, 1839.

Rody the Rover or the Ribbonman. Dublin: Duffy, 1845.

The Squanders of Castle Squander. Synoptic version *London News*, Vol. XX, No.541, supplement, January 1852—Vol XX, No 557, May 1 1852; rpt. London: London Illustrated Library, 1842.

The Tithe Proctor. London and Belfast: Simms and McIntyre, 1849.

Valentine M'Clutchy, the Irish Agent. Dublin, London and Edinburgh: Duffy, 1845.

'Wildgoose Lodge' as 'Confessions of a Reformed Ribbonman.' *Dublin Literary Gazette or Weekly Chronicle of Criticism, Belle Letters and Fine Arts* Vol.I, No. 4, 23 January 1830—Vol. I, No 5, 30 January 1830

'Taedet Me Vitae', *The Nation,* 30 December 1854, p.249